That Time of Year

That Time of Year

Robert O. Stephens

www.ivyhousebooks.com

PUBLISHED BY IVY HOUSE PUBLISHING GROUP
5122 Bur Oak Circle, Raleigh, NC 27612
United States of America
919-782-0281
www.ivyhousebooks.com

ISBN: 1-57197-397-4
Library of Congress Control Number: 2003095469

Copyright © 2004 Robert O. Stephens
All rights reserved, which includes the right to reproduce this
book or portions thereof in any form whatsoever except as
provided by the U.S. Copyright Law.

Printed in the United States of America

For Ginny, who supported me all the way.

Next Year in Cromwell

Next Year in Cromwell

 As soon as I saw it, I knew that train was in trouble. On the downgrade and coming around curves, its wheels were squealing against the rails, and in the cars you could see people straining against the seats.
 When it was gone, I realized the train had only two passenger cars and an odd lot of empty boxcars, to judge from the open doors. Where was the rest, the other passenger cars and the freight cars?
 I was on the gravel road that passes Cluster's Pond and overlooks the railroad cut. Since I was going down to the valley anyway, I thought I'd better take the road that follows close to the track and see what came of that race. Even before I got to the level I could see ahead where the train was tipped over to the left with the right wheels still on the track bed. Lucky, I thought. I expected worse.
 I stopped the car on the roadside and walked across the narrow field to the railroad right-of-way. Several men in suits and one woman with her hat askew were beginning to step down from the canted cars. They looked scared, all right. A little farther along I

thought I saw a familiar figure and walked on to him. He was in a suit too, but his necktie was loose, his coat was sagging on one side, and he was fanning his face with his crushed hat. I recognized him about the same time he saw me.

"Well, I'll be, if it ain't Will Ford," he called. "I thought I was fried chicken back there."

I had met Simon Dunaway earlier at Zeke Morgan's jail cell, when he and I both visited Zeke.

"Looks like you took the fast train," I said. "What happened?"

"That train lost her brakes as we began the downgrade at Simpson's Draw, and I thought we'd go all the way to China 'fore she stopped. Lucky that curve was a easy one, or we'd be down a hillside."

"Didn't they check the brakes before they began the run?"

"They checked 'em, all right, but now I wonder what for. Even 'fore we got to the draw I figured out we didn't have the whole train behind us. Somewhere back there they got uncoupled. Wish I'd seen when." By that time he was really fanning.

"There's a crew station a couple of hundred yards up the track," I said. "Let's get the engineer and send a trouble signal. Then maybe you can explain what's going on."

"Right. Lemme tell Brother Tommy what we're doin', and he can get the folks lined out while we're gone. They're some rattled."

Simon could talk with me because we had a common interest in Zeke Morgan. I was Zeke's lawyer, and Simon was Zeke's friend and his partner in a locally notorious religious cult. So after we got the dazed engineer to the crew station, we sat on the bench, and as Simon gnawed a plug, I asked, "Why do you think this wasn't an accident?"

Simon's answer was a long one, as most of his are, and I had to fill in some parts from my own experience.

His story and mine began three months earlier, when I was hired to defend Zeke Morgan on a murder charge. Zeke was accused of killing Julius Meadows, the banker in Cromwell who held Zeke's note on the farm Zeke ran on the eastern edge of Ireland County. Zeke's farm was lost to foreclosure by the bank. He was known locally around Cromwell for a fiery temper and, so some people said, had threatened Meadows if his note was not extended. To make matters worse, Zeke was known as a follower of Walter Cornelius, who ran some sort of religious movement a couple of counties away. Zeke and several folks like him were the targets of concern by prominent ministers in town and by several of the leading merchants. Heretics, the ministers called them, and the merchants thought the shouting and hurrahing of the believers would scare business away from town. They especially feared that the Eastern and Southern Railroad would run fewer trains through Cromwell. So when Meadows was found shot in his office, Zeke was the one they went for.

It looked for a while like Zeke had no friends in town and might have to prepare his own defense if the circuit judge didn't get around soon to appointing a defender. But late one afternoon, as I was sitting in my office trying to work out the right phrasing for Matt Gompton's will, a boy came with a note asking me to come see Joshua Walker that evening after nine o'clock. Josh Walker was the biggest lumberman in town and, as it turned out, a friend of Zeke. His house was one of the handsomest on Poplar Avenue, with lots of gables and wide verandas. It also had a small side door masked by a number of tall shrubs, and I could tell by the dim light that it was the door I should go to.

Walker answered the door himself and pulled the shade after I came in. "I want to hire you to defend Zeke Morgan," he said even before I had settled in the chair across from his desk. The lamp shade hid his face as he leaned back in his chair, and I couldn't tell by his expression what his attitude toward me was. He still had on his coat and tie as if he were in his lumber office, and he had wasted no time on friendly small talk.

"Why me?" I said.

"Because you haven't been here in Cromwell long enough to be infected by the thinking of the town like the other lawyers. They think they already know the answers or know what the answers better be. Also, you're Jonathan Ford's son, and I'm betting he taught you to think right. Too bad he's not here now."

Then he leaned forward, and the light showed a heavy face, serious and even sad. "But I want my name kept out of it. Passions are running high in this town, and I don't want my friendship for Zeke Morgan to hurt my business. You can say you've been hired by friends of Zeke and keep your own counsel about particulars. You also need to recognize you're going to lose some friends by defending Zeke."

"What kind of case does Zeke have?" I asked.

"That's for you to find out. You'll have to do a lot of work finding out Zeke's exact situation before you ever get in front of a jury, more than you will in court. I think Julius Meadows was shot by somebody else, and you'll have to find out who killed him and why."

Then his voice became warm, almost gentle. "Besides, what I know of Zeke Morgan, he wouldn't rob or ambush a man. True, he's got a short temper and sometimes speaks before he reckons the effect of his words. But he's got a streak of charity in him that helps more than hurts. He helped me once when I was out estimating timber and fell down a ravine. He got me out, looked after me, and took me to a doctor even when it turned out I was on his land and in the wrong area. For a man who's so jealous of his property, that was an amazing thing to do."

So I agreed to defend Zeke Morgan, and the fee Josh Walker offered and I accepted meant he wasn't trying to buy cheap. He wanted a full defense and damn the cost. But keep his name out of it, he warned again, and don't come see him unless it was absolutely necessary. A couple of days later I notified Billy Eustis, the county attorney, that I would be defending Zeke. He raised his eyebrows but said nothing while I filled out the forms. I told him I would see him soon to review the county's evidence from the scene of the crime.

∽

When Joshua Walker said I was still new in Cromwell, I knew he meant I was back in town after a long absence. I had grown up in Cromwell in easy circumstances. My father was a lawyer and in his later years was the resident attorney for the Eastern and Southern. But he wasn't a native of Cromwell. Mama was and knew all the right people and was related to half of them. Her people, the McDonalds, had run a good-size farm in the county before the war but found during the troubles preceding the war that farming was a poor man's way to live. They scraped together what money they could, moved to town, set up a general store near the railroad, and prospered. About the time the county began to recover from the war, she met and married John Ford, and I came onto the scene in July 1888. But I was their only surviving heir. Two sisters died in infancy of diphtheria. Mama didn't have the heart to try for more after that.

After I went to the state university and studied history, my father thought it was time I read law and followed in his steps. Law didn't look right to me then. I wanted to follow up on the big question still being discussed in the colleges about religion and science. With more study, I might try to become a college professor of religion or maybe a minister. Mama liked the minister idea. Papa didn't, but he agreed to pay for more study. Before long, I was in Germany at Göttengen University reading biblical criticism with Professor Julius Wellhausen.

Germany in 1910 was not a friendly place to people like me. The professors acted like pompous gods, and the students cringed around them but snarled at each other and sneered at me. My main escape from that scene came when I met Lisette Anders. She was the daughter of a prosperous pharmacist and was as charming in her blonde way as any woman I had ever met. She hinted at intimacies that were always just beyond reach. I wondered how she would be as a professor's or minister's wife and thought of my relatives' and colleagues' shock. Then Claus von Lakenberg came on the scene. He was a Hauptmann in the Imperial Army, was from an old Prussian Junker family, and was arrogant. Urbane but stiff in manners, he charmed Lisette and let me know that Germany was Europe's future. The Imperial Army, he said, would lead the Fatherland to dominance in the world. I tried to tell Lisette that Claus was too aristocratic for her and she could at best become his mistress, but not his wife. That didn't seem to bother her. Then came the letter from Judge McCloud, telling me that both Papa and Mama had died in an auto accident at a railroad crossing and I should come home. I did and visited their graves and wondered what Papa would have said about my wandering. A little later I had markers erected for them among the stand of monuments where most of their family and friends were gathered. I remembered what one of my northern friends from the university had said: the first thing you do when you come home is go worship your ancestors.

Papa had left a large estate, more than enough to support me while I tried to find a way to live in Cromwell. I moved into my parents' house and lived in a wing with my books and oil burner stove to heat coffee and fry eggs. I decided to try the law as Papa had wanted. Judge Andrew McCloud, a longtime friend of Papa and Mama, agreed to let me read law in his office and explained the subtle reasonings. He was strong on interpretation and strict about jurisdictions where laws and decisions applied. At times he sounded more like a judge applying austere principles to the sad affairs of men than like a pleader for men's weaknesses to a jury. After little more than a year, I passed the bar exam and put out my shingle. Work came slow and mostly dealt with wills, contracts, and property line disputes. That was why I was surprised when Joshua Walker wanted me to defend Zeke Morgan.

While I was studying with the Judge, I was often invited to dinner at his home. At the table, we avoided law talk with his family but had good discussions about politics and religion over the snap beans, pickled beets, and baked chicken. His wife, Miss Maud, knew how to keep the talk easy as she urged you to have more boiled potatoes. Then in her late forties or early fifties, I'd reckon, she still kept some of the mannerisms of a young woman and could compete with her daughters in charm, with an arch smile or a sidelong glance. Daughters came second for her, though. She worried about their son Richard, not long ago graduated from West Point and now stationed near the Mexican border in Texas. Out of nowhere, she would ask if you thought Richard was getting enough to eat.

Their younger daughter Emma was engaged to Harry Bains, one of the more promising tobacco buyers in town. She was blonde and pretty in a conventional way, with curly hair, ready to talk pleasantries but quick to retreat from a frown or an opposed view. I thought she would be a submissive wife for Harry. Kate, the older daughter, was taller than most women, had a well-rounded figure, wore her dark hair around a lively, slightly freckled face, was quick to smile, and was always ready to speak her strong opinions. She and the Judge sometimes crossed views. Handsome, I reckon you'd say she was, instead of pretty. Though quite attractive, she was not married, and you could sometimes see the look in Miss Maud's eyes, wondering if they had a spinster in the family. Kate's past was the problem. She had come home from normal school under circumstances not talked about outside the family. Some folks in town whispered she had had quite a fling at normal school, some said she'd had an affair with a man not good enough for her, and some thought she had actually been married and divorced while away from Cromwell. It was that rumor of divorce that kept away the eligible men in town. She lived at home and worked as librarian at what was called the town's library, a brick building once used by the railroad as a storage house but built in the generous style of a more leisurely time. Not an unpleasant place to spend your hours.

Judge McCloud was judge now by courtesy, as he had retired from the circuit court three years before. He still kept a law office and handled a case occasionally but didn't depend on his practice for money. He and Miss Maud owned several properties in town and out in the county. He was at that stage in life when he could spend time in reflection, remembering his days as a young man, hardly more than a boy, in Longstreet's Corps and wondering how he survived. He was ten or more years older than Miss Maud and had spent years getting over the war before he married. He sometimes talked about his and others' puzzling over God and fate and why the South lost the war. He scoffed at the Lost Cause people, though, and applauded the recent progressive actions in the state legislature to support public education, especially education for women. Time women learned to do better than their mothers and grandmothers did, he said. But he talked more and more about his religious questioning, to the discomfort of Miss Maud. He was afraid, he said, that the big churches in town were getting too comfortable in their doctrines and recent prosperity. They failed to satisfy a lot of people's yearnings and opened the way for the emergence of backwoods cults and strange behavior. He wondered what effect those restless yearnings would have on some women and the colored folks. Kate had her own views on that question.

∞

When I went to see Billy Eustis, I found the sheriff's report he showed me was pretty skimpy. About all it said was that Julius Meadows had been shot in the chest with a Colt .45 and that miscellaneous papers were found on the desk and floor of his office. No doors or windows had been broken. I thought its lack of detail might have been deliberate, to allow an argument that Meadows had been expecting a visitor. Zeke, the prosecutor would claim.

I must have had the Judge's talk in mind as well as Josh Walker's when I went for my first visit with Zeke Morgan in the county jail. Jeb Billings, the bailiff, was surly and acted like I was invading his territory. "What you want to see him for? Defendin' ain't gonna get him outta here." I told him I'd be visiting Zeke a lot, and he'd better get used to it. After more grumbling, he unlocked Zeke's cell door and found a chair for me. He closed the door with a bang and left.

Zeke swung his legs around to sit on the edge of the bunk and looked me over. I told him who I was and that I had been hired to defend him.

"I know you," he said. "Who's payin' you?"

"Some of your friends who want to keep their names out of it."

He seemed to accept that answer as expectable. "All right," he said like he was agreeing to something. "Hope they know what they're doin'." It made me wonder who he thought his friends were.

We sat in silence a couple of minutes, and I took the time to look him over. He was a good-size man with a face still red from the sun, dark eyes that stared, a face shaved clear of mustache or whiskers, and grizzled hair that stood out from his head. His hands, clapped over his knees, were large and bony. His shirt and trousers were clean and ordinary, the kind a farmer might wear when not working in the field or doing chores. I couldn't tell whether his expression was hostile or dubious, or maybe just sad. He wore his face long.

"We need to work up a defense for you," I finally said. "You've been charged with the murder of Julius Meadows, and it looks like the county attorney and the town have already decided you're guilty. We've got a lot of minds to change, and we need solid evidence to do it. Let's go over your story and see how it fits against what the county attorney is saying."

I wasn't surprised when Zeke claimed he was innocent. He said he was home with the grippe when Meadows must have been shot. No, he had never owned or used a pistol, just a shotgun to scare off varmints. He said Meadows had agreed orally to extend his note but had never put the extension in writing. He wondered if Meadows had changed his mind and why. Not good, I thought. Land transactions needed to be in writing.

Zeke began to open himself more when I asked him to tell me how he got involved with Meadows. He sketched a larger picture of his life and times than I expected. There was a storyteller behind that solemn face. He had lived on his farm for almost ten years. His wife had died not long after they moved to the farm, and since they had no children, he worked the farm just enough to get by and hold the land. Some years his tobacco crop failed to make enough to pay the mortgage, and he had fallen behind. That was when he had to ask Meadows for an extension. Some people in town, he said, who thought they knew about his business, wondered why Julius Meadows ever gave him more time. Mostly, though, they talked about how, after his wife died, he got involved with the Amosites, or some called them the Cornelians. They meant followers of Amos Caruthers and Walter Cornelius.

Amos was a backwoods preacher two counties away. About ten or fifteen years before, he had stirred up a lot of interest among the country and small-town folks with his preaching about the power of the Holy Spirit at arbor meetings and market days. What made him attract more than the usual casual attention such preachers get was his talk about how all the Jesus worshipping that had gone on for almost nineteen hundred years had been made null and void by the new coming of the Holy Spirit. You can imagine how that suited the preachers in the town churches. Somehow Amos Caruthers got himself in trouble with the law and got shot one dark night. The lawmen were never able to find out who did it. His followers circulated rumors that Amos was a victim of the Jesus people in town and, so Zeke said, started meeting secretly in believers' homes while the town preachers warned their congregations against the heresies of Amos Caruthers. He'd been removed from this world according to God's justice, they said.

Then before long, Walter Cornelius came onto the scene and began organizing Caruthers' followers and starting new groups of Amosites. It soon wasn't clear whether the new believers were followers of Amos or Walter. There were rumbles in the backcountry of disputes between the two groups about who had the true spirit. As I listened to Zeke, I wasn't clear which bunch he was involved with.

He said the truth was out there and I had to find it. We shook hands and I called Jeb, who was still grizzling, left the jail, and went out to start looking.

To find out where we stood on the property question, I went to the courthouse to examine Zeke's land records. I had known Wayne Bosley, the county clerk, since we were in school the same years, but we were never close friends. He had his friends on another street and, according to the Judge, Wayne got his job through family political connections. He had to let me see the records all right, but he provided no help. It was hard to tell whether he was resisting or being unaccommodating. After rummaging through dusty files, I found the title to Zeke's land with the mortgage attachment made out to Julius Meadows. Then a surprise: a small plot of the land extending into adjacent Brand County with a separate title had been excluded from the mortgaged land. I wondered why the exclusion and why Zeke hadn't mentioned it. Was it a family cemetery? I also found records of owners of the land before Zeke and saw that the land had been bought earlier from a seller in Texas. The reservation on the small plot had continued from one buyer to the next. The Texas holder had been one Joshua C. Morgan. I didn't mention to Wayne what I'd found.

Background, I realized, was what I needed, and I thought I knew where to find it. I called on Judge McCloud at his office and asked him what he knew about Zeke Morgan and his farm. The Judge said it would be better to discuss the matter away from the office. He invited me to supper at the McClouds' the next Tuesday.

At the supper table, the Judge was more relaxed, and the family was in a talkative mood. The late evening sun was coming through the lace curtains, and the room and table felt large. Miss Maud was at her end near the kitchen, the Judge at his near the parlor door, Emma and Kate opposite me, and I could feel Richard's half-presence on the long side where I was seated. Miss Maud sometimes looked past me as if Richard was sitting there.

"All I can tell you about Zeke Morgan," the Judge said, "is that he's a decent man but has a fanatical streak. He's always paid his debts and kept his promises. That didn't keep him from getting into hot arguments about the Amosites, defending them. Maybe making enemies."

"Well, I wonder if there's any connection between Julius Meadows' death and Zeke's religious disputes." Kate smiled, and her look said she meant more. Her filmy shirtwaist did more to reveal than conceal the curves of her neck and shoulders and waist.

"I was going to say," the Judge went on, "Zeke did more than defend. He attacked, scorned, sometimes insulted folks for not being able to see the new way. Got to be a thorn in the backside of some mighty high folks in town."

"Mr. McCloud!" Miss Maud said in mock shock. Kate and Emma smiled.

"Harry says lots of the storekeepers downtown are really upset about what happened to Mr. Meadows," Emma reported. "Harry says they think Zeke Morgan ought to be hanged like a killer for disturbing the peace of this town with his wild talk and then the murder."

"Well, I'm glad Richard is away from all this upsetting business, even if he is down there with those Mexicans, riding wild," Miss Maud interjected. "Zeke ran Richard and some of the boys off his land several years ago. They were hunting, Richard said, and straggled onto Zeke's place."

"My guess, Miss Maud, is they got into forbidden territory." The Judge was making a peace offering. "Zeke was secretive. You'd start to ask him close questions about those Amosites and Cornelians, and he'd clam up. Must've been hiding something about them."

The talk went on and the day got dark. Auntie Bess had long before taken the dishes off the table and rattled them in the kitchen. The Judge wanted to know how the law business was coming along, and I said passable but didn't mention Josh Walker's interest. He and Miss Maud reminisced about the old days with Mama and Papa and their croquet games on the side lawn. Kate and Emma smothered yawns. I looked at my pocket watch, apologized for staying so long, and went out into a fine summer night. It was Kate's kind of night, I thought.

Next morning Kidd Saunders came to my office. He was one of the more aggressive lawyers in town and had important connections. He settled his burly body in my one other chair, leaned an arm with gold cuff links on my desk, and got down to business.

"Will, we need to talk. You're upsetting lots of folks by defending Zeke Morgan. He's a pest, and the town wants to be rid of him. We don't need a long trial that gives Zeke a chance to shout in public his wild doctrines. He's bad for business and bad for folks' beliefs. Several important ministers, who I won't name, want him and his heresies to go away. And there are good business people, who again I won't name, they're afraid that Zeke and his ilk will keep the Eastern and Southern from running more trains through here. We need those trains if we're ever going to be more than another backwater town."

I wondered what plans for the town required so many trains but kept to the question at hand. "Zeke's entitled to a defense."

"I know that. Hell, any lawyer needs cases. But you don't have to make a circus of it."

"Zeke's entitled to a full defense."

"Depends what you mean by a full defense. The facts are against you. Everybody knows that. The law's against you, too. The law in this town is what the jury says, and the jury is going to find Zeke guilty."

"The facts are still to be discovered."

I had known Kidd Saunders only at a distance. Now I saw him up close. He had a full head of dark hair and a face red from blood, not sun, with a crisp army-style mustache above a sardonic mouth, not smiling now. His white collar and cuffs with the trim-cut gray suit and dark cravat set off his red face. He had the watchful eyes of a bargainer. Lots of folks would think him handsome in a forceful way. Talk was he had political ambitions. I could see he was willing to force me.

"You're not established in this town yet, Will. Carry through on Zeke's defense and you'll never be. Too many important people are watching you to forget what you're doing. But you plead guilty with extenuating circumstances and get Zeke off with prison time instead of hanging, a judge and jury and other folks might begin to see things your way."

"I still have lots of questions to answer. Among them is why so many folks are anxious to get Zeke away from here. So far things don't add up."

He stood up. "You've been warned," he said, picked up his hat, and went out.

About noon, when I was walking up the street to the State Cafe to get dinner, Ed Braswell stopped me. Ed ran the town's weekly newspaper. *The Cromwellian,* he called it. He had a wry, dry sense of humor, and I had the idea he laughed up his sleeve at some of the notices of missionary circle and poetry club meetings he printed. I once asked him which Cromwell he named his paper for. He said time would tell. Whatever his private views were, he knew who his subscribers and advertisers were. He was careful that way. This time he asked in hearing of several on the sidewalk if I wanted to put a notice in the paper about setting up my practice. Be good for business, he said. Then in a lower voice he said, "Don't bust yourself, Will, by bucking the power in town. They can be mean. I tried it once and learned my lesson." Then in a louder voice, "Come by if you want to put it in."

I had a hard time concentrating that day on Jake Tilley's contract to buy a plot of land on Cook's Creek. I had to decide soon what was the best place to look next. Late that afternoon, getting on to suppertime, the errand boy from the library brought a note from Kate. Said come see her at the house late afternoon the next day. I gave the boy a quarter and told him to say thanks to Miss Kate. I hoped the quarter would help make him our friend instead of Kidd's.

∞

When I went to the McClouds' the next day, the east porch was full, the Judge at one end, Miss Maud and a group of women at the other. Kate was nowhere in sight. The Judge and his cigar had clearly been sent to the far end. "Evening, Judge," I said as I went up the steps.

"Come sit, Will. Nothing finer than a breeze in the shade."

"No sir. That's the right way to wrap up a day."

We talked a few minutes, and I excused myself to make manners with the women at the other end. The Judge waved me on.

Miss Maud looked up from the beans she was shelling. "Come in, Will, and have a chair. I think you know all the ladies here." I went down the line of rockers, shaking hands and getting smiles and "Nice-to-see-you's." Some smiles and greetings were more guarded than others. I suspected Zeke and I had been the topic of talk before I came. A couple of the other women had laps full of beans, and several were doing needlework.

"So, did you and Mr. McCloud have a good man-talk?" Miss Maud tried to get the talk going again. I told her we agreed on the weather and a few other big things.

"I hear that Tom and Mary Lou Davison finally agreed on that new child's name," Miss Bertie said, trying to help. "Thought he'd be out of diapers before he got a name."

"Heard that too," Miss Ina Ruth said. "Named him David Dwight for his uncles on both sides. Guess he won't have trouble rememberin' his initials. I'm glad they didn't name him junior after that first junior that died. I'm against namin' a child to take the place of another child. Seems like they tryin' to get back the one they lost."

"Well, I hear Mabel Layton is expecting again. How many is that they got now?"

"How is she going to be president of the missionary circle if she's going to be staying inside?" put in Miss Bertie again.

"They've plenty of folks at Sawmill Baptist to run the circles. I hear Brother Lawson is really pullin' them in."

"It's those hot sermons he gives. Shakes 'em up and makes 'em walk the aisle."

"I hear he's pretty hot on the Amosites, too." Someone realized I was there, and a couple glanced sideways at me. After a moment's awkward silence, the situation was rescued by Kate's arrival. She smiled and greeted the women, and they smiled. A couple looked awkward, like they weren't sure how to treat a compromised woman.

I offered to help Kate with the bag of books she had under one arm. We stopped to say hello to the Judge and went around to the side door near his end of the porch. I could hear one of the women ask Miss Maud, "Is Will courtin' Kate? Well, I never!" Kate glanced at me and winked.

Inside, she said, "That's good cover for what I want to show you." She pulled a small package from the book bag. "Let's go to the gazebo to look at these." So we left the women on the porch to look across the shady yard and street and talk some more before they went home to see about supper for their menfolks.

The package held several cheaply printed pamphlets and thin books. "I found these in the back room of the library," Kate said as she handed them to me. "They never were put out for circulation." I looked at the dust on them.

"They look like biographies of Amos Caruthers. I looked them over quickly and stuck them in the little bag. Mrs. Bennington was in the front looking at women's magazines and called me. I didn't want her to look for me or start asking questions."

I thumbed through them. A page or two looked like storytelling, all right.

"I wondered if these had any connection to Zeke Morgan. They're some kind of Amosite writings. I don't know how they got into the library holdings. Came before I did, I guess. Margaret Lanham kept the place before I took over, but she opened the library just when she felt like it, and the place was a mess. I doubt she knew what was there. Anyway, I can't see her as an Amosite."

"Can I take them home and read them?" I asked. "They might say something useful."

"That's why I brought them. You'd better keep them out of sight, though. I don't know if anybody else knows about them. Or thinks they're safely hidden."

I looked at her in the late afternoon shade of the gazebo. Her lips and eyes were smiling. She looked pleased to be in on a secret. I thought it was a face a man would be glad to gaze into in lots of settings. The shape and slope of her body as she sat on the bench made a study in grace.

"We ought not waste those ladies' ideas," I said.

She laughed and nudged me in the side. "You've got reading to do. What kind of lawyer are you, working up a case on me?"

We sat and talked some more until Miss Maud called out the side door for Kate to get ready for supper and asked me to stay. I said I didn't want to wear out my welcome and went back to my rooms to read some pamphlets.

They were about Amos Caruthers, all right, but not biographies. Amos was the central figure, and there were several episodes about his life happenings, but mostly there were stories about marvelous things he was supposed to have done or said, and I began to feel shivery. They weren't talking about a backwoods preacher. They were talking about some kind of divine spirit that spoke through Amos and used his body a while. The things said about him weren't what you could verify as historical evidence but things that pointed up his possession by that divine spirit. Things that should have happened whether they did or not. I wondered if he would recognize himself in the writings.

One pamphlet was written, so it said, by Lemuel Barnes, a former Presbyterian missionary. It called for worldwide proclamation of the teachings and example of Amos Caruthers. It had the form and sound of a catechism. Another was written by "Mason Brewer, M.D." and claimed all kinds of mysterious healings by Amos. According to that one, Amos must have gone from one catastrophe to another. I found right interesting one done by an old soldier, Lucas Cates. He claimed that Amos had foreseen the end of the world as we know it, all brought about by gigantic battles described in considerable grisly detail. Millions would die, and Amos's spirit would be left to brood over the remains. A woman wrote another, if the name Estelle Collins, mentioned incidentally, could be credited. She claimed that Amos had a vision that woman preachers would be the great carriers of his spirit. And all of them claimed they were written through divine inspiration.

I looked over the pamphlets again. No printer or publisher was named, and the type and paper indicated they probably hadn't come from the same source. But they showed some signs of editing by various hands. A patch here and there had a different style, and the transitions sometimes didn't work. It might stretch your belief to think the writer named was in every case the writer in fact.

But where was Zeke Morgan in all this? Had he put the pamphlets in the library? Were they there waiting to be discovered at the right time? Right now I had more mysteries than discoveries. I had a hard time getting to sleep that night. On the edge of sleep the faces of Zeke and Kate and the imagined faces of old Lem and Mason and Lucas and Estelle kept parading by with secret looks.

Early next morning before the sun was over the trees, I headed for the office to finish those contracts before going to the jail to see Zeke again. As I passed the McClouds' I saw Miss Maud working in her garden. She had flowers, but also vegetables. Even though her family had been in town for a generation, she still remembered country ways and had to have her growing things. She had Mose Banks off in the corner doing some heavy work. We tipped hats, and I gave her good morning. She said she was sorry the ladies had not been more cordial. The town was just too tense, she thought, and hoped this Zeke Morgan business would go away before Richard came home for Emma's wedding. Weddings were such nice occasions, she said, smiling. I agreed they were and said I needed to get some work done too.

Jeb Billings was still in his morning grumps when I got to the jail but said the traffic was picking up. Zeke already had one visitor. Zeke introduced his caller as Simon Dunaway. I tried to remember where I had heard his name. Was it connected with those pamphlets? Dunaway was large and looked somehow worn around the edges but had a good-humored smile and blue eyes you would almost call merry.

"Glad to meet you, Mr. Ford. I came by to cheer up Zeke. I'm glad to see he's got another friend like you. We need all the friends we can find these days."

After a bit more small talk, something about getting those papers to the right people, he called Jeb and let himself out. I wondered what "we" he was talking about.

Zeke had a puzzled look. He must have learned from Dunaway that the friends he thought were paying for his defense had not talked to me. After his openness the other day, he acted cautious and maybe secretive.

I told him I had looked up his land records and asked about the mystery plot jutting over into Brand County. I asked why that plot had been exempted from the mortgage. He kept shifting about on his bunk, crossing and uncrossing his legs, and wouldn't give me a straight answer.

Finally he said, "You need to talk to Mr. J. C. Morgan in Waxahachie, Texas. He can tell you."

"That's a long way to go for an answer. Can't you tell me?"

But he wouldn't. Seemed to get more uncomfortable the more we talked. I tried going over again the events before and during the time Julius Meadows was shot. In terser form, he told the same story he had told before. But he did recollect one point.

"I mind now, 'bout a week before I got the grippe, I seen somebody crossin' the land. He, or maybe they, got away in the thicket before I could get up to 'em. Had hobnail boots, I could tell that. Wish I was more of a tracker."

It wasn't much and just raised more questions. I thought I'd better try at the other end of the puzzle and find out how things looked from the Meadows' angle.

Kidd Saunders was the Meadows' lawyer and provided about as much help as I expected. Meadows' papers were not available. Tied up in probate, he said with a nasty smile. "When you going to give this up, Will? It's all against you."

I'd had some cards run off with my name and "Attorney-at-Law" printed on them. I sent one with a note to Mrs. Cornelia Meadows, the widow, asking for permission to call. Wanted to be proper. After a couple of frosty days in midsummer, she returned my card with a message on the back: "You may call at ten o'clock Tuesday. C. M. M."

I was at her door at ten o'clock Tuesday. Her maid let me in and showed me to a sunny parlor. Mrs. Meadows was waiting on the sofa. I'd not met her before. She was a handsome but severe looking woman in gray, not mourning black, with her hair done up in what I took to be classic Roman style. I tried to remember the pictures in my history books. She offered me coffee from the silver pot on the low table and asked what was the purpose of my call.

I told her I was Zeke Morgan's defense attorney. She said she knew. I said I was trying to find out what exactly went on between Zeke and Mr. Meadows and wondered if he ever mentioned business to her. I tried to suggest she must have had an interest in being familiar with her husband's business. She said, rather formally, that

Mr. Meadows was all business, went by bankers' rules, and made no exceptions. Up to that point Zeke was a zero in her remarks. She could have said the same about anyone. Then as I was getting ready to leave, she came down to particulars. "I will say, Mr. Ford, that Mr. Meadows said he enjoyed his meetings with Mr. Morgan when he went there to assess his property." She left hanging in air the question of how Zeke could have presumed on her husband's charity.

Before the maid could show me out, a young woman stepped out of one of the rooms opening to the hallway. She was attractive, no doubt about that, and had her hair done in that same classic Roman style.

"Mr. Ford. I'm Julia Meadows. May I talk with you before you leave?" The house suddenly didn't seem so severe.

We sat on the shady piazza with several lacy green potted plants around us. Her blonde hair hanging from the back of her Roman coiffure swayed gently as she moved lightly. Her face and blue eyes were lively. She said she was home from Randolph-Macon because of her father's death. It was also summer vacation, I remembered.

"I know why you came, Mr. Ford, and I doubt Mama gave you much satisfaction." I nodded in agreement.

"Daddy talked with me, too. Sometimes I think more than with Mama." I wondered if she had listened to the talk in the other room.

"I think you might like to know that Daddy once told me he wondered if Mr. Morgan knew what was on his land. He didn't say more, but that made me wonder what he knew." I asked a few questions about the occasion for his remark, but she really didn't know more. She wasn't finished talking, though.

She said I should call her Julia. Miss Meadows was too formal, and Miss Julia was too old for her. She missed her father a great deal. She missed reading Latin with him. Her father was really a classical scholar but hid that from his business friends. He sometimes saw himself as a reincarnated Roman of the Republic and acted like a paterfamilias, but she could never remember to call him Pater. He was Daddy and a friend. I might have noticed that both Mama and she had Roman names. In his mind Julius was a true patrician of the Republic, both Roman and American. He deplored the turn of the nation to imperial ways as the Romans had turned. I thought of the Philippine war. She said Julius thought it was no wonder that mystery cults flourished when the nations became imperial. She wondered what mystery cults he meant. She didn't know of any Cybeles. She wished she could study classics in Germany the way I had studied there. I wondered how much else the town had said about me. She hoped we could talk some more and I could tell her about German universities. Not an unattractive prospect, I thought. The audience would be better than the subject.

The maid came out on the piazza and said Miss Meadows was wanted inside. She stood, smiled up at me, shook hands, and said she hoped we'd meet again. I noted she cut a pert figure in her gray silky dress as she went inside.

That evening I had to drive out to Jake Tilley's to clear up some details on the contract. As I came back into town in the dark, my headlamps caught some dark figures as I turned the corner at Harrington's Feed Store. Looked like three men beating on a fourth pushed against the wall. I held my lights on them and shouted I was ready to shoot. Hoped they didn't know I carried no gun. The three ran into the dark, and after looking around for a minute I went to see the one slumped against the wall. It was Rufe Johnson, the porter at Meadows' bank. He was bloody on his arms and had a bloody bruise on the side of his head but didn't look hurt badly. Must have used his arms to protect his head.

"Mistah Will, is that you?"

"Rufe, it's Will. Are you hurt bad? Do you need to go to a doctor?"

"Nah. Jus' get me home if you will."

As I carried Rufe to his place, he said the men who hit him claimed they were punishing him for immorality. Said he was living with his dead wife's sister and her children. Told him to leave town or else. Then he said he was no longer porter at the bank, had been fired. When I asked why, he said he wasn't sure but maybe he knew too much. He remembered that Meadows' office had been broken into a little bit before he was shot. Sheriff Callahan had said burglars had been looking for money, but he had seen the safe and it was all right. Soon as Kidd Saunders took custody of the bank after Meadows was shot, they fired him. Now maybe firing him wasn't enough. They wanted to get him out of town.

As I let Rufe out at his place, I told him he ought to keep low for a while. Couldn't tell who was around the next corner. Next morning I found both headlamps on my car had been smashed.

So, what a day. Seems I had found out more about Julius Meadows than about Zeke Morgan. Julius at least looked defendable. He liked talking with Zeke. He thought something was on Zeke's property, maybe something Zeke didn't know about. And somebody thought something was in Julius' office and didn't want Rufe talking about it. My guess was that Julius did extend Zeke's note, and did it in writing, and somebody broke into Julius' office to get it but didn't. Then somebody tried again and got Julius instead. Who was that somebody, and why was that extension so valuable to anybody but Zeke? Kidd Saunders seemed to be the front man, but who was behind him? And somebody didn't want me looking around corners.

∞

I thought it was time to make another late-night call on Josh Walker and see if he was willing to pay to follow up on what Zeke had said about seeing J. C. Morgan in Texas. I took a chance on finding him there without sending a note ahead. It worked. He was at his desk and dressed like he was ready for work.

"You did right, Will, coming without getting anybody else involved. I don't know who's passing reports on you or to who. But you're being watched. Somebody is afraid of what you'll find."

I told him about the strange plot of land over in Brand County, how Zeke had been evasive about the exemption on the mortgage, and how he finally said J. C. Morgan in Waxahachie, Texas, could tell me. So did his hire extend to cover a trip to Texas?

"'Course it does, Will. I want you to get to the bottom of this. I'll get some cash for you and send it in a plain envelope. No return address, no checks. You'd best not let anybody know where you're going. Fact, you ought not to buy a ticket to Texas from here. Ticket agent might be in on the plot. Just get a ticket to a town big enough they don't know you, and get the ticket for Texas there." After the headlamps, I saw his point.

"Guess you know," he went on, "there's a lot of unfriendly talk about you in Cromwell. I hear it and let them talk. I hear it when builders and carpenters are talking among themselves at the company. You seem to be a threat to lots of folks, and I'm not sure they know why. They seem to quote Brother so-and-so or Pastor whatever. The preachers are down on you. So watch your back."

The plain envelope came two days later. I went to the library to look up where Waxahachie, Texas was and try to figure which line would get me there. Kate was at the desk but gave a nod toward someone in the reading room and treated me as librarian to citizen. I played the game. I looked at so many books even she couldn't know about destination Waxahachie.

Walker's warning had put me on edge. I hadn't realized that opposition to my defense of Zeke was so wide or deep. Kidd Saunders must have been right when he said Cromwell was against me. Before I left for Texas, I thought, I'd better see the Judge. He moved about in circles that Josh Walker missed. He might know who was making things happen. And since I was a known caller at the McClouds' for Kate, so the women thought, talking with the Judge might not be suspect.

So I went to the McClouds' at courting time. Didn't tell him, of course, about Josh's warning or my Texas trip. But I did tell about the smashed headlamps without getting Rufe's story involved. The Judge pulled a long time on his cigar and said yes, he'd heard talk by several merchants that I was making Cromwell look bad, especially to the railroad people. Cousin Malcolm McDonald at the general store, he remembered, had said I was becoming an embarrassment to the kin. He hadn't heard any ministers talk about me but wouldn't be surprised if they did. Well, he did remember Mr. Barton from the Methodist Church speak sorrowfully about the poison spirit in town and wonder if it ought to be mentioned in his prayers.

"I wouldn't be upset about the headlamps, Will. It could be a prank by some of the young hellions. They might resent you have a car and they don't."

I could tell that the Judge didn't know any particulars. Maybe folks thought he was too close to me to tell him their secrets. Anyway, now he might keep his eyes and ears open.

I asked Kate if she would like to watch the moon from the front porch. She laughed and said she didn't know I had gone sentimental. But she went. We sat in the rockers until the moon got over the porch roof. She asked what I was doing with all those books at the library. I almost told her about Texas but said, like a joke, I had just been trying to see her. That really made her laugh. Then she said, "Let's go inside."

In the sitting room, she pulled a parcel of pamphlets from that book bag. "Here are some more papers I found in the back room at the library. Again no known donor." She was serious now.

In the lamplight, we examined the pamphlets. Like those she had found before, these named no printer and were on cheap paper. Different though—these named no author or presumed author but all looked to be by the same hand. They didn't sound like the writer knew about what old Lemuel and Mason and Lucas and Estelle had written. In fact, they sounded like they had been written before the others had been. They were about Amos Caruthers, though. Instead of stories, they presented arguments that Amos was the body of the Holy Spirit, not just a speaker for it or him or her. They were tight, well-reasoned arguments, the kind the Judge said lawyers ought to prepare but seldom do. The pamphlets all but said Amos didn't know how special he was but did say it was up to folks like the writer and the readers to tell the world about their special revelation. Some of the pamphlets went into particulars about how to tell about and act according to their special knowledge and called on the spirit of Amos to give them power. They began to sound like law giving.

Again I began to get shivery. I looked up, and Kate was looking at me. Her face was serious. "They sound like something Walter Cornelius wrote," she said.

How do you know about Walter Cornelius? I thought.

She must have read my look.

"When I was at Normal," she said, "a group of the girls talked about Walter Cornelius. They were from good families, not backwoods types. They were probably just saying what they'd heard at home. Anyway, they told about how he tried to take over the Amos followers and then push them out while his people took charge. He made something different from what the movement was at the beginning."

All right, I thought. That's pretty general. You seem to know more. You seem to know the man behind the style.

"What was Cornelius like?"

Kate was vague about any personal knowledge of Cornelius. She talked about politics of the Amosites and Cornelians, always what somebody else had said. The more she talked, the more general the knowledge. I left that evening feeling like another mystery had jumped up at me.

∞

Next morning, to follow up on the Texas lead, I went to see Zeke Morgan again and ask him how to find this J. C. Morgan in Waxahachie. Jeb's only comment this time was, "Here again?" Zeke was already shaved and had on fresh clothes. Looked like he was expecting someone, and I knew it wasn't me. Zeke was more helpful than last time I came and gave me a ready answer.

"You need to see Mr. C. K. Bean. He's a lawyer there and can tell you how to find Mr. Morgan. Morgan lives out in the county, I reckon."

While I wrote that in my little black book, he asked, "How's your search comin' along? You goin' to get me outta here?"

"Too early to tell," I said. "Lots of loose ends to follow out. For one thing, how well did you know Julius Meadows? Did he talk much with you? Anything more than talk across the desk about your note?"

"We talked some, time he came out to the farm to look it over."

"Just once?"

"Coupla times maybe. He was all right. Seemed like a decent man. A little stiff, maybe, but straight." He grinned. "I didn't have no doubts about him carryin' my note. Thought we might be singin' the same tune."

"Did he ever ask about or look at that piece of land over in Brand?"

"He looked once. Said it looked good."

"Know what he meant by that? It wasn't part of the land he had a mortgage on. Why did he look?"

"Just curious, I reckon. He's a banker—or was. Always seemed to be lookin' at the future of things."

About that time, the cell door clanged open and Simon Dunaway came in.

"Hey! Will Ford, ain't it?"

"That's right," Zeke said. "You know each other already. I remember now."

I wondered what the connection was between Zeke and Simon. Besides "old friends."

Simon soon let me know. "Zeke, I bring you greetings and good wishes in prison from your friends in Bristol."

"Thank 'em for me, will you?"

"Mr. Ford, good to see you. I was just goin' to tell Zeke how all the folks in Bristol are followin' his case. They his friends and fellow believers. All true followers of the way revealed by great Amos."

"Amen," said Zeke.

Simon was on a roll and didn't stop. "They know the way of true believers is filled with sorrow in this world. They know the persecutions of the righteous. They know Zeke is on trial for his faith and are with him in spirit right here in this prison. They—"

"Simon, let him talk."

"Yes, a'course. Let's be practical. How's Zeke's defense comin', Mr. Ford? You learned yet who done it?"

"Not yet. This town is clammed up. Everybody talks, but not to me. They've got their minds made up. Going to be hard to find a jury that won't convict Zeke. Some talk I pick up, they'd like to convict his lawyer, too."

Simon laughed long at that. "Watch out, you'll get to be one of us 'fore it's over."

"I remember you talked about great Amos. What about Walter Cornelius? Are you folks Amosites or Cornelians or both?"

"Ah, Cornelius! I'm gettin' my doubts about him. He's one of us, and then he ain't. Some folks is callin' him a usurper. That's a fancy word for tryin' to take over things."

"You said folks in Bristol are following Zeke's case. Do they know anything about your doings, Zeke? Like where you were when Meadows was shot? Or what they know about your land?"

"Maybe they might."

"It's worth a try, Mr. Ford," Simon said. "Why don't you come over and I'll show you around. They might talk to you if I come with you."

So I decided to go to Bristol and talk with Zeke's friends. That's when I saw the runaway train and met Simon again, sooner than I expected.

∞

While we sat on the bench at the crew station, Simon told how the train had a bunch of Amosites on board. They had been to a gathering of Amosites from other parts of the state. Now somebody was trying to get rid of them, too. I realized the danger and the plot were bigger than just with Zeke at Cromwell. And the Amosites were more widespread than I knew.

As we waited for the engineer to come back with word about help on the way, Simon talked on. He told how he and others wrote pamphlets calling on the Amosites to resist the ministers of the big churches and their fellow persecutors in the government. They saw the combination as an ungodly plot to bring about the destruction of the world. They had visions foreseeing the end of the world and called on true believers to prepare for the end. They saw demonic forces rising in the nation and in Europe. Simon wondered if there was some safe place from the cataclysm to come.

As I listened, I thought there was a cagey brain and maybe more learning than first appeared in his folksy manner. Cataclysm. Not a weekday word.

I wondered if the pamphlets could give any clues about Zeke's involvement with the Amosites. Or the Cornelians. "Would I be able to see some of those pamphlets?" I asked.

"Don't know why not. Fact, I'd like you to. But be warned, they might bring you to the true light."

"I'll take the chance. When can I get them?"

"I'll send 'em to you. Plain envelope, no return address. Don't want the folks in Cromwell to know what you're readin'. Just write your box number on this slip. No name needed."

I decided to make the best of my chance meeting with Simon. He could lead me to those Amosites in Bristol, and I wouldn't have to be so obvious in looking for them. "Can you take me to your friends in Bristol?"

"Meet me there in two days. I need to help the folks on the train right now." He gave me directions on how to find him.

When I got back to Cromwell, I had a visitor. I felt a shadow at the door of my office, looked up, and saw Wayne Bosley standing there. He seemed to be looking around the office more than at me.

"Wayne," I said, "what will the county clerk have?"

"I come with a question, Will."

"What can I answer? You're not looking for legal advice, are you?"

"No, official this time. Did Zeke Morgan give you any papers about his mortgage with Julius Meadows that should be officially recorded?"

"What kind?"

"Whatever. Any letters or documents that might be legally binding." He's fishing, I thought.

"Don't remember any. Kidd Saunders says all the papers are tied up in probate. I'll probably have to get a court order to see them myself."

"I'm talking about papers in Morgan's possession. I could get a court order to secure them."

"That's Billy Eustis' department, isn't it? Prosecution and defense have to share discoveries, don't they?"

"That's for you lawyers to say. I just need to keep the official records complete."

"I appreciate that. Actually I do. I'd like to find a paper like that, too."

"I may be getting back to you. The bank's attorneys may petition for an order to search Morgan's papers."

"Good luck to them. I'd like to be in on the search."

"Right." He stood there a minute more as if he wanted to say something else, then turned around and left.

Two days later, I was in Bristol and found Simon's rooming house without any trouble. It was in a neighborhood of small houses: some were neatly kept, some had seen better days, and some larger ones had been made into rooming houses. Some of the houses looked like farm houses built in town. They and some of the people in the yards had a country look about them.

"Here you be, all right." Simon met me in the parlor and introduced me to his landlady, Mrs. Rogers, as "a friend." She looked at me with a question in her eyes and said she hoped I had a good visit. She had probably noted my lawyer suit and thought I didn't look as countrylike as most of her roomers.

The first Amosite Simon took me to was Jeremiah Clegg. Jeremiah sounded like his namesake, that wild-eyed prophet in the Old Testament, and looked like him too, I'd think. He came the closest I'd ever known to someone having fire in his eyes. He was a long, thin man with big hands, big feet, and big ears that were partly hidden in long, wild hair. We found him in a small house at the end of a dirt street. Somehow you got the feeling he'd been pushed back there. He was ready to talk, though, once Simon told him I was Zeke Morgan's defense in Cromwell.

Jeremiah had had trouble with the law. He'd been persecuted into jail, he said, and hated preachers and police. He had written his pamphlet while he was in jail and was ready to talk about it, too. He explained how present tribulations of the righteous were the work of demons in government and religion, and he looked forward to their fiery ends when judgment came. He had lively visions of angels making them suffer and called on true believers to resist preachers and police. He looked forward to some kind of divine interruption of the evil world and looked forward with considerable satisfaction to the destruction of the present world. I could tell this world was not his home and was glad to get away when Simon said we had to move on. No help for Zeke at that stop.

We stopped at a corner cafe for smoked pork sandwiches and coffee. Simon munched his bread and meat and for once was not talkative. I contributed to the silence.

Our next call was on the Reverend Reid Bethune, retired pastor of a good-size church across the state line. We found his house on a tree-lined, brick-paved street in one of the better parts of town, a neat bungalow with flowers in the yard and books on the shelves and tables. He was both gentle and genteel, you sensed, with a kindly smile and a courtly manner. But his eyes were sad. Simon introduced me again as Zeke's defense attorney, but added that I was interested in Zeke's fellowship with followers of the way of Amos. Reverend Bethune smiled sadly and said he hoped he could help.

The reverend told how he had ministered to several churches in the nearby states since his graduation from seminary decades before. As he moved from one church to the next, usually with a step up in prestige and salary, he became increasingly dissatisfied with his work and his congregations. His people were just going through the motions, saying what they thought they were supposed to say and finding nothing real in their spiritual lives. He was afraid that was true for him, too. He began to feel his ministry was a sham. Then he met Amos Caruthers and got a new vision and a new sense of purpose. Amos, a man of obscure backcountry birth, had a message and a presence that complacent folk in the towns needed to bring them alive. But they and their ministers resisted the new way. Unlike Jeremiah Clegg, though, he urged readers of his pamphlets to endure persecution by the authorities and have faith that their way would win out in the end, for they were the chosen few. The key, he said, was for them to help each other.

I saw he was ready to talk more, and he was interesting all right, but I needed to know about Zeke Morgan.

"He was a close friend of Amos, I believe, and visited him not long before he was killed, martyred I'd say. But what their business was I wouldn't know. I was here in Bristol when Amos died. One of the brothers later mentioned Zeke's visit."

"Would you know anything about Zeke's land or the mortgage on his land?" I asked.

"Not really. I had the idea Zeke thought his land was something special. But I never knew why. Maybe because his wife was buried there."

"Did he ever say anything about the mortgage on his land? Was he worried about losing his land?"

"Not that I could tell. We didn't talk about mortgages. He never acted worried about his land. Never mentioned that."

"Did he ever talk about trouble with the law in Cromwell?"

"He said he'd had a few run-ins with lawmen because he got folks excited about his preaching on the streets. They ran him off and told him not to come back. He laughed it off, though. I urged him to teach the way quietly and avoid breaking the law. He said he'd think about it."

"Did Zeke ever say he was being persecuted because of his preaching?"

"Oh, yes. He thought the town ministers and sheriff were all against him. He didn't mind, though. Said he wouldn't mind being a martyr but needed to get his other work done first."

"What other work?"

"He didn't say. I didn't ask."

Simon seemed to think we'd spent enough time with Bethune. Said we had more bases to touch. Bethune smiled at his analogy and said he hoped we scored. We made our manners with the courtly man and left.

Instead of taking me to other writers of pamphlets, Simon took me to more pamphlets. We went to a dusty office at the back of a feed store, and Simon spread out seven pamphlets on a table that had served as somebody's writing table, with pens and ink pots at the back. I asked what they were. He pointed to three, or maybe five, and said they were more testimonies about Amos. Some were too fanciful to believe, he said, and some were just plain wrong. The brothers and sisters needed to sift through them and decide which were worth keeping. Pray about it and decide, he said. They needed to gather the believers and come to a general agreement about them. He didn't expect agreement to be easy. Different believers had different views on which writings showed the right way to present Amos and his teachings and what he meant. Some wanted the meanings to determine what the facts should be. Disputes had grown hot at times, and Zeke was in the middle of the disputes and showed his temper toward the brothers and sisters.

"Does that mean Zeke had enemies among the brothers?"

Simon gave a wry chuckle. "They sure had hot words at times. But not enemies, I'd say. Jus' less lovin' toward him. Folks do color their views with talk about the man. You don't like his arguments, you don't like the man. You lawyers know about that, don't you?"

"Would any of them have anything to do with Zeke and his land or his mortgage?"

"I doubt it. Folks in Bristol don't have much to do with Cromwell. Too far away. It's a long trip for me to visit Zeke."

"You said the other day you brought greetings from Zeke's friends in Bristol. That sounded like somebody here was keeping up with his case. What friends did you mean?"

"Brother Bethune mainly. And he has friends among the believers. But I might've laid it on a bit thick to cheer up Zeke. Not all the folks in Bristol sent greetings. They know about him as a test case. What happens to him might happen to them. There's opposition here, too."

"Like what?"

"Folks get their notes called at the bank. Some don't get no more credit at the store. Some get pushed off the sidewalk. Some get their houses or gates splashed with paint. Preachers tell their folks to shun the brothers. Little children get taunted at school."

"Sounds like Cromwell."

"Right. It's more general than you'd think."

I could tell Simon had done and said about all he could today. I asked him to keep in mind the need to clear Zeke and let me know if he learned anything about who killed Julius Meadows and why. He said he would send the pamphlets in a plain envelope. I asked him to let me see the disputed ones too. We shook hands, and I headed for the station to catch the 6:15 train to Cromwell.

I had hardly gotten settled in my office the next day before the errand boy from the library brought a note from Kate: "New developments. Come to supper at six. K."

The Judge looked a little grim, I thought, when he met me on the porch. "Glad to see you, Will. Come on in. We need to talk." Miss Maud said she hoped I had a good trip. Emma, she said, was having supper with Harry's family and talking about the coming wedding. Kate came into the parlor with a mischievous gleam in her eye. She also looked great in a late summer dress that hinted at curves beneath it. I lifted my eyebrows and she grinned.

After the Judge had rushed through a blessing and the serving dishes had been passed around the table and we were looking at full plates, the Judge asked how my trip to Bristol went. I told him how Simon took me to Jeremiah's and Reverend Bethune's and let me see some Amosite pamphlets but said it didn't look like anything definite came from the trip. Lots of background information, though.

"We've had sad times here, Will," the Judge said. "Tell him, Kate, what's happened."

"The library's been closed. The trustees say they want to renovate the building and make it worthy of Cromwell. But they also want to purge it of undesirable materials and get new books with help from the Carnegie Fund."

"What does that really mean?"

"They're looking for Amosite writings and using the renovation as an excuse to find them and get rid of them."

"Let me guess who's behind it," I said.

"You don't need to. Kidd Saunders is leading the way, with several of the big ministers cheering him on. Including our own."

The Judge was getting purple by this time. "That I cannot understand. How could our Mr. Bascomb lend his authority to such an outrageous undertaking! He's never been one to stifle spiritual inquiry. He's let himself become a tool of Saunders' political ambitions!"

"Now, Mr. McCloud, watch yourself," Miss Maud cautioned. "You'll work yourself into a stroke."

"She's right, Papa," Kate said. "It will even out after a while."

"And my daughter has been shut out of the library," the Judge went on. "She's been put on leave of absence while Saunders has his own people in there poking around and throwing out."

"It happened pretty fast," I said. "I haven't been gone that long."

"Yesterday morning Kidd and Mr. Bascomb walked in without warning and said the trustees had decided to close the place for repairs. I was told I was on leave of absence until further notice. They locked the doors as I left."

"Sounds like it had been planned quite a while," I said.

"Sure does." The Judge hit the table. "And I hadn't heard a lick about it. Where are my friends these days? Why didn't somebody tell me what was going on?"

"Please, Mr. McCloud!" Miss Maud was getting alarmed.

"When I walked by there yesterday afternoon, the builders already had scaffolding going up, and several people were going in and out of the back door." Kate was near tears.

"Some of Kidd's cronies," the Judge said. "He's trying to make a political issue out of the library. Last night he made a speech at the town merchants' dinner. Said we need to get rid of books that will taint our children. Several ministers were there leading the applause."

"He wants to run for the state assembly," Kate said. "And he knows how to get the voters excited."

We sat there silent for a minute. Auntie Bess came up behind Miss Maud. "All right if I take off the dishes now, ma'am?"

"Yes, thank you, Bess. I'll serve the pie later."

We sat at the table another half hour. The coffee was better than at Simon's corner cafe, and the talk got lighter as the evening darkened. The Judge had cooled down, and Miss Maud was telling a funny story about the army that Richard had written in one of his letters. The Judge must have been nursing his grudge against preachers involved with Kidd Saunders. Reverend Thaxton, he said, was not much of a preacher. He used the Joshua-at-Jericho approach. Just marched around the subject seven times and blew loudly.

"Papa, that one's got more whiskers than the Smith brothers," Kate said, but smiled.

"That's my Kate," he said. "My most honest critic."

I wasn't sure how much Kate had told the Judge and Miss Maud about the pamphlets she had found in the back room at the library. I thought I'd better get off the library subject before I said too much. I couldn't tell them about my Texas trip plans. But I needed to let them know I'd be out of town. So I said I had some business down state and would be gone several days and not to worry. "Hope nothing exciting happens this time while I'm gone," I joked. I wished later I hadn't said that.

We finally ate that pie. I thanked them for the supper and the news and went home to get ready for my trip. I found myself wishing I didn't have to wait so long to see Kate again.

∞

Later the next morning I had a visit from an older woman almost in tears. I hurried around the desk to clear a chair for her.

"I'm Ella Poteat," she said between dabs at her eyes.

"Yes ma'am. I remember your boy Hogan. Played first base on the high school team. Hope he's doing well."

"Doing fine, thanks. But he's not my worry. It's my husband Cal—Calvin you may remember. I can't find his will. He's had a stroke and can't talk or move. I keep askin' him where's his will, and all he does is just look at me. I know he can't last long. One of these days he'll just breathe one more time and stop. Then everything'll be bottled up. We have bills and taxes to pay or we lose the place. You know how the law is. Everything gets put in the man's name and wives get left with the leavin's."

"The state provides ways for folks who die intestate."

"I know that. I saw what happened to my sister. It took forever to get her property cleared, and the courts got most of that."

"Sometimes it comes to that if your affairs are tangled."

"What can I do? Could we make a new will and have someone sign and notarize it?"

"It would still be better if you could find the will. Do you know how your husband thinks? Could you ask him some yes or no questions and interpret his looks as yes or no until you get an idea about where to look?"

"That might work. Well as I know, he had papers scattered about in places, and I'd have to think of places I'd put papers if I was in his place. He was a friend of Zeke Morgan's. That's why I come to you. They talked some about Amos Caruthers, and he read some of Zeke's papers about Amos. I can't find them papers, either. I thought maybe you might know where to look, seein' how's you're defendin' Zeke. Cal might've put the will with Zeke's papers."

I wondered for a moment if she was fishing too, but figured she was more worried about wills than mortgages. Then I wondered if Cal had put those pamphlets in the dusty corner of the library, where Kate had found them.

"I haven't seen any papers of Zeke's yet, Mrs. Poteat. If there were any, Billy Eustis probably searched for them, and he's obliged to share them with me if he found any. I'll keep in mind your worry if I get to see any papers. Meantime, you'd better try to think like your husband. What would he do? I'd say you've got a job of interpreting to do."

"I reckon you're right, and I'll give it a try. Not much else I can do." You and me both, I thought.

"Good luck then, Mrs. Poteat. We'll stay in touch."

"Thank you, Will. I wish you luck with Zeke." She gave me a sad smile and left.

∞

After a couple of days while I finished up some contracts, I caught the train to Raleigh. Jeb Billings and another train watcher saw me off at the station. Jeb asked when I was coming to see Zeke again. Zeke kept asking after me, he said. I told him that was between my client and me. I wouldn't be gone long.

At the capital, I waited in the station cafe until the slow time between trains to get my ticket. There was no line at the ticket window, no familiar face nearby, and the agent was nobody I knew. So I used some of Josh's money to buy a ticket to Atlanta. I would buy the rest of the trip from there. Somehow I kept thinking back to Cromwell instead of what might lie ahead in Waxahachie. I knew faces in Cromwell. J. C. Morgan and C. K. Bean were just names, like Waxahachie. I tried to imagine what Zeke Morgan was thinking as he waited for his trial. I couldn't decide whether he had been calling for me or whether Jeb's comment was another of his taunts. I wondered what Kate was doing while the library was closed. Probably finding out who among her school friends were still friends.

The ride to Atlanta was almost pleasant. The green countryside slid by and showed the effect of late summer rains. We rolled through small towns with their unpaved streets and stopped several times at mill towns with their red brick factories and high windows to take on freight. The dining car attendant came through the coach to announce lunch in ten minutes. They had lunch and dinner, not dinner and supper, on this train.

In the dining car, I sat with a businessman from Atlanta. We both had the daily special plate of pork chops, snap beans, and rice with gravy. I wondered where they picked up fresh snap beans for a rolling eatery like this. I asked the waiter when he came to refill our coffee cups. "In Bal'more, suh. They brings 'em to the station. We loaded two hampers." He poured the coffee with a flourish, smiled genially, and hoped we had a good dinner. You're from down south, I thought.

Since there was no line waiting to be served, the man from Atlanta and I lingered over our coffee. He had introduced himself as Ralph Shaw, in textile machinery. He said Atlanta was moving right along since the exposition a few years ago. It had brought in good business. Money people up north had seen the opportunities and were building factories where the cheap labor was. He was worried about labor unions coming in, though, and hoped the factory hands would see how the owners would look after them. Didn't need any outside agitators, he said. Didn't want unrest like they were having up north. No Socialists need apply, he said. He hardly asked about my business, and I didn't burden him with details. I left extra on the tip for our down-south waiter.

In Atlanta I bought the ticket for Waxahachie, with changes in New Orleans and Shreveport. Since the run to New Orleans would be overnight, I got a Pullman berth. The porter helped stow my bags and agreed to give me an early call so I could see the morning come into the low country. Sometime during the night we rolled through Montgomery and Jackson, and I could hear the voices outside the train.

As we rolled into Louisiana, I looked across the wide, flat fields, many still wet with a night rain. We passed through Covington, with its big houses and high pines like a canopy over town. "Rich folks running from the New Orleans heat," the porter said.

It was hot in New Orleans, all right. The palms on streets and in courtyards, together with the fancy iron grillwork on the older buildings, made it feel like a foreign place. I tried the Creole seafood and rice and had French coffee in a restaurant near the station and thought how different it was from dinner at the McClouds'. Kate would have liked it, I thought. She had a zest for new things. I walked for a couple of hours while I waited for the ride to Shreveport. Even the English sounded different here. Sort of had a

French lilt. I tried some more of the coffee, heavy with chicory, and watched the blacks move along the pavement with the whites, most dressed in summer whites with bright-colored sashes on the women and bright bands on the men's hats. Parasols shaded them from the sun, but the moist heat clung to everybody. The waiter said there would be music nearby after dark. Dixieland, he said, and moved his fingers like a piano player.

On the run to Shreveport, we went through several heavy stands of pine as we climbed into red clay country. Near Mansfield I could see oil derricks through breaks in the pines and pools of oily water near some. The man across the aisle said wildcatters from Beaumont were looking to new fields to explore. The rigs at Beaumont were beginning to fall into the hands of big money men. The little men had to reach out now. He said he was in the oil lease business. Had to find the owners of likely sites and get them to sign leases on a contingency clause. I told him I had some interest in the law and wondered how the contingency clause worked. He said it worked in the fine print. Always read the fine print. I said I had had some experience looking into land titles. How did they work in Louisiana? He said the Napoleonic code was a pain. Always look for the exception clause. Texas was looser about marking property lines. The law usually saw things the company's way. He relit his cigar, much to the disgust of the woman sitting behind him. She scowled and fanned.

At Shreveport the change was a quick one, and I hoped my bags made the transfer. The conductor had told me they had the bags near the door of the luggage car for a quick handoff. Going into east Texas late in the day, the train rolled through more piney woods, now with the sun slanting through the trees. The country was green and the weather hot. We put windows up and down, depending on which way the train was heading, to keep out cinders. I hoped there was a hotel or rooming house open in Waxahachie when we arrived late. Spending the night in a waiting room at the station was not a pleasant thought.

As it turned out, the train was a local and stopped at most stations even during the night. It was almost morning when we rolled into Waxahachie. I stood on the platform and saw the early light in the sky over the town. Down the platform, I saw my bags and didn't wait for a porter to get them. In the station I asked the agent about a hotel and he sent me to the Planters' House. At the hotel I waited while the night clerk came out of the back room, and I heard water flushing. Yes sir, they had rooms available. How many nights? Please register here. The restaurant would open at six. Would I like a cup of night-brewed coffee? I said I'd look down the street until the restaurant opened.

That was a better move than I expected. Not far down the street I saw C. K. Bean's sign and his office next to the bank. From the outside it had a prosperous look, with recently painted blinds to shade the morning sun. Back at the Planters' House restaurant I had some fresh-made coffee and ham and eggs and biscuits, then went to my room, settled my clothes in the wardrobe, shaved and freshened up, and waited to call on C. K. Bean.

I sent the hotel porter, burdened with a heavy tip and a note asking for an appointment. He could see me at ten o'clock, came the reply. The town had come alive with farmers pulling their wagons and shoppers turning into stores as I walked to Bean's office.

He was a large, beefy man with a heavy mustache and shrewd eyes. He had a woman typing off in a corner of the waiting room. His manner was courteous but noncommittal as we shook hands, not greatly impressed with another lawyer from back east. When I said I was interested in finding Mr. J. C. Morgan, though, his manner changed to interest, and he invited me back into his private office.

"Just what is your business with Mr. Morgan, sir?"

I told him I had been hired to defend Zeke Morgan on a murder charge, that a land title with reservations on it was involved in clearing up facts of the case, that Zeke Morgan had given me his name as a lead to finding J. C. Morgan, and that Morgan knew about the exception on the title, having been a former owner of the land in question.

"Is that all you need from Mr. Morgan?"

So I told him about Zeke Morgan being involved with the Amosites and about the way folks in Cromwell were trying to railroad Zeke into a hanging or a long prison term because of his Amosite preaching. I said that following out leads on the Amosites looked like my best chance to defend Zeke.

"I know about the Amosites, even this far out in Baptist and Campbellite country. You know, don't you, that Mr. Morgan's Christian name is Joshua Caruthers? He was kin to Amos Caruthers. Collateral family, I believe."

"No. Zeke didn't tell me that."

"Well, it's so. I can see now, Mr. Ford, that you do need to talk to him. I have another client coming in at eleven, but my afternoon's free. You'd better let me take you out to Morgan's. You'd not likely find it on your own. I'll stop by the Planters' at 1:30 to pick you up."

Bean's car was a Haynes Tonneau much like mine, and as we followed the dirt road to Morgan's place, we compared notes on the cars. The ride was easy, he said, and the chassis worked well with the springs to cushion against unexpected potholes and rocks in the road. He wished the steering was more reliable, though. I wished the headlamps were brighter and more focused. Then he began talking about how the county ought to take care of its roads. It relied too much on railroads, he said, and left large parts ignored. Farmers needed better roads to get their crops to market, and the oil business was beginning to move into the county and would need roads to get the oil to shippers.

As we followed several back roads, I thought it would be good to get some road signs too. Joshua Caruthers Morgan's place was better than the roads leading to it. A white clapboard house with wide porches and wide gables, it had the look of being well cared for. Fences around the house and outbuildings were painted, and the gate swung easily. Bean went up to the house first while I waited at the car and threw sticks for the dogs to bring back. After a while Morgan came out with Bean and invited me in. We sat on the porch and drank lemonade while I told him my story and ended by explaining how the title to Zeke's land was becoming an important part of the investigation. The reserved plot was especially important.

J. C. Morgan looked enough like Zeke to be his brother instead of his cousin. Same red face and dark eyes, big bony hands, and lanky. But without the zealot stare. Maybe because Bean vouched for me, he was more open in his talk than Zeke had been.

"That land has been in the Morgan family for a long time, Mr. Ford, close to a hundred years. Seems like when one Morgan died or let go, another one would take it up. Zeke took it over when I came out here. Soil's better here, and I'm glad I came, but I left good things behind, too."

"What good things?"

"That piece of land you're askin' about. Amos Caruthers was born on that plot over in Brand County. His folks have held on to that plot ever since Amos began to spread his message. First, they thought he might have to hide out there. Then after he was killed, his followers wanted to have it as a special place. Venerate it, you might say. That's what Zeke was hangin' on to it for."

"So does Zeke hold that Brand County plot too? It was excluded from the mortgage he signed with Julius Meadows. He's the banker who was shot. By Zeke, Cromwell folks say."

"Yes and no. He has title to the land, all right. But it has a lien on it that keeps it from bein' sold or taken."

"Who holds the lien? I didn't find any record of it in the county files."

"That's the catch. Walter Cornelius has it. You've heard of him, ha'nt you? And he's out of the country. I'm not sure how he got it. Through some third person, I reckon, and through some slick dealin'. He's like that, you know."

"Why does Walter Cornelius hold the lien, then?"

"Don't rightly know. I'm sure he's got somethin' in mind. He looks ahead. Whether he's for or against Amos's folks I couldn't say. Seems one way sometimes, different way another."

"Mr. Morgan is one of the county's best men," C. K. Bean said. "And he's very careful about clear titles and clear boundaries. You know we still have problems about old Spanish land grants. Back then they measured distances in donkey steps. Later in plow lines. It makes for complicated cases sometimes, and you have to know what laws you're workin' with and what are their jurisdictions."

"You said Walter Cornelius is out of the country. Where? And can he be reached?"

"He's down in Mexico. Just outside Monterrey. Some folks say he had to get out of the country to stay out of jail. I don't know about that. They might be makin' him out worse than he is."

I thought for a moment. Josh Walker had been willing to pay for me to come to Waxahachie. I reckoned he'd be willing for me to follow the trail to Monterrey.

"Could you tell me how to find Cornelius in Monterrey? I'd better not stop now."

"I think I got somethin' about him in the house. A letter a fellow wrote after seein' him there. Just a minute." He went inside.

"Looks like you got yourself a long trip," Bean said with a wry smile. "I don't envy you. It's hot as blazes gettin' there. And the Mexes aren't always friendly. You speak any Spanish?"

"Would French or German help?" I asked. He laughed.

Morgan came back out with information from the letter jotted on a slip of paper. Not real specific, but better than nothing. As we said goodbye, he said tell Zeke he'd be thinking about him.

C. K. Bean and I rode back to town watching the late afternoon sun color the clouds pink. The sky looked big, and the land looked flat and big. I thought about how much of it I'd have to cross. Bean wished me luck as he let me out at the Planters' House.

Miss Maud had asked me several times to write to her Richard down on the Mexican border and had given me his address. I still had his address and used it to send him a telegram asking him to meet me in San Antonio or Laredo if he could get furlough. Next day his answer came: MEET YOU ALAMO HOTEL SAN ANTONIO SEPTEMBER 15 RICHARD. That left me three days to get there and meet him.

∞

The train to San Antonio rolled through open grasslands and fields with some stands of timber left from the piney woods to the east, then through limestone hills covered with lower trees as we neared the city. I had no trouble getting a room at the Alamo Hotel, settled in, and bought a Spanish phrase book for tourists to study. I took time to walk around the city and watch the mixed crowd of Anglos, Mexicans, some Germans from the hill towns, and a good many army types from Fort Sam Houston. There seemed to be a good bit of army activity, trains of supplies running from the depot out to the fort, some groups of soldiers in khaki moving through town. A lot of Spanish and German spoken in the streets as well as English spoken with a drawl. A desk clerk at the hotel said tourists would come with cooler weather.

Richard came into the lobby of the hotel still dusty from his trip. He had come with a detail and had a couple of days before he had to return with his troops. The trip was duty and didn't count against furlough time. He was saving that to go to Emma's wedding, he said. We agreed to meet for dinner.

Richard was a couple of years younger than I was. That counted for a big difference when we were boys, but as we grew older we had found more things in common. We had played baseball on the same team and memorized German verbs together. German was strong in the high schools then, the language of Kultur, the teachers said. He had been involved more in sports than I had and did well in mathematics. He was a natural for West Point, and I had gone to the state university to read history. West Point had translated his leadership in sports into military leadership. He liked leading his troops and was ready for action, he said.

At dinner he was full of army talk about chasing Mexican bandits away from the border. Something was brewing down there, he thought, maybe another revolution. He laughed at some of the old-style army leaders and told how they had a hard time getting used to new weapons. They kept the machine guns back with the artillery instead of with units on the line. He hoped the generals were learning.

I told him about my plan to see Walter Cornelius in Monterrey and asked about travel in Mexico. He said the border was open and I wouldn't have any trouble crossing over. No passports or visas needed, but farther in I might have to give some official-looking type five dollars on the train. He'd probably put it in his pocket, he said.

I told him Miss Maud had once said Zeke Morgan had run him and some other boys off his land. What did he remember about that?

"Right. I remember now. I was with Johnny Masters and Ronnie Blake. We followed a deer through a break in the fence and came up on four men with surveying tools. They saw us and ran off in the trees. Before we could follow them, here came Zeke Morgan with a shotgun and shouting something. We got out of there quick as we could. I wonder now if he thought we were surveyors."

"Did any of you have on hobnail boots?"

"No. You know the kind of boots we hunt in. Just brogans."

"Zeke once told me he found hobnail boot prints on his land but couldn't track them."

"Not ours."

"So what do you know about Walter Cornelius? He has a lien on part of Zeke's land, the part over in Brand County. So says his cousin in Waxahachie."

"You know you're getting into touchy territory, don't you? Not talked about outside the family. Kate was mixed up with Walter Cornelius some way. I'm not clear how. I was away at the Point then.

She worked with him and his people when he was writing something, and she helped get it published. I heard guarded talk between Mama and Papa about her being engaged, but I don't know what became of it. That's history now and best forgotten."

"I see."

We paid the bill and moved out into the lobby. Richard lit up a cheroot. I said I didn't know he smoked. He said it's part of army life. Got it from the British, he thought. Now there was a professional army—the British. He wondered how they would deal with bandits on the border.

He invited me out to see the fort the next day. I saw the big red brick buildings that looked older than they were. I thought the army was there to stay, all right. On one of the wide green lawns, he introduced me to several officers' wives who acted like they would enjoy more of his company. He laughed when I said that. Can't think that way until you make captain, he said. I thought of Lisette and Hauptmann von Lakenberg. As I left, we said we'd see each other in Cromwell at Emma's wedding.

∞

Richard was right. Crossing the border at Laredo was little more than a change of trains. The flat, low-brush country we had passed since leaving San Antonio was barely interrupted by the streets of Laredo. The town was dusty and hot, with cottonwoods along some roads and near the river. An army group with their white tents was camped outside of town. The agent at the station said the train to Monterrey had different gauge rails from that running on the north side of the border.

The Mexican coach car had something of a European look about it. More decorative designs and plusher seats than the Missouri Pacific coaches I had ridden, but a bit worn around the edges. Several Mexican families with lots of women and girls in frilly dresses and seats full of hat boxes and packages and Papa sitting aloofly away from their chatter took up most of the car. The conductor spoke a little English and liked my attempts to use Spanish phrases learned from my little book. He said the families would get off at local stops and go to their casas. One roughly dressed gringo sat by himself, chewed tobacco, and spat into a cuspidor. We struck up a conversation as we passed each other going to the water closet. He said he was in oil and was headed for Vera Cruz if the trains made it and the bandits didn't stop us.

In the late afternoon, we were still passing through dry scrub and cactus. Most passengers had pulled down shades against the sun, and the sway of the coach had put most of us in a stupor. A couple of the women were taking sips from cups of bottled water and fanning themselves. In the distance I saw some groups of horsemen riding across a low hill and wondered if they were the bandits everyone talked about. But they left us alone.

Toward evening we stopped at Sabinas–Hidalgo. Some left the train, others got on. The man with the uniform was one of them. He was soon in our car and stood in the aisle by my seat.

"¿Destinación?" He looked short and dark.

"Monterrey."

"¿Tiene credenciales?"

The conductor came up and said something fast in Spanish.

The uniform shrugged and said, "Cinco dólares." I paid. The conductor winked at me and went up the aisle. The oil man had a handful of papers and his money already out. The uniform took the money and ignored the papers.

The train began to climb into higher elevation as the evening came on and we neared Monterrey. When I stepped out of the coach at the depot, I could feel the chilly night air. I had my choice of several boys to take my bags to a horse-drawn taxi. They all seemed to be shouting and crowding in. I hugged my arm against my wallet in my breast pocket. I gave my bag carrier a couple of pesos, and he grinned. Probably gave him too much. The taxi man and I agreed on a fare to the Hotel Europa, thanks to my phrase book. We bumped down the avenida lit by ornate gas lamps.

In the Europa with its ornate lobby, I got a room from a desk clerk whose English was almost as good as my Spanish. The room was large, with french doors opening to a balcony overlooking a plaza. The bed was big, too. Con la cama matrimonial, the desk clerk had said with a leer. The plaza had gas lamps on all sides and several trees with their leaves moving lightly in the night breeze. Walkers crossed the plaza, some talking, some laughing. The mountain they call Saddleback, with its two humps and a swoop in between, loomed darkly in the distance. Kate would like the view, I thought.

I slept well but woke early. Not as early as the crowd on the plaza. They must have gotten out before daylight. A good many were headed down one of the streets leading off the plaza to what looked like a market. Time for me to get started too, I reckoned.

I had the breakfast of dark, rich coffee, crusty rolls, and some kind of green tropical melon in the hotel dining sala and went to the desk clerk to see about a guide to help me find Walter Cornelius' place. Different clerk this time. He spoke English with a liquid Spanish glide over the hard parts and wanted to be helpful. Yes, there were English-speaking guides available. He sent a boy for one. Señor Sordo came in with the boy, shook hands, and asked how he could help. I showed him my written directions. While he studied them, I looked him over. A middle-aged man, somewhat short, with eyeglasses and scanty graying hair, dark coat, dark cravat, white shirt, trousers a little baggy, face thoughtful. Maybe a bookkeeper or genteel clerk. Probably all right.

"Yes, Señor Ford, I can take you there. This place is out of city and will take a little time. We will need to go in my cart. Is too far to walk. I will need to charge you for use of transportation. Is acceptable?"

We agreed on terms and went to his cart, a two-wheel affair with cushioned seats and good springs, wire wheels with rubber tires, pulled by a horse that looked steady but not fast. As we started rolling in the open cart with cool morning air around us, I thought this might turn out to be a pleasant ride. The only catch was whether

Cornelius would be at his place or I had wasted a long trip. There had been no way to send an overture.

Señor Sordo was right. It did take a little time or more to drive to the village where Cornelius was supposed to be. After the avenidas with their trees and three-story houses close to the street came smaller houses near the edge of town. Adobe walls and red tile roofs. Farther on we saw clusters of hovels made of sun-dried brick and with roofs made of brush laced together. In front of some places, figures sat in blankets. "Indígenas," said Señor Sordo with a pained look. Out in the open country, the road went past houses in the gray distance marked by lines of tall, slim cedars.

Sordo's habits as a guide came out as we rode. The old Camino Real running north into what is now American territory was near. The site of the battle with the army of the Yanquis was not far away. Santa Anna was a fool, he thought. The Yanquis were strong but not honest. I told him I thought my grandfather had been in that battle. My father had said so, but his memory of the War Between the States had blurred earlier events, and my grandfather, killed in the war, had not been around to tell his story. Sordo was pleased to learn that some soldiers from that earlier war had returned home and named towns after Mexican places, like Monterrey and Buena Vista. I didn't tell him how they mangled the names.

He asked, if it was not indelicate to ask, what my business was with this Cornelius. I said I was a lawyer and had to clear up some land titles with him. No mention of Zeke Morgan's troubles.

"Ah, un abogado," he said, pleased. He knew various abogados in the city. An honorable profession.

Cornelius' village was small, but he had a large house and grounds and was there, his servant said. I sent in a note mentioning Zeke Morgan and J. C. Morgan and asked if I could have an hour of his time. Cornelius himself came to the gate to invite me in. I introduced Señor Sordo and asked if he could wait inside for me. Cornelius invited him in to wait in the patio and have a chocolate while he waited. Sordo said he had a newspaper to read.

Cornelius looked like a gaunt scholar, not yet middle-aged, but with obvious energy and a strong and oddly accented voice. His eyes had a snap to them, his nose Roman if I remembered my history books, his mouth sardonic. He ushered me into a large room—his study, I guessed, from the books and papers scattered about. The room overlooked a long terraced garden with more of those tall, slim cedars lining it. This is like a Roman villa, I thought.

"Well, Mr. Ford, it's been a while since I saw someone from back east. I hope you bring good news. Would you like coffee or chocolate while we talk?"

While we waited for the maid to bring coffee, I told about Zeke Morgan's troubles and said I was Zeke's lawyer. I went right to the point about the mystery plot of land and its exclusion from Zeke's mortgage. J. C. Morgan had said he, Cornelius, held a lien on the plot. So what was the story on the lien?

"You do get to business directly, Mr. Ford. I've gotten so used to our Mexican friends circling the point I'm confounded by a direct approach."

"Sorry," I said as I stirred the coffee and tasted one of the little cakes the maid had brought.

"To be equally direct, let me say I hold that lien to keep that land from being taken over by the Eastern and Southern for a spur line to the quarry in Brand County."

"I hadn't heard there was to be a spur."

"I have my informants, and they're usually right. I'm sure somebody, probably J. C. Morgan, told you Amos Caruthers was born there."

"Yes."

"That place is special. Holy ground. Not to be desecrated."

I thought, here we are two thousand miles away, and he's guarding it like it was under his hand.

"Will you be able to protect it in court if it comes to that?"

"I'm in temporary exile here, but I'll come back when I'm needed."

"Why exile?"

"That's a long story. You sure you want to hear it?"

"If it concerns Zeke Morgan's defense, I do."

So he told me how he had seen the light about Amos Caruthers, better than most had. Amos was not just a backwoods preacher. He was the embodiment of the Holy Spirit, the incarnation, the realization of hopes long deferred. He brought new life to people if they would just recognize it. The old religion was wearing out. Reduced now to sterile legalisms without spirit. He, Cornelius, was a scholar of tradition and could see the true significance of what Amos embodied. Too many of Amos's followers saw him as a voice of the Holy Spirit but not the Spirit himself. They needed to be corrected. He had written a handful of tracts to show the real Amos and cut away the false teachings.

"I think I've seen some of them," I said. "Kate showed them to me." I dropped the name on purpose.

"Kate? Kate McCloud? You know her?"

I said her father, Judge McCloud, was my mentor, and Kate lived in Cromwell. Yes, I knew her.

"Wonderful woman, Kate. I worked with her when I wrote those tracts." He didn't explain.

"And the tracts?"

"I saw that arguments were not going to be enough. We needed stories to teach. That's when I encouraged Simon Dunaway to get some of the believers to write lives of Amos. That's to build up a cult myth, you know. People can fasten their minds on a story, remember it, even build on it. It's been done countless times before."

"I've seen some of them, too."

"Good. You've seen more than I thought. Kate show you those too?"

"She found them stuck in the back room of the library in Cromwell. She runs the library there."

"Good again. We've got more secret followers than you and most people might think. Good men. Good women, too."

"The Cromwell folks are tearing up the library now. Trying to find those papers. Kate's been suspended."

"Persecution. Kate's getting it too. That's what got me out here. Persecution, sir. The preachers and police threw me in jail back east, put me to trial on false charges of misusing believers' funds. But the plain folks saw through it and let me go. I knew it was only a matter of time before they snared me on something else. So I came out here. Beyond the reach of their law. An exile from my own people."

"What else could they get you on?"

His mouth drew down in a sardonic smile. "Bigamy, sir."

I'm sure I must have looked stunned.

"You find it hard to believe? My enemies don't. To make the story short, I had a wife back east in my younger days. We had a marriage of sorts, but were never close. She refused to go with me when I went to Germany to study with the great professors in their universities. I was gone for years. We lost interest in each other and finally stopped writing. When I came back, she chose to stay with her family. I felt I had no wife. She would not consider divorce. Then when I began to work with the Amosites, I met Kate McCloud. She was my secretary and became more than important to me. My work and Kate were my life. Having no wife in a real sense, I asked Kate to marry me, and she said yes. We had a happy few months together. Then she found out about Margaret and left me. She had our marriage annulled. That's when my affairs became part of the public record and my enemies seized upon it. They have been in correspondence with Margaret's family and are waiting to pounce. Hence my exile."

I didn't know what to say to that and sat silent. Cornelius continued.

"But I'll come back. Meanwhile, my exile helps protect the movement from further persecution while our enemies try to get at me. And I hold the lien on that holy ground safe from their grasp."

Finally I could talk. "You must find it hard to be so far away and have to wait."

"I am not out of touch with events. Even though the Mexican mails are slow, I keep in correspondence with those who tell me what happens. Simon Dunaway is good about that. And I am not idle. You see about you many papers. In exile, I am writing a history of the movement. One day it will vindicate all that we do."

After Cornelius' revelations, I couldn't think straight. The guarded talk I remembered about Kate began to take on new meanings. Zeke's secrecy about that land in Brand County took on a new light. But how could it clear Zeke of the murder charge? It was all a mix-up. And I had to get back and work up a sound defense. That November court date was looming closer.

I must have been mulling over all that as Señor Sordo and I rode back to town. "You are quiet, señor. Was the visit not satisfactory?"

"Pardon my silence. The complications are greater than ever. I need to return as soon as possible."

"We will hurry then." He flicked the reins, but señor horse moved at his own pace.

I had to wait a day for a train north. I walked the streets and plazas of Monterrey, even saw the new Government Palace, but my mind was back in Cromwell. My connections took me on a more northerly route than I had come, but that was all right. No need for Waxahachie now. As we rolled through the Appalachians, the misty clouds hung low beneath the mountaintops and the autumn leaves drooped from rain. The train chugged slowly on the grades, and I knew I would arrive in Cromwell well into the night.

When I stepped off the train, the night agent said welcome back, but his eyes slid away. The freight master waiting on the platform nodded but gave a funny look. I had to wait a half hour for the night taxi to return from a run, and folks at the curb seemed to stand back from me. I wondered what had happened while I was gone.

∾

News travels fast in Cromwell. I had hardly finished breakfast the next morning when a boy brought a note from Kate. Zeke, she wrote, had been taken from jail by night riders and lynched. The night I had left town.

I hurried to the McClouds'. Kate was waiting. "Where have you been, Will? We had no way of reaching you!"

After she had calmed down, I told my story and she told hers. But I left out the part about seeing Walter Cornelius. She found it hard to believe I had been to Texas. I didn't want to add the Cornelius complication. She was near enough to tears.

The story Judge McCloud had brought home, and others had said the same, was that Jeb Billings had managed to be away from the jail at the time three men with neckerchiefs over their faces had pushed into the jail. Sol Jenkins, one of the town's habitual drunks, had been in another cell and had seen and told. The night riders had not seen him or had ignored him. They had not spoken but had moved quickly and seemed to know what to do. Zeke had shouted for help, but no one came. They rode off with Zeke. Next morning a farmer approaching a crossroads saw Zeke hanging from a tree there and hurried into town to tell the sheriff.

"Did the sheriff find out who the three men were?"

"What do you think? He went through the motions of an investigation and reported the night riders were not from Cromwell. Case closed."

"What about Zeke's body? What happened to that?"

"Some people from Leland came. Said they were Zeke's cousins and claimed his body. They were taking him to be buried in their family graveyard, they said."

"How did they know?"

"News travels. We knew. Word must have traveled up the road very fast."

I sat there trying to imagine Zeke's burial. What kind of people stood around that grave? Zeke hadn't said anything to me about cousins in Leland. But he had held back a lot.

"I keep thinking, Will, about similarities between those night riders and the fanatics who shot Amos Caruthers. Do you see them?

And the so-called investigations come out the same. Killers unknown."

"Strange, isn't it?"

"And what about your case? No accused to defend now."

"I'm thinking things have changed a lot. The case has turned inside out. The unknown people who've been attacking Zeke are going to be on the defensive. Now they have something to hide. They'll be worried. And they could be dangerous."

"Will, take care of yourself. We don't want anything to happen to you."

"I can make it look like I'm off the case. I'll file a motion tomorrow to take the trial off the docket."

"I hope you're right. I—we couldn't endure losing you. Things just didn't seem right while you were gone."

"I doubt it would come to that. Things should ease up now."

And they seemed to ease. Kidd Saunders came by the office for a friendly visit—friendly for him. He said he was sorry about what happened to Zeke but was glad the town would be spared the trial. He was sure we'd have another trial when the sheriff found the lynchers. He hoped I wouldn't be defending them. We laughed, for different reasons, I suspected.

I was probably perverse, but I asked anyway if he'd heard of any success in finding them. He said no, but he had every confidence in Sheriff Callahan. Then he hoped I would find my place in the life of Cromwell. It was going to make its place on the map of the state.

The Judge asked me to supper a couple of days later. They wanted to hear all about my trip to Texas. "Be sure to tell about your visit with Richard. Miss Maud will want to know every word he said. And tell her how good he looks."

At dinner I couldn't believe how good Kate looked. Her blue eyes sparkled, and her face was alive with mischief. I suspected she and the Judge were in connivance to put on a good show for Miss Maud. The truth soon came out.

"I hear Richard looked peaked and puny when you saw him," Kate said. "Isn't he getting enough beans and biscuits?"

"No, Kate," the Judge started in. "It's the alkali water down there. Does terrible things to a man's insides."

"I think he's found the answer, Judge. Those big black cigars he smokes keep him from feeling anything else. He's getting black as those cigars."

"Not Richard!" Miss Maud was aghast. "He must be handsome in his uniform when he comes for Emma's wedding. Black, my foot! I think you're all just jealous of him."

"Now, Miss Maud. Will wouldn't tell a lie. He's just trying to give us a factual account of his travels. Tell us some more, Will."

So I told about the wide open lands in Texas. The Judge was interested to hear what the man from Atlanta had said about labor and what the Louisiana man said about oil leases. He liked to hear what C. K. Bean told about problems in fixing property lines. Even Miss Maud liked the part where Richard said how much smarter the younger officers were than the generals. I would have liked to tell Kate about the quaint streets of New Orleans and the plaza in Monterrey, but that couldn't be talked about. Besides, I thought it might be too personal. Emma came in as I was finishing. She and Harry had been to a church social. Harry was just the most thoughtful man, she said. Never left her for a minute to go smoke cigars with the men outside. She wondered why we laughed so hard.

Then I told them I had more traveling to do. I planned to go to Leland to see Zeke's cousins and pay respects at Zeke's grave. I would drive my car this time. Miss Maud's face lit up.

"You'll go through Jacksboro to get there, won't you, Will?"

"Yes, ma'am. It looks like the best way."

"I wonder if you could take the girls with you to Jacksboro. We have some family things, jewelry and such, I need to send to my sister Nettie. We've had them on hand since Aunt Nora's passing, and I've meant to take them to her. The girls could take them and visit

Nettie while you're in Leland. Kate's not working, because the library is closed."

"Yes, ma'am. Be glad to. The road's a bit rough in places, but we'll manage." They want to know where I'm going this time, I thought.

Kate said, "Mama, don't you think you should have asked us first?"

"Seize the moment, Kate. You do want to see your Aunt Nettie, don't you? Emma, you can stand to be away from Harry for a few days, can't you? I do want to have this chore off my mind."

∽

So we planned to leave the day after the next. When the day came, though, Emma was ill and couldn't go. Miss Maud began to have second thoughts. "I don't know if it would look right, Kate going off alone with Will. People could talk." The Judge said they talked anyway. Besides, feelings were easing up since there wasn't going to be a trial for Zeke.

The day was bright and clear as Kate and I started the run to Jacksboro. I had the top open so we could see the fall trees and low hills and enjoy the fresh air. I said I hoped Emma was not going to be seriously ill. Kate rolled her eyes and said, "Female trouble." She said she had the jewelry for Aunt Nettie in a small bag tied inside her dress. The larger things were in her bag in the back. Before long she began to talk about Cromwell. She really believed now that religious fanaticism was behind Zeke's death, and she thought it wasn't over yet. The townspeople really did hate the Amosites and were not above killing people because of the ideas in their heads. She thought several of the ministers in town were in on the plot against Zeke and the Amosites. She was sure that the move to repair the library was a ploy to destroy those pamphlets she had found and was glad she had hidden them in the Judge's library. I reminded her I still had some of them. She thought some of the churches were becoming obsessed by other people's sin and were out to impose their views on folks. She had heard recently that a woman friend of hers had been denounced publicly from the pulpit for reading paperback novels. How picky could you get! The preachers were shouting against liquor and divorce and telling their congregations to get the laws tightened up. Elect the moral people like Kidd Saunders. She laughed, but not for fun.

By midafternoon we were getting into steeper hill country, and the car was working hard to make the grades. I stopped at a shady spot near a house set back from the road to put some more water in the radiator and hoped we would make it to Jacksboro before dark.

We were just heading into a narrow stretch of road between two steep banks when I heard a crashing in the woods to our left. Out of the corner of my eye, I saw a big boulder rolling down and tried to stop. It hit the front left wheel and bumper and rolled on to the other side of the road ahead of us. We were half in the drainage ditch. I turned off the motor and looked toward Kate. Her hat was off, and she was hanging on to the seat. Her dress was rumpled and pulled halfway up her leg.

"You all right, Kate?"

"Just shaken out of my composure. How about you?"

"Let's get out of here before something else comes down." I thought I heard a rustling in the bushes above us and wished I had brought Papa's old service revolver.

I got the bags out of the back while Kate kept a watch on the ridge above.

"So where do we go?" Kate asked.

"There was that house about five miles back where we stopped for water. It looked lived in. Maybe we can get help there. Can you walk that far?"

"Let me get my other shoes from my bag. I thought I would be using them to walk in Aunt Nettie's garden."

We started back the road we'd come. I kept looking over my shoulder but saw nothing. Then it occurred to me. "What are we going to tell the people in the house? We aren't a married couple. They might be picky about that."

"They don't know. We can say we're husband and wife. I have Aunt Nora's old wedding ring in that little bag. Her children didn't want it buried with her."

"Well, maybe it'll work. But what will we do about staying overnight together? Married folks do that, you know."

"We'll manage." She gave me a sidelong look.

So I looked the other way while Kate opened her dress and found the wedding ring and put it on. We walked on. The grade was downhill, but the bags were getting heavier all the time.

The folks in the set-back house were an older couple, Clay and Leola Justus, both past their prime but still getting along, they said. "We seen you when you stopped to water that machine," Clay remembered. I told them how the big rock had rolled down the bank and hit the car. Did that happen much on this road?

"Does if it's pushed," he said.

"Why do you say pushed?"

"'Bout noon we seen three nasty lookin' strangers ridin' up the road. Didn't look this way. Didn't act like they wanted to be knowed. I told Leola they look like they up to no good."

"Jus keeps his eye on things," Leola said. "Don't much get by him."

I asked if we could stay the night with them. We'd head back to Cromwell soon as we could find a way. They seemed more than pleased. The house was too quiet since the kids left home, thought Leola. Clay said the boys had gone downstate to find work. Can't hardly make it on a hardscrabble farm no more. One girl lived in Jacksboro with her husband and baby. He worked at the mill, and she would too, soon as the baby got old enough. It was a hard life in the mill, but it paid wages.

At supper with Clay and Leola we had smoked ham, collards, grits with gravy, corn pone, and coffee. The way Clay looked at the grits and gravy and then at Leola, I guessed the grits were something extra for the occasion. Kate helped Leola with the dishes, and I sat with Clay on the porch in the cool evening air while he puffed his corncob. "Outta my patch," he said as he crumbled the tobacco into the pipe.

"We turn in early 'round here," Clay said when the smoking and dishwashing were done. "You folks take the boys' room up them steps. Got a double bed. Fine quilts. No springs though. Rope-tied bed. Good feathers in the tick."

Leola gave Kate a lamp, and we carried the bags up the steps. The moment of truth had come. "I'll just study that corner while you get settled," I said. I heard clothes coming off. Then the squeak of ropes as Kate got in the bed.

"Now hand me a couple of those quilts, and I'll make a pallet by the bed."

"For heaven's sake, Will, get in the bed! They'll be listening downstairs for the squeak of the ropes. You'll give the show away. Now get yourself ready and get in. I won't bite." I thought Kate sounded amused. She talked low but plain.

So I took off my outer clothes, turned off the lamp, and got in bed with Kate. I had a difficult time trying not to touch Kate, but she didn't mind how much those warm soft curves got close to me. Sometime during the night I felt her shaking and realized she was laughing softly. Or was she crying?

"You all right?" I whispered.

"Just hold me." I don't know how much those ropes squeaked that night.

∞

Sounds below told us getting-up time had come. I hated to do it, but we got dressed and went down.

"Sleep good?" Leola asked. "Jus gone to do the milkin'. We'll eat soon as he comes back."

We had coffee, grits, and stewed apples when Clay came back. "Outta my patch," he said and helped himself to more apples. Leola poured a pottery mug big as a bowl full of fresh milk. Both Kate and

I drank until our lips were wet with the cream on top. I thought she winked as she lifted the mug another time.

After breakfast, Clay took Kate and me in his mule wagon to the train stop at Loftin, maybe ten or twelve miles away. Before we left, Kate and Leola hugged like sisters. I thought I saw Leola wink at Kate. I wondered what they had talked about while they were washing dishes. As we rode to Loftin, I tried to remember who knew about my trip to Leland. Who did I tell? I thought only the McClouds knew. Clay said he would pull my car machine to his place if it would roll. He had a pulley hoist he could fasten to his wagon and lift the front end. He'd used it to move fallen timbers over the rocks. I tried to pay him for the hospitality and ride. He said the stay at his house was their pleasure. I could pay him later when he had the car machine moved. We'd need to get it somewhere it could be fixed. He took my ten dollars, though, when I asked him to get something nice for Miss Leola.

On the train to Cromwell I asked Kate to marry me. She looked out the window a long time. I said she had her reputation to think of. She smiled and looked out the window some more. I told her finally about my visit with Walter Cornelius and what he had said about her. Yes, she had gotten the marriage annulled. Was she still in love with him? She looked out the window some more.

Finally, she said, "I don't know if I should, Will. I like being friends, but marriage is something else. You're a rational man. Sometimes I think too rational. Sometimes I tremble at the way you calculate things. I'm a passionate woman. It was Walter's passion that drew me to him. He had his flaws, I know now, but he had fire."

"I thought things were strong for us last night."

"That was last night. We have so many things to find out if we're close on. Money. Religion. Time. Sex. Patience. Sense of order. How we face trials and losses. How we deal with sickness. It's just so big." She dabbed at her eyes and then smiled.

Then she turned to face me. "I want to tell you how it was with Walter and me. You deserve to know. But I won't explain to those people in Cromwell. They can talk and guess all they want. They wouldn't understand anyway."

"I'm listening."

She said how when she went off to Normal, all the girls had to take a course in ethics. But the class was taught by a retired preacher and was really a review of biblical ethics, not much different from what they had heard for years and years in Sunday School. Not exploration, just indoctrination. The emphasis was on believing first and understanding afterward. When some of the girls asked probing questions, like why it was all right for Sarah and Leah and Rachel to send their handmaids in to sleep with Abraham and Jacob—wasn't that adultery too, even if the handmaids had no choice?—the teacher always answered that was what the Bible said, and it meant what it said. It was the holy book and not to be questioned. Finally she and several other girls just rolled their eyes and stopped listening.

When Joy Arnold, one of the girls from Virginia, began to tell Kate and others about a new religious movement in the area, they started to meet several evenings during study hours to hear more. They heard about a man named Amos Caruthers, who claimed to have had a visitation, not just a vision, by the Holy Spirit and had been empowered to speak with a new voice. Literally a new voice. He sounded different from other men and spoke with an authority no one could resist. He helped others, women as well as men, to speak with that new voice and to do things they never before thought they could do. It was like they had been changed into new and powerful people. Instead of cringing before God and cowering for their sins, they each had a new and original relationship with God that had nothing to do with old sacrifices and guilt offerings and other persons standing between them and God or telling them what God wanted. Then Caruthers disappeared, and his followers were left stunned until a new leader appeared. Walter Cornelius gave new life and new force to the Amosites, as they were by then called, though some thought he was trying to take over. That was when Kate and the other girls came into the picture. Joy told them that

Walter was coming to Bellville to rally believers and asked who wanted to go. By then Kate and several of the girls were more interested in the Amosites' doings than they were in their studies, so they cut classes, got on the train, and went to Bellville.

"It was crazy, I guess," Kate said with a wry smile, "but we were already in pretty deep. Anyway, we went."

Walter was as magnetic as they had hoped, and they couldn't get enough of him. They skipped meals and sleep to be around him, and when he asked them to form a circle at Normal, they jumped at the chance. Kate was chosen corresponding secretary of the circle and spent more time writing reports to Walter and asking questions than she did on her studies. Her grades began to suffer, and the Judge and Miss Maud wanted to know what was happening. She gave them evasive answers that only partially satisfied them.

Walter had been impressed by Kate's reports and questions and wrote to invite her to work with him and the other Cornelians, as they were getting to be called, to help prepare pamphlets showing how Caruthers was the embodiment of the Holy Spirit. She was to help edit the papers and get them printed. He didn't tell her what a mess they were in.

She spent a weekend pondering the new direction her life was taking, but she went without telling the Judge or Miss Maud. Walter and his people put her to work right away, and she plunged in without looking back. She lived in a rooming house with several of the women believers and worked early and late and never got around to writing to the Judge and Miss Maud where she was or what she was doing. Finally, they made the trip to Normal to check on her and found she had left. The dean of women was even more upset than they were, she found out later, but had delayed telling them Kate had left until she found out something definite to tell them.

That was when they met Joy Arnold, who had come back to get her things from school. Joy told them Kate was in Jamesboro working with Walter Cornelius. They weren't happy about that development, but at least they knew where to find her.

When they appeared in Jamesboro, Kate knew she had come to the time of decision. They pleaded with her to come home, and Miss Maud kept saying what would Richard think about his sister. He was at West Point then. But she had begun to change—she was half in love with Walter, half in love with his work, and the two loves fed each other. She loved because she could believe. In spite of the Judge's pleas and Miss Maud's tears and her own tears, she told them she had made her choice and was happy with it. The best they could get was a promise to write and to call on them if she needed them.

So she went back to working with Walter and helping send out those pamphlets and soon was helping him write letters of advice to distant groups. Before long she had worked herself to exhaustion and came down with what they feared was pneumonia. She was sick for several weeks, was nursed by the women at Jamesboro, and was visited often by Walter.

When she began to get well, Walter came to her one day, asked the other women to give him a few moments alone with Kate, and asked her to marry him. He'd realized how much she meant to him personally, not just for her work, and wanted her to be beside him always, in work and in living. She said yes, and there was much excitement among the workers, but she thought some of the women looked askance at her. Maybe jealous, she thought.

Anyway, they got married in a civil ceremony and were blessed afterwards by the brothers and sisters without benefit of clergy. Walter said he'd bow this time to the state but not to the preachers. They were the people he still blamed for Amos Caruthers' death. They had their honeymoon in a riverside cottage owned by one of the believers. Kate said she could feel their spirits rise together during that time, though she sensed somehow that Walter was experienced in matters of intimacy. She wanted their feeling of perfect union never to end. She finally remembered to tell the Judge and Miss Maud about her marriage and about how happy she was.

That happiness crashed after three months. One day the elders of the group sent word to her and Walter that they wanted to see them immediately. They left the work table still full of papers and soon stood before the elders. Brother Simon Dunaway said they had learned Walter had been and still was married to one Margaret Foster Cornelius and with great regret decided they had to take action. Walter had to choose his work or Kate. He couldn't have both. Walter tried to explain how his union with Margaret was meaningless and dead, but the elders said they had enough trouble with the authorities without giving them power to strangle the whole movement. That was when Kate made another of her big decisions. She said she would petition for an annulment of their marriage and get off the scene for the good of the movement. That was when she made her call to the Judge and Miss Maud.

Kate and Walter said their tearful goodbyes. Walter said he would never marry again even if Margaret finally agreed to a divorce. Kate said she would go back to Cromwell and learn to live there but would keep Walter in her heart. Looking ahead to the prospect of living in Cromwell, she thought she might never marry again. Probably wouldn't have a chance as a disgraced woman in Cromwell, though Kidd Saunders had been helpful, maybe even protective, when she got work at the library. But if she did marry, it would be with deliberation, not passion.

She had learned since coming back to Cromwell, though, that she still dreamed about Walter and knew her emotions weren't dead. She just had to keep them inside and go through the motions of life in Cromwell. Music had become the way she lived her emotions, even when she had to sing church music.

"So that's why I say wait and see. I just don't know."

"Let's make it prayer for judgment continued then."

She laughed. "You didn't say you love me." I said I did love her. Didn't she know how hard it was for a man to say that?

I got off the train two flag stops before Cromwell and telegraphed the Judge to meet Kate. She would explain. I caught the next train.

That Time of Year

∞

Back in town, I looked through the mail, then decided I had better check in with Josh Walker. I went to the side door after nine o'clock that night. The light was on in his home office, and he was in his business clothes. He motioned me in and pulled down the shade. "Thought you'd come around soon."

I told him what J. C. Morgan had said was the secret about Zeke's holding in Brand County and how I had tracked Walter Cornelius to Monterrey to find he held the lien on that piece of land. He smiled sadly. But now that Zeke had been taken out and lynched, defending him was no longer the question. The question still was who had shot Julius Meadows and why. He said I should find out that. It would clear Zeke's name. Zeke deserved it.

"And don't forget you're still under suspicion here," he added. "Zeke's death didn't change that. Folks may smile, but somebody is afraid of what you'll find out."

I told him about the boulder on the road to Jacksboro. "You see what I mean?" he said.

He said Zeke's farm had been taken over by Meadows' bank, but the bank had made no move to sell it. He wondered why the trustees were holding it. There was still that exempted plot, I said.

"That's right. The trustees may have to do some fancy legal maneuvering to get at that. International claims and such. Cornelius may well have to come back to hold on to it." I didn't tell him Walter's other reason for not wanting to come back. He said he would continue to pay while I searched out Meadows' killers. "We owe it to Zeke," he said as he let me out the side door.

Later the next day, Kidd Saunders came by the office. Smiling, he asked if I had thought more about what place I wanted to find in the community. He was thinking about running for the legislature and could use me to help work up his campaign. The pay would be good. He had his backers. Having me in his campaign would mollify those who thought he had been too harsh about Zeke. May he rest in peace. Or he had connections with the Eastern and Southern. He could get me on as counsel with them.

The railroad might not welcome me, I told him. I expected to press claims against the railroad because of my folks' deaths. I expected to go to Richmond soon to file claims. "I wouldn't do that, Will," he said. No smiles then.

Before he left, Kidd asked, "By the way, where is your car? Haven't seen you riding around town lately. You need a car to do business in Cromwell. Can't ride the train everywhere." He let his well-tailored self out the door.

I still needed to get back to Clay's and see about my car, but I couldn't help feeling I needed to see Kate, even if she had turned me down. I still couldn't figure her out. Affectionate one day, remote the next. Interested in my life, then aloof. We needed to talk. Seriously. I stopped by the McClouds' and asked Miss Maud if I could call that evening. She said of course, I was always welcome. No hint about the broken trip to Jacksboro.

When I got to the McClouds' that evening, we sat in the parlor and had little cakes and tea. The whole family was there, including Emma this time. The air seemed formal, and I was glad I had worn my dark suit. I made an almost formal apology for failing to deliver Kate to the family kin in Jacksboro. Kate sat there and said nothing. Miss Maud said, "We know the circumstances were beyond your control, Will." Emma looked at her hands in her lap. The Judge had a poker face. I said I had been concerned for Kate's safety. I began to squirm. Miss Maud said they would eventually get the keepsakes to Aunt Nettie, old wedding rings and all. I saw amused glances jump from one person to the next in the circle. What had Kate been telling them? I wondered. I said I would need to go back upcountry soon and bring my car to town for repairs. The Judge said I could probably have it put on a flat car at Loftin and brought in. I said I hoped Mr. Justus would be able to get it to Loftin.

Auntie Bess came in to take away the cups, saucers, and plates. I jumped up to help collect them and take them to the kitchen. Miss

Maud called, "She'll get them, Will," but I kept moving. While she rattled the dishes, Auntie Bess muttered, "Rufe want to see you 'fore you leave. In the alley." I thought I'd see him soon.

When I went back into the parlor, I looked at the Judge. "Sir," I said, "I'd like to ask you and Miss Maud a question." They all became silent.

"Yes, Will?"

"Do you remember any of the circumstances at the time of Mama and Papa's accident? Where were they going? What was their business?" I'd asked those questions soon after I came home, but the answers had been blurred by our grief.

"Why do you ask, son?" The Judge stood. I could feel a relaxation in the room. It was like when the judge steps down from the bench.

"I think I should file a claim against the Eastern and Southern. For loss of life and property. Something's not right about the stories I've heard. What were they doing at Dawson's Crossing? Everybody says that's a dangerous place. Long slope to the crossing. It was even closed at one time, wasn't it?"

"You're right to think so, Will," the Judge said. "We had questions at the time never got answered."

"What questions?" Kate came over to stand with us.

"For one thing, they must have been detoured to go to Dawson's Crossing. But why did they detour? Sheriff Callahan went out there and said his men couldn't find any detour signs. That doesn't mean there hadn't been signs. For another, why didn't John's brakes hold on that slope? Wasn't rain or ice to make the surface slick. True, the train can come right fast around that curve at the crossing, but if you're looking, you have room to stop."

"Are you saying something was wrong with Papa's brakes?"

"No one knows. No one was there. Not that we know. But Roy Willard down at the garage repair says a brake cable could be cut so it would snap if you jammed hard on your brake. Of course he wasn't there, and the car was so mangled after the locomotive finished with it and it was brought to town, couldn't no one tell how it had been before the wreck."

"All that depends on Papa getting to the crossing just as the train came. How could that be?"

"Don't know exactly. If there was a detour sign, might have been a flagman held him and Wilma till the right time. Flagman might have heard a signal. Or even the train's whistle as it came up to the crossing."

"That's a plausible case, all right," I said. "But what were they doing near Dawson's Crossing in the first place?"

"Maybe I can say something about that." Miss Maud came up. "Wilma told me about a week before the accident that she was going with John out near there to talk with some landowners. The railroad wanted a right-of-way across their land, and they didn't want to give it. John expected tempers to be hot. She was going along to help keep them cool. She said wives and womenfolk would likely be there too. She'd try to get the women to cool down their menfolk."

"That's right. I remember now, her saying that. It fits with what I heard. Seems your daddy was sympathetic with the farmers. Got into a dispute with the railroad directors about it. They said he was looking after the wrong folks' interests."

"Was he?"

"He was trying to work a bargain with the farmers. Reckon the railroad don't like bargains."

"Couldn't they just fire him? That's better than killing."

"Those negotiations had gone on a long time. John had already got some give by the farmers if the railroad would change its route and go between farms instead of through them. But the railroad men said that was too expensive. John said it got to be a choice between the life and work of the farmers and the profits of the railroad. He was going to advise the farmers to refuse the company's offer and he would help them. Reckon that's when the railroad decided he had to go—without telling him, of course."

"How did the deal come out?"

"It's still hanging fire, last I heard."

I said there was a lot of hard evidence to collect. But I still meant to file that claim. I thought a civil claim might have a good chance of being settled out of court. A claim of criminal action would end up in court with a bunch of railroad lawyers working against me.

Kate walked with me to the front door. "Will, I want you to come back to us. They were scared tonight about what happened to us. It's not you they're angry at. It's themselves. They blame themselves for getting us on that road to Jacksboro. They thought things were getting better here. Now they don't."

"I thought maybe they were angry about what happened at the Justuses'. You wearing that ring and the fix we were in."

"They thought it was hilarious. I told them most of what went on. Maybe not everything. They had a good time thinking about your embarrassment. They can laugh at you because they like you. And we didn't fool Leola, you know. She caught on fast. If Clay didn't catch on, I'm sure she's told him now."

"I thought he did keep a real poker face on that mule wagon. Bet he was laughing up his sleeve."

She hugged me as I left.

I got back to the alley behind the garden. There were a couple of small shedlike buildings near the paling fence. I thought I saw a deeper shadow behind one. That had better be Rufe or I was in trouble.

"Evenin', Mr. Will," he said softly. "It's Rufe. Nobody else here."

"Good. Auntie Bess said you wanted to see me." I kept my voice low too, and eyed the shadows.

"Wanted to tell you what I heard today." I waited.

"Maybe you don't know, I got a position at Mist' Hardin's hardware. After the bank let me go. He's a good man, Mist' Hardin."

"Yes."

"I was workin' in the alley backa the store. I hear voices. Then I begin to listen. Voices come outta that back room where they keeps the ropes and wire. Thought I heard some a them voices 'fore. Then

I reco'nized the sheriff's voice. He was sayin' they did a good job on Zeke. Reckon that's Mr. Morgan. Now they needs to finish the job."

"They say any more?"

"Jus' laugh some and say they ready."

"They know you were there?"

"No, suh. I done got 'hind that pile a crates."

"How come you to recognize them?"

"Reckon they the ones beatin' up on me."

"You better take care. They might come at you again."

"You better take care, Mr. Will. I thinks they talkin' 'bout you."

"Thank you, Rufe. I 'preciate the warning."

"I owes you."

"Good night. Let me know if you hear anything more, will you?"

"I do that. 'Night, suh."

The next day I was walking down Elm Street and stopped to look at the revolvers on the wall near the front at Hardin's. The thought of keeping a gun handy was not much to my liking. But by now I was beginning to look into the shadows. Then I felt someone next to me. In the window's reflection, I recognized Dr. Washburn. Longtime family doctor. Had dosed me through whooping cough and just about all the other diseases kids get. He stood close.

"Good thing to be looking at, Will. You might need one."

"How are you, Doctor?"

"Fine. Just keep looking at the guns."

"Yes?"

"You need to watch your back, Will. I keep hearing talk about you. Not friendly talk. Funny thing how folks think a doctor won't tell what he hears. Say it right in front of me sometimes. Talk about how 'when we get Will Ford out of the way.' That don't sound good to me. Or good for you. You don't watch out, you'll be beyond my patching up."

"Anything special mentioned?"

"Just you. Didn't hear particulars. General threat's bad enough."

"I think I might be buying a gun soon."

"Just remember what I said." He walked off and was already saying hello to somebody else.

I still had to get my car back from Clay's. I rented a horse from Willard's and started off in the opposite direction before I doubled back to the road to Clay's. I kept looking back over my shoulder but didn't see anyone following or watching. The fall weather was still clear and the air cool. The trees looked a little more peaked than when Kate and I saw them. Have to admit I thought about Kate a long time on that ride. But I was glad she wasn't with me this trip. I carried a Smith & Wesson .38 in the saddlebag. I had taken Doc's advice. Roy Willard threw in the saddlebag for the trip. Must have seen the gun in my pocket.

Clay had done what he promised. The car was waiting beside his house. "Didn't have no trouble," he said. "Them mules is strong. Your car machine ain't the same now. Somebody went through it. Pulled out the seats and jimmied the lock on your carryin' box. Motor runs good, though. I tried it. Rigged a few a them wires, and it lit up."

"You've got the touch, Mr. Justus," I said. "You the one should have a machine."

"We get along."

I went to the door to speak to Leola and thanked her again for taking us in. I said Kate sent her thanks, too. Maybe she didn't send them, but I knew she wanted to. Leola laughed and said, "You better hold on to her."

As Clay and I pulled the car to the railroad and Roy's horse followed alongside, I asked him if he had any notion when the car machine had been gone through. He said sometime during the night we were there he heard hoofbeats on the road coming away from where the machine was. I wondered why I hadn't heard them. I noticed he was faintly smiling.

The Judge was right. I had no trouble getting the car lifted onto a flat car by one of the freight hoists at the station. It would have to wait a day or two for pickup. The agent asked, "Did you hit it or it hit you?"

"Some of both," I told him. I had been hit all right, by recognitions bad and good.

I settled up with Clay and told him I still owed him and Leola. Maybe he'd need some lawin' sometime, he said. We shook hands, and I started back to Cromwell on Roy's horse. As I rode, I looked back at recent happenings and judged that whoever was doing them, Sheriff Callahan and some of his boys if Rufe heard right, somebody was vicious but inept. Maybe that was their weak point. The boulder hadn't done its work. They lynched Zeke but left Sol to tell about them. They muffed the job on Rufe. And they let him and Doc Washburn hear them. I also had my doubts about Kidd's lawyering. Had he searched Zeke's land title and seen how the Brand County property was excluded from the mortgage? He couldn't get at that property by foreclosing on the farm in Ireland County. Cornelius held a lien on that plot. But who got the property after Zeke died? Wonder what they were looking for in the car? What do I have they still want? The pamphlets Kate gave me, I reckoned. Sheriff Callahan, though, wasn't the kind to yearn for religious pamphlets. Somebody behind him wanted something else.

Back in Cromwell, I asked Roy Willard to hold the car when it came in. I had another business errand and would see him about repairs when I got back. I asked if I could use the horse another few days. "You want the saddlebag, too?" he asked. I said it might be a good idea. I didn't say where I was going this time.

I still wanted to get to Leland and visit Zeke's grave. This time I went alone and by horse. The fall rains were about to set in, so I took my slicker and needed it before I got to Leland. A small hill town, it was, that had seen better days. The houses were white against the gray hills but unmarked by plant smoke. No mill here that I could see. Progress had passed it by, the boosters would say. They had a room and boarding house—Sojourners Inn it said on the sign out front—and I told Mrs. McGraw I'd like to stay two nights. "Fine," she said. "I'll have to ask you to pay in advance. Supper's at six."

When I went to the dining room at six, there were three people at an eight-place table. Two older men with coats and ties and a fortyish woman in a starched shirtwaist. The table linen looked clean, and the plates and cutlery were set out like they had been measured. Mrs. McGraw kept a proper place, I thought. I introduced myself and said I was from Cromwell. The woman said she was Miss Houston and worked at the bank. One man said he was Jack Wright and was retired. Didn't say retired from what. The other smiled and said call him Monty, he was from Montgomery.

"Chicken pie tonight," Monty said. "I smelled it."

The chicken pie was tasty and the crust worthy of a fruit pie. The snap beans were just right, not cooked to death. The sweet pickles were crunchy. When the peach cobbler and refills on the coffee came, I thought four people were missing a good meal. No one had made a move to leave, so I asked how to find the Morgans in town. Mr. Wright said there was a passel of them in Leland.

Just then Miss Houston looked up from her coffee. "Morgan? Cromwell? You must be looking for Zeke Morgan's folks. What a shame about him."

"That's right, ma'am. I'd appreciate it if you could tell me how to find them."

Miss Houston was helpful. From things she said, I judged the bank was the information center of town. She knew who was around and who was gone and when they'd be back. Probably knew how much they owed at the bank, too. She said I'd find Zeke's cousins out on Mimosa Road, big brick house on the left. In walking distance if it didn't rain. I said my horse was down at the livery. She looked like she was about to say "I know" but didn't.

Next day about midmorning I found the right Morgans in the big brick house. Somehow they knew I was coming. The rain had stopped, but the clouds still hung around overhead. I told them I had been Zeke's defense lawyer. They said they reckoned so. I said how sorry I was about what happened to Zeke. One of the cousins, a severe looking hefty woman about sixty, said, "How come you didn't stop that happening?" It was more a challenge than a question. I said I'd been in Texas looking into Zeke's connections with the Texas Morgans and the Amos people.

That broke it loose. It soon became clear they weren't in favor of the Amosites. They lamented Zeke ever got mixed up with them. "That Caruthers side did it," the hefty woman said. "They're tryin' to start a new religion! Who they think they are!"

"And then go off to Texas when things get hot!" said a younger, sharp-faced woman.

"They didn't step forward to claim him when the time come," said another. "Reckon he didn't leave them nothin' in his will if he had one."

"It don't do us no good here to be kin to Zeke Morgan. Folks say he's a murderer." No, I thought, but blood is thicker than religion here.

"Now, Patty," said the old, bulky man hunched in a rocker with his walking stick between his knees. They called him Grandpa. "They never proved Zeke killed a man. Mr. Ford here was out to prove he didn't. They killed him. Some folks say he was a martyr, just like the saints in Bible times."

"Pshaw! I never believed that," said the hefty woman. "He got hisself in trouble over religion."

A bluff, red-headed fellow they called Herb spoke up. "Mr. Ford came here to do right by Zeke. Wants to visit his grave. I say let's go out there."

It turned out we all went out there to the town cemetery, even hefty. They grumbled, but they went. Zeke had a pleasant plot overlooking the approach to town. "They wouldn't let him be buried in the churchyard," said hefty. "Holy ground's not for heretics. The preacher said that. And I agree."

"Who did the service?" I asked.

"Our preacher did. But he used the time to talk about keeping our faith pure. Didn't say many kind words for Zeke," Herb said.

"You going to put a marker?" I asked.

"Will when we can get together on what to say. 'Rest in Peace' is about as close as we can get."

So, Zeke, I thought, I hope you can rest in peace with this bunch squabbling over you. It doesn't look likely.

I put a toy dove on Zeke's grave, one I had picked up in Cromwell and carried in the saddlebag with the Smith & Wesson.

"What's that for?" asked Patty.

"A remembrance."

As we started to turn away, Grandpa asked, "What do you believe in, Mr. Ford?"

"The law," I answered.

"That's not what he meant," said hefty. "Don't you have no faith?"

"Let's get out of here," Grandpa said and led the way.

∞

Riding back to Cromwell the next day, I got to wondering what I did believe. I smiled to think how I had once thought of being a minister or teaching religion. How far had I come? Did Germany do it? I could read the Bible some more, but I knew now the Bible meant what you wanted it to mean. All the Sunday School lessons and catechisms they whipped into us kids and the sermons we heard later made sure of that. You couldn't come to it clean of ideas about what it was supposed to mean. Maybe I should read some more of those pamphlets. But Cornelius had already said he had put the interpretation on Amos Caruthers. Maybe I really believed in Kate. Now, she was a shifting text if there ever was one. How about the law? The Judge had already shown me how slippery that was. The law meant what the man doing it said it meant, and he could change tomorrow. A judge in the railroad's pocket could throw out Cornelius' claim on that land any time. Watch the limits of application, the Judge kept saying. Then I remembered to look over my shoulder.

I got back to Cromwell just before suppertime, left the horse with Roy's stableboy, and started up the street toward home. Near where Willow crosses Oak Street, just outside Oak Street Church, I met Dr. Paul Dade Norman coming down the steps after checking the lock on the main door. He walked toward me with his hand out for a shake.

"Will Ford. Good to see you again."

"Evening, Dr. Norman. How are you?" We shook. I wondered if he could see the Smith & Wesson in my left pocket. Probably not.

"Never better. Hope you are."

"Nice evening."

"It's a good evening to tell you what's on my heart, Will. I've been working on my sermon and thinking of the spiritual condition of my members. They are upset, sir, not at ease in Zion as the Bible promises. It's this Zeke Morgan business and the heresies he was preaching about that Amos Caruthers, all that business about being the voice of the Holy Spirit and distorting the truths of Scripture."

"Yes sir. He said it, I hear."

"He was confusing the people, trying to make them believe things the Bible don't say. He was trying to make something new out of what's long been recognized as God's own revealed truth. Inspired by divine revelation and closed to further additions. A curse put on anyone who would add to, take away, or change the divine record. That's in Revelations. And it's been good enough for the faithful for near onto nineteen hundred years."

"Yes sir."

"My point is this, Will. Now that Zeke Morgan has been gathered to his reward, which I doubt was very happy, you are the one keeping folks upset. Can't you just let the matter drop? Let Cromwell be happy again."

"Zeke never did get that trial to vindicate himself."

"He would have stirred up people more. You know how he was. An unholy fanatic. He would have attacked the community of the faithful instead of defending himself. He wanted to be a martyr."

"That happened to some folks in the Bible, as I remember."

"That was before revelation closed. Now we have the eternal word and the doctrines drawn from it."

"Weren't most of those doctrines worked up in the sixteenth and seventeenth centuries? Some maybe in the eighteenth. And with an old understanding about how the Bible was written and put together. This is the twentieth century."

"Ah. I see it now. I regret to say, Will, your mind has been poisoned by those German doctors. All skeptics and nonbelievers."

"Even Dr. Schweitzer?"

"A brilliant man, but godless. Maybe you should go off to the middle of Africa, too. And take your poison with you."

"I have a few things to do here first."

"Take care, Will. God is not mocked."

"Yes sir, I'll do that." He walked away without shaking hands.

∞

When I went to Roy Willard's the next day to see if the car had come in, he said, "Who fixed the wires on your motor?"

"Come again?"

"The wires on your motor. That's a clever job. Better than the factory does. You do it?"

"Oh. No, Clay Justus, the fellow up the hollow, did it."

"I'd like to get him to work for me. I could use a man with a touch for motors like that."

"Maybe he would. I'll ask him next time I see him."

I asked him if he could fix my car. He said he could now. He'd gotten some new equipment that would do it. He was preparing for the future, and motorcars would be a big part of it. Horses were going out, cars coming in. Roads were getting better all the time. But he was thinking beyond cars. Trucks, that was what was going to beat the railroads. Trucks could go where railroads couldn't. All over Ireland County, for instance. Trucks weren't real reliable yet. Too many breakdowns. But they'd get better. And he'd have the stuff to keep them going.

I told him I hoped he was right. If I ever had any spare money, I'd place my bet on him. Besides, the railroads were due a comedown. They acted mighty big these days. Even with those antitrust laws on the books.

About that time Rowe Hardin came up. "I heard what you were saying, Roy, and I'm with you. I'm looking forward to the day when trucks can carry my freight. Railroad rates are eating me up."

Roy turned to me. "You know Mr. Hardin?"

I said I had recently bought something in his store but had dealt with his clerk. I knew of him, though. One of my friends, Rufe Johnson, worked for him.

"Rufe's a good worker. Shame about what happened to him at the bank."

Hardin talked some with Roy while I waited to get Roy's estimate on repairs to the car. I noticed Hardin stood by the car while Roy looked under the front end. Then he came back and stood by me.

"I noticed you need new headlamps. I have some new models that might work better for you. Brighter. Take a better focus. Why don't you come by the hardware and look them over?"

Later that day I went by Hardin's. He must have seen me come in. He came up, shook hands, and invited me into his office. Then he closed the door. Strange, I thought. I looked around and didn't see any headlamps at hand.

"I wanted to talk with you, Mr. Ford," he said and settled, tiredly I thought, into his chair. "I hope you have a few minutes to talk." Here it comes. The call to be a good boy. He was a deacon at First

Church and a man of considerable influence in town. Maybe in his fifties but looked older. One of the pillars, I'd say. The dark suit looked natural on him.

But he talked about himself, not me. "You probably don't know it, but I have cancer. Dr. Washburn says it's only a matter of time and not much of that. Knowing so, I have set about to put my affairs in order."

I said I was sorry to hear it.

Among affairs to be set right, he said, was his conscience. He knew about what had been going on and wanted no more part of it. He was ashamed of his church and his minister. They were willing to destroy others in the name of their religion. To protect their religion.

"Like Zeke Morgan?"

"Like Zeke. Like you too, if you aren't careful."

"I've thought so too. But it wasn't your minister or your deacons who got Zeke."

"They were behind it. Sheriff Callahan is their agent. They and some of my fellow merchants know some dirt on the sheriff and make him do as they want. What's the dirt? I don't know exactly. Liquor running, I suspect. We keep finding drunk people in this dry town, and the sheriff never can seem to find out where the liquor came from. The preachers keep preaching against liquor, but the liquor still comes in."

"That figures," I said. "Who are the sheriff's goons? Not his deputies. Somebody would talk."

"Callahan has some backcountry men as his night riders. Few people in town would know them. They're a sorry lot, I'd say."

I remembered Clay's description of the riders on his road.

"That's not all, Mr. Ford. Kidd Saunders is using the church men and the sheriff to build his political reputation. He wants to run for the legislature. And go higher from there. I imagine you've heard some of his speeches. He's not a modest man."

I said I knew what he'd said when he closed the library.

"What you don't know is that Kidd is trying to get title to Zeke Morgan's land and sell it to the railroad to run a spur out to that quarry in Brand County. I'm one of the bank's trustees and know how he and some of the trustees, my friends I thought, are keeping that land from foreclosure sale. They'll sell it to the railroad when the time comes, and he'll make a killing."

"Why haven't they done it, then?"

"There are still legal technicalities. The railroad lawyers are working on them now."

"Whew!" I said. They're still trying to find out about the exclusion on the mortgage and the lien, I thought but didn't say.

"I'm not surprised you're stunned. It's a sorry mess. I feel better now, though. You're in their way. They're afraid of what you'll find out. Or have found out. You're a threat to them and their plans to get that land secured before other landowners find out. You'll need to watch out for yourself."

"Thanks for the warning."

"I'll let you know if I find out anything more. In the meantime, let's look at those headlamps."

So now I needed to check out what Hardin had told me. Roy had my car fixed in a couple of days, with the new model headlamps put on and connected. I could go where I needed to go now without that saddlebag. I had found a way to strap the Smith & Wesson on the inside of my leg and hoped it wouldn't shoot off my ankle. With some timely aid at hand, or foot, I could maybe draw the hidden goons out into the open. I didn't like being bait, but now I knew I had been anyway.

The first question to answer was how Sheriff Callahan and his boys knew Kate and I were going to Jacksboro. I tried to think back. Who knew why I was going? Let's see, I had asked Reverend Basil Carraway about who had done a funeral service for Zeke. I remembered asking Clyde Rogers, the undertaker, who had held Zeke's body until the Leland cousins had come to claim him. I wondered if I had mentioned my plan to Josh Walker. So I decided to test them to see which of them was the connection.

I wondered what the Judge would say about my acting as bait. Or better, about getting into violence. He had always said the law will find the criminal, give it time enough. After his time in the big war, he'd said fighting didn't solve anything. He had refused to get involved with the night riders during Reconstruction. The killing was over, he kept saying. Still, I had to try.

First chance I had, I stopped by Reverend Carraway's house and found him in the yard cutting the dead roses from his bushes. We had been speaking acquaintances for years, even before I went away to Germany. He still thought I might go into the ministry and asked if I was still studying my Bible. Our joke was that I was shocked by the gamy stories. He asked the same questions this time, but I managed to let him know I was going back to Leland to see Zeke's cousins. Since they had been the ones to claim him, I wondered if Zeke had written them letters about plans to move away from Cromwell. He asked why I would want to know, now that Zeke was with his fathers. I said the property still needed to be settled. He understood property.

This time I drove toward Leland on the Jacksboro road and in full view of anyone who might look. But no easy talk with Kate this time. I looked often in the mirror on the dash, looked ahead to possible ambush points, and looked for hoofprints in the dusty places. On the way, I stopped at Clay and Leola's. She said I had to come in for coffee. How was that nice Kate? While we had the coffee, I told Clay what Roy had said about Clay bringing his touch with motors to work for him. "We still gettin' along. We likes it here," he said. "If the crop don't make next year, maybe I'll come down." I said I'd tell Roy. I even went as far as Leland, but not out to the Morgans'. Didn't see any of them in town, but I did cross paths with Miss Houston. We howdied, and she asked if I was eating at the Sojourners again. I said I was just passing through this time. I'm sure the Morgans wondered what I was doing when she told them she'd seen me.

But the trip was without excitement, good or bad. I reckoned Reverend Carraway was not the taleteller. Clyde Rogers would be next, I thought, as I pulled up in front of the house. When I started to open the door, I saw an envelope stuck under the door. From Kate. Come to Sunday dinner. That meant after morning services at their church. Kate and Miss Maud had asked me several times to get back in the church habit. I had found excuses often enough. Reckon my distaste for Mr. Bascomb was behind the excuses, even before the library was closed. This time I went and sat with the Judge, Miss Maud, Emma, and Harry in their pew. Not their pew by name but by courtesy. The pillars of the church would probably have fallen if anyone had taken their pew. Kate sang in the choir. Miss Maud nudged the Judge several times to keep him awake. I noticed he said "amen" when he lifted his head. Good man, the Judge.

Sunday dinner at the McClouds' was high dinner. Auntie Bess had on a frilly apron when she brought the dishes, and the Judge took his time saying grace before he carved the ham in paper-thin slices. "Let you do it next time, Will," he said. No thanks, I thought, that's an art it took years to perfect.

After dinner, Kate took my arm as we went into the parlor. "We've missed you, Will. Is anything wrong?" I told her I had finally made the trip to Leland and seen Zeke's folks. I told her what they said about Zeke. She smiled wryly. I didn't mention the second trip.

In the parlor, the Judge called on Miss Maud to play something on the piano. She begged off, her hands were stiff and besides, Emma could play better. Emma tried to beg off and said let Harry play. That got them laughing. Kate asked me if I remembered the time when Harry and Richard, then about ten, played a duet at their recital. They didn't start or finish together, and piano playing hadn't been the same in Cromwell since. Both had taken to baseball and hunting after that. Miss Maud insisted Richard would have been a wonderful player if he had just practiced more, he had such talent.

Emma did play the piano prettily, but without much flair. Kate was the singer in the family and had a rich voice. Soon we were grouped around the piano singing Cohan's "Mary" and then "Whispering Hope." We almost harmonized. About that time the doorbell rang. Auntie Bess came to the parlor door and said, "Mr. Saunders, ma'am." We stood still and looked questions at each other. Miss Maud was up to the occasion. "Please invite him in, Bess."

Kidd Saunders had chosen Sunday afternoon to call. After Miss Maud had invited him to sit and we had sat, mostly on the edges of our chairs, Kidd said he had come to let Kate know the library repairs were almost complete, and she could take up her duties before long. Kate was equal to the moment, smiled, and said she looked forward. Kidd and the Judge and Harry discussed the fall weather and decided the November rains would set in soon. He complimented Emma's playing and said it sounded fine even outside. He hardly looked at me, and I wondered if he had not expected to see me there. Miss Maud offered him coffee and cake. He thanked her and accepted and stayed some more. He and Harry agreed business was coming right along. Some folks were making fortunes in tobacco. Finally he said he had to go, and the Judge and Miss Maud walked with him to the front steps.

"He was lonely," Kate said as we sat again in the parlor. She reminded me how his wife Mary Louise had died when their baby was born. The baby too. That was while I was away. He had gone through a long grief before he took hold again. That was when he took up with the railroad and began pushing for Cromwell to prosper. He probably had no private life and found Sundays a lonely time.

I said, well, she could get back to the library soon.

"Maybe that's what I'll do, but I'll need to make some decisions soon." I asked what decisions she meant.

"We both know that library work is temporary. The library here is not big enough or supported enough for me to spend my life there. And I couldn't go to a bigger library or teach school. The trustees wouldn't give me a good reference. My past is cloudy enough that someone would always find a reason to keep me from a good position. I've been thinking maybe I ought to try nursing. I could go to that hospital in Richmond and train to be a registered nurse. They're not so picky. Good character there means being able to take responsibility and be cool in a crisis. I can get character references for that. You'd write one for me, wouldn't you?"

I said I would if she really wanted it, but I hoped she had other plans. She didn't pick up on that. By the time I left, my mood was as gray as the late afternoon.

Next day I let Clyde Rogers know I was going out to Zeke's farm to locate the old cemetery. I named the day and said I would travel alone. No-show again for the sheriff's boys. The cemetery was spooky enough. I looked for Amos Caruthers' grave but couldn't locate it. Several old, old markers were lying on the ground and so faded you couldn't tell what they had said. I wondered if one of them marked Amos's place and only Walter knew which, if any. I circled the cemetery several times to look for boot prints but saw only mine.

It must be Josh Walker after all, I thought. I hated to think he could be playing a double hand, but I had to check it. So I made another late evening call to the side door. Josh was there in his business suit again. I told him about my trip to Leland to see Zeke's folks and their talk about Zeke. He said he was sorry to hear a man's kinfolks didn't recognize his worth, but he wasn't surprised. He'd seen it before. I told him I thought I had better go out to Zeke's place and look over the boundary markers. If the bank was still holding on to the property, there must be some question about just what they had. There might be an answer there. I thought day after tomorrow would be good enough weather to make the trip. It looked like the weather was breaking. He said do it and let him know if I found something useful. He reminded me to be careful and asked if I carried protection these days. I reckoned he might have heard I'd bought the Smith & Wesson at Hardin's, so I said I kept it mostly at the house and didn't think I'd need it on a daylight trip.

His question about carrying protection bothered me some, and I wondered if it had double meanings. This time I wore field clothes and carried the gun in my coat pocket, handy if needed. I also hired one of Roy's horses instead of taking the car. I might need to take to the fields instead of keeping to the road. The horse would be useful too for getting through the rough places. But as it turned out, I didn't need the protection. I needed answers. When I got over into the Brand County plot and started looking for boundary markers, I came across an odd looking pile of brush. After crouching in the bushes and looking and listening, I pushed aside the brush, and there was a cache of whisky crates, most of them full. Must have been ten crates, each with a dozen bottles, except for eight or nine empty slots in the top crate. Then I looked over the ground around the brush pile and saw boot prints not like mine. Off in a far bush, I saw an empty bottle. I studied the boot prints a while to see if any had marks you could trace. Best I could tell was that one pair was deeper on the outside than the inside. Maybe a bowleg.

I listened some more but heard only small sounds like squirrels and birds moving about and acorns dropping. I worked my way back to the horse and started to Cromwell. The early dusk came on as I rode, and it was dark by the time I got to Roy's. "You asked that Clay fellow yet about comin' out of the hills?" he wanted to know. I said he wanted to see how his next crop made out. He said he hoped I had a good hunt.

It looked like I had struck out. I couldn't remember telling anyone else I had planned to go to Leland. I puzzled about that for almost a week. I made another night call on Josh Walker and told him about finding the whisky. He said that helped explain the sots in a dry town, all right, but he wasn't sure what it had to do with Zeke. He knew Zeke wasn't a drinker and didn't think he peddled whisky or he'd have had money to pay off that mortgage. Keep looking, he'd pay for my time, he said.

～

I met the Judge on one of his walks, midday now that the late afternoons were darker and colder. He said come to supper tomorrow evening. I said I was getting uneasy about eating so often at his house, but I knew I didn't want another comedown from Kate. He said he was asking for the womenfolk. They liked to have another man to talk to. Besides, Emma was going to eat with the Bainses again. That wedding was going to be talked into eternity.

At supper, I must have looked like I was somewhere else. Miss Maud asked what was bothering me. I decided to tell them what I had been doing to find out who told I was going to Jacksboro and Leland. While I was telling about the tests of Carraway and Rogers, without mentioning Josh Walker, the Judge got a funny look.

"Will, my boy, I'm the one you're looking for. I told Kidd Saunders you and Kate were going to Jacksboro and Leland. Thought he ought to know, as Kate was out-of-pocket for the library. Notice of absence, so to speak. We were waiting for notice the library would re-open."

"Oh, Papa!" Kate said with a gasp. Miss Maud sat stunned.

"And he used that knowledge to endanger my daughter! And my young friend here!" The Judge was working up to a fury.

"Now, Mr. McCloud! Watch yourself! You don't want to have a seizure!" Miss Maud had risen half out of her chair.

We sat silent a minute to gather our thoughts. Then Kate said, "Papa, didn't you tell Kidd about Mr. and Mrs. Ford going out to meet with those landowners at Dawson's Crossing?"

"Good Lord! I did! I remember now. Kidd asked me what was going on with that land deal, and I told him." He was getting red in the face again. "And he used me to plot the deaths of my old friends John and Wilma!"

"Mr. McCloud!" Miss Maud said again.

"I just can't believe it!" The Judge looked like a man in deep sorrow. I thought I saw tears in the corners of his eyes. His head drooped. Kate went around the table and hugged him.

"It's all right, Papa. You didn't know."

He just sat there.

I glanced at Miss Maud. She had a faraway look in her eyes, like she was trying to remember something. "Let's go sit in the parlor. Bess will take these things away."

In the parlor she said, "Let's have some tea to settle our nerves." She went into the kitchen to put on the kettle while Auntie Bess rattled the dishes.

When she came back and sat facing the Judge, she got that faraway look again. "I was thinking about Kidd's visit the other Sunday. Strange, wasn't it? He didn't need to come tell Kate about the library. Maybe Kate was right. He was lonely. But I had the feeling he was somehow apologizing. Without saying so, of course."

"What are you saying, Mama?"

"I wonder if things have gotten out of control for Kidd. Maybe those people who do his dirty work are rougher than he expected. I had the feeling his talk about the library opening soon was a kind of apology to Kate. I wonder if he thought his ruffians were going to jump Will after he let Kate off in Jacksboro. That's not much comfort to you, is it, Will? You know he hardly spoke to you that day. He's still your enemy."

"I expect so."

"But I feel he thinks things are getting out of his control."

"Not bad, Miss Maud." The Judge was rousing. "You may have seen what we didn't. Trust a woman's feelings, Will."

I wondered about that. She was probably right, though, that Kidd was still against me.

We drank some tea and began to talk about other things. Kate said she hoped Congress would hurry up and pass that women's suffrage amendment. There were some people she wanted to vote against. The Judge said he didn't think you ought to vote with your emotions. Kate said there were reasons enough. What do you think, Will? I said I was with the Judge. Trust a woman's feelings. The Judge said that was a good lawyer's answer. I ought to go into politics. Miss Maud said she could hardly wait for her boy to come home for Emma's wedding.

The whole family was at the train station when Richard came in a couple of evenings later. Harry and I came along to help carry his luggage, and he brought a pile. Must have been half of Texas there. Miss Maud hugged her hero and hung onto him. Tall as she was, Kate had to stand on tiptoes to hug his neck. Emma settled for a waist hug. Even the Judge gave a quick embrace before wringing Richard's hand. Standing behind Richard, I could see tears in the Judge's eyes and wondered if he was thinking about other soldiers coming home. Harry and I stood back to wait our turn. "Hello, traveler," Richard said as we shook hands.

After we helped get the luggage into the front hall, Harry and I left Richard to the family and didn't see any of them for a couple of days. No doubt he was telling them all about chasing Mexican bandits and his life in Texas, or as much as he wanted them to know. Richard had arrived in civilian clothes, tall and hard, brown and lean, with sun-streaked dark hair, but I saw him in uniform a few days later as Miss Maud showed him off in town. Three days after his arrival, Harry and I were called to feast with the returned prodigal son and his family. It was a lively supper, with much of the talk beginning to veer towards the coming wedding and jokes about how Harry didn't have much freedom left. He said he'd resigned himself to his fate. Almost nothing was said about the Zeke Morgan and Kidd Saunders business. As I got ready to leave, Richard went to the door with me, lifted his eyebrows, and said, "Let's get together."

Two mornings later, Richard came to the house before I went to my office. We drank coffee while he talked about having to get bigger clothes if the women didn't stop feeding him so much. Then he said he wanted to hear what had been going on with the Zeke Morgan case. He'd heard a word dropped here and there and thought the family was keeping back things from him. Didn't want to spoil his holiday, he reckoned.

I brought him up-to-date, including my talk with Walter Cornelius in Monterrey. So that's how it had been with Kate and Cornelius, he said. The family sometimes never told him everything. He was upset about the boulder on the road to Jacksboro and amused about the night at Clay and Leola's, though maybe I didn't tell everything either. He probably could fill in the blanks. He wasn't worried about Kate taking care of herself. I told him about my attempts to flush out Kidd and the sheriff and about the Judge's sadness. He said he wanted to help. What could he do? I told him my plan, and he said count him in.

So I went to Kidd's office and told him I had some memoranda from Julius Meadows to Zeke that would set things straight about the mortgage and foreclosure. I thought they would set aside the foreclosure on Zeke's farm. Kidd demanded them for the probate. I said I was waiting for a handwriting expert to authenticate them. I could see he was upset and left.

That night Richard came to the house with the Judge's old service revolver. Came in the back way through the unused part of the house. I went out my usual door, got in the car, and drove off. A couple of blocks away, I parked under some dark pines and circled back to the house and waited in the rhododendrons. I checked my Smith & Wesson. I reckoned it was about nine o'clock.

After what seemed a long, long time as the cold and damp came up through my boots, I saw three dark figures come around the house. Probably had left horses in the back, as I hadn't heard a motor. They went to one of the windows on the side porch, cut the screen, and raised the window. They muttered a moment, something about "got a candle," and crawled in. In another moment, I saw the flare of a match and the light of a candle cupped by hands. I crept up to the window, careful to miss the squeaky board, and looked in. Two had started shuffling through papers I had left on the table while the third held the candle. "Move fast," he whispered.

Then I heard Richard's voice from the back door opening. "Hold it there. Real still. I got you covered." They froze. In the shadow, I thought I could see one at the table let his hand edge toward the side away from Richard. A knife there, I thought. They'll try to drop the candle and jump him in the dark. I spoke from the window.

"I got a gun pointed at you too." One turned to look at me. I crouched to come through the window. I saw him start to lunge as the light went out. I was expecting that and shot as he came. At almost the same time, Richard shot. I heard two thumps of bodies falling. Richard struck a match on the doorjamb, and the flare showed the third figure straightening from a crouch and raising his hands. The man I had shot was lying on the floor and groaning. The other was lying on his side, holding his leg and cursing. Richard stepped over to the light switch and flicked it on. I saw the man I had hit had blood at his right hip joint. Must have hit bone. Richard's man had a thigh wound. I hoped he hadn't hit an artery. We wanted these men to talk, not die on us.

Richard turned to the third, took his gun from his belt, and frisked him for a knife. "Search those two for guns and knives. I'll keep watch." I got guns from both and a knife from one. One gun, I saw, was a Colt .45. Then he turned to the third, now standing against the window with his hands still up. Richard pointed his revolver at the man's groin. "If you like that thing between your legs, start talking fast, Or I'll shoot it off." The man dropped his hands and grabbed his crotch, terror on his face.

They talked all right. All of them. The two who'd been shot begged us to get a doctor. No doctor till you talk, we said. Their stories clicked with what we already knew. They were from out in the county, near the crossroads where Zeke's body was found, and worked for Sheriff Callahan. Yes, they had grabbed Zeke and strung him up. Yes, they had rolled the boulder on the Jacksboro road and searched the car for papers. Yes, they had put Mr. and Mrs. Ford out of business at Dawson's Crossing and bragged about the timing. Yes, they were to find the papers for Mr. Saunders and take them to him and the sheriff. Out at the whisky place in Brand County. Yes, they had shot old Meadows when they were looking for papers in his office. He hadn't ought to been there, but they took care of him. Now, for God's sake, get the doctor.

I looked them over. They were a pretty scummy lot. Looked dirty and had the instincts of hyenas, if I remembered Papa's old natural history books with pictures of strange animals. The one with the thigh wound, I thought, was bowlegs. He'd leave a new track now. The one with the hip wound was feeling the pain more now. His teeth were chattering. I fetched a bottle of Lydia Pinkham's from Mama's medicine cabinet and poured some down his throat. The laudanum would help.

Richard tied up the third man with some sash cord from the back room. "Now go get Doc Washburn. I'll watch these yahoos."

As I hurried down the street to Dr. Washburn's, I could see lights coming on in several houses and a couple of men standing in their yards with their topcoats on and looking in our direction. They must have heard the shots. "What's up, Will?" one called. "Gun went off, no trouble," I called and didn't stay to explain.

Dr. Washburn was used to getting night calls, I reckoned, and didn't take long to get dressed. When he saw me, he looked relieved. "Glad it wasn't you," he said. "Tell me as we ride." I told him Richard was waiting with three of Sheriff Callahan's roughs. Two had been shot but not too bad to talk. We needed to follow up with a ride out to Zeke's place and needed to keep them quiet and out of the way. "Think I might have something in the bag to keep them quiet," he said.

Back at the house, he looked them over. No hemorrhage there, he said as he poked at bowlegs. He put bandages on the two and shot them with morphine. I told him about the Lydia Pinkham's, and he laughed. Then he turned the needle on the third. The man cringed.

"This'll help calm you," he said and jabbed before the man could dodge. By the time we got them to his car and mine, they were beginning to fade. We took them to his office where he had slabs for patients. "You go on. I'll watch them and give them some more if they come out of it."

I went to my office and used the telephone to call Sheriff Burton in Brand County. Thanks to the phone company, they had begun to keep operators on night call. I had to ring a long time to get Martha Bateson to answer in Cromwell and even longer to get the Brand County operator to get a call through to Sheriff Burton. I told him who I was. Yes, he knew about me. I asked him to meet me at Zeke's place in his county. I had found a whisky cache there and had reason to believe the whisky runners were there tonight. He liked the idea of catching some whisky boys. It would look good at the next election. He said be careful. Those whisky boys were ready to shoot. He'd had one of his deputies hit by them. Yes, I thought, and you'd be strict about jurisdiction. An Ireland County arrest over there wouldn't stick.

Back at the car, I asked Richard if he thought we needed help at the cache. Depended on how many there were, he said. Then I thought we needed an impartial witness when we faced up to Kidd and Callahan. They might claim false arrest. I mentioned the Judge, Rowe Hardin, and Josh Walker. They had sway in Cromwell. Not the Judge, Richard said. He was not as quick as he once was and, given his anger at Kidd, might lose his temper. Hardin was probably too weak. He might do better later as a witness to conspiracy at a trial. Walker would be about right. He was a night worker anyway. And he pulled a lot of weight in Cromwell.

The light was still on at Josh Walker's, and he opened the door like he was expecting me. I said who Richard was, and Josh said he was glad to see him home and shook hands. I told him what had happened at the house and what we needed to do now while Dr. Washburn had the sheriff's men in medical custody.

"Good that you've brought matters out in the open. Fine work, Will Ford. Let's finish up this business for Zeke." He went to get his gun, then turned. "You check with Burton in Brand County? We don't want to get hung up in legal technicalities now." I said the sheriff would meet us. "Good again."

On the road to Zeke's, I pushed as fast as night sight allowed. Those new headlamps from Hardin's helped. Even so, we had to dodge a mule and two cows standing on the edge of the road. Why aren't you in the pasture sleeping? I thought. Only crazy people are loose at night. I hoped Kidd and the sheriff hadn't given up the wait for their boys. I figured Kidd would be anxious enough to wait for results.

We walked the last couple of hundred yards. I was glad I had scouted the place earlier. I knew we should come up through the brakes so Kidd and Callahan wouldn't see it was us until we faced them. They were expecting three, and we were three. Hard to tell differences in the dark. I hoped they didn't have a signal. I had forgotten to ask the goons.

As we were breaking through the last screen of bushes, Callahan jumped up from the log he'd been sitting on. "What the hell took you so long?" Then he saw who we were. Kidd had been leaning against a tree. He straightened up.

"Josh Walker! What the hell you doing out here in the middle of the night?"

"Came to see you, Kidd."

"Where's our boys?" the sheriff said. "You in trouble when they come."

"Shut up, Cal," said Kidd.

"They're sleeping it off," Richard said. "We came to get them some more." Sheriff Callahan couldn't help glancing at the brush pile.

"We've done nothing wrong. You people are interfering with private business," Kidd said. "You're trespassing. This property belongs to the bank, and I'm its trustee."

"You're in Brand County, and I'm its sheriff," said a voice behind them. They swung around. I pointed to the brush pile.

"Boys, check that brush pile." Sheriff Burton pointed, and two deputies started pulling off brush.

"What's there?"

"Likker, Sherf. Lots of it," one said.

"Well, Cal. Mr. Saunders. Looks like you're in serious trouble. Possessing liquor in Brand County is a serious offense. This is Brand County, you know."

"Wait a minute, Sheriff," Kidd said. "I have nothing to do with liquor. I'm here to see about bank property. You better talk to Sheriff Callahan about liquor."

"Like hell you don't!" Callahan exploded. "You're in it deep as I am."

"Shut up, Cal."

"You'll need to come with us, Mr. Saunders, and explain what liquor is doing on bank property. You're its trustee."

Kidd turned to Josh Walker. "You going to let these Brand County people arrest somebody from Cromwell?"

"I'm here to witness for Zeke Morgan. You remember him, don't you?"

Kidd looked from Josh to me and back to Josh. "You've been paying him to track me."

"And proud of it."

"You're the one in trouble. Folks in Cromwell will have your hide. Your business too."

"We'll see."

Sheriff Burton straightened up and spoke formally. "Mr. Reuben Callahan, Mr. Kidd Saunders, I arrest you for possession of illegal liquor in Brand County. Take them away, boys."

After the deputies had led them away, Burton turned to Josh, Richard, and me. "That's a good night's work. How did you know? You were right on the mark."

"We have three of Callahan's boys in custody in Cromwell. They talked," I said.

"How'd you get them in custody? Cal was out here."

"Medical custody. They're shot up some. Lead and morphine."

"Oh?"

"We'll explain come daylight. What about this liquor? You going to hold it for evidence?"

"Right. I'll have one of the boys watch it tonight and pick it up in the morning. And count the bottles before I leave."

Sheriff Burton had Kidd and Callahan charged with illegal possession of liquor in Brand County. They were released on bail. Somehow Burton managed to make the process last several days while Callahan raged and Kidd threatened. But Burton knew his county, and Brand knew its jurisdiction. Meanwhile, Callahan's boys had talked too much before witnesses to recant. For some reason they were more afraid of Doc Washburn's needle than they were of jail. I didn't want to ask why. The Judge and Josh Walker, and soon Rowe Hardin, leaned on Billy Eustis as county attorney to call a grand jury and indict Hiram Howell, Joe Bob Martin, and James Swayne on the charge of abducting and murdering Zeke Morgan, with Reuben Callahan and Kidd Saunders indicted as accomplices. Kidd and Callahan were released on bail pending trial. I knew the fight had just begun. They were going to try to swing Cromwell in their favor. I wondered if Billy Eustis would work up an airtight case or cave in to town pressure. A county attorney needed to show convictions when the next election came, but not if he tried the wrong people. Maybe the key would be whether Kidd and Callahan were convicted first in Brand County. That might cut away a lot of their support. Their trial might be as much political as criminal.

I asked Richard if he was likely to get in trouble with the army because of his part in the shooting and arrest. He laughed. The army had gotten used to rough stuff lately and was more interested in leadership than in civilian niceties, he said. I hoped he was right.

While Ireland and Brand Counties disputed over jurisdictions, Emma and Harry were married at the McClouds' church. Miss Maud beamed when she saw her daughter, shimmering in white, come down the aisle on the Judge's arm and even more when she saw Richard standing in his dress uniform as one of Harry's groomsmen. The Judge managed not to look at Mr. Bascomb during the vows and prayers but kept from scowling. Kate said later there had been a finger shaken in his face. Kate, I thought, was truly regal in blue but kept tactfully back in her place. Harry and I were there too, of course. The crowd was somewhat smaller than might have been expected, the McClouds being currently out of favor with some. The town's feeling about Kidd Saunders was already building up. But Emma and Harry were in their own world and left soon on their wedding trip to Niagara Falls. Richard left soon for Texas.

Kidd Saunders and Sheriff Callahan appealed to the ministers in Cromwell and represented themselves as victims of a conspiracy by the Amosites. They had been trapped into compromising circumstances that could be readily explained, they said. The sheriff also claimed he was the victim of territorial jealousy by Brand County and had been falsely arrested by Sheriff Burton for political reasons. Cromwell had to stand by its own. By the following Sunday, several ministers delivered sermons against the Amosites and preached scorn on Cromwellians who betrayed their town. They didn't name names yet, but everybody knew they meant me, the Judge, and Josh Walker. When they came to the exhortation part of their sermons, they called on the faithful to vote Not Guilty if they were picked for jury duty. There were lots of "amen's" to that, I heard. *The Cromwellian* had an editorial about the travesty of justice in our fair city.

Feeling was running high against the three roughs the sheriff had used for his dirty work. The town saw them as county scum, not their boys, and soon a gap began growing between town and county folks.

A couple of fistfights broke out when farmers came to town. The three night riders rightly believed that the sheriff was throwing them to the wolves to save himself. So they talked and talked. The sheriff had sent them to derail the Bristol train, they charged. The town wasn't as interested in that as Simon would be, I thought. When I remembered Jeb Billings's peculiar absence from the jail the night Zeke was grabbed and lynched, I reminded Billy Eustis how likely he was to lose his prisoners to a similar raid. I'd heard talk about town how they ought to be taken out and strung up. I appreciated the irony when Billy got a court order permitting him to move them to the next county opposite from Brand for their own protection. I wondered if Hiram, Joe Bob, and Jimmie recognized it too.

Then the Eastern and Southern got into the fight when it assigned C. K. Whittington to defend Kidd and Callahan. Billy Eustis went pale when he heard that. "There goes my case," he said and threw up his hands, his secretary reported. Whittington was one of the railroad's sharpest lawyers and had a string of victories in and out of court when the railroad and some strikers had come down to shootings and beatings. The railroad wanted Kidd to win his case so he could carry out their plans to get that route to the quarry. That meant steady, regular profit to them. The ministers wanted him to win so they could get him elected to the legislature and push their plans to tighten up divorce laws and prohibit the sale and consumption of liquor. The laws of the state had to be like the laws of the Bible, they said. God wanted it that way.

I wasn't feeling very hopeful about developments any more than Billy Eustis was. He had come to me several times to get details about Zeke Morgan and Julius Meadows he might use to support the confessions of the county boys. J. C. Morgan and Walter Cornelius were beyond reach for testimony. Simon Dunaway might come from Bristol, but what he could say wouldn't have much influence on a Cromwell jury. C. K. Whittington had already shown in other cases he could get witnesses who would say what he wanted them to say. If we only had some written evidence.

Then came a knock on my door late one evening. I looked through the window before opening the door. Rufe Johnson stood in the shadows and spoke low. "Mr. Ford, it's Rufe. Comin' for Mr. Hardin."

"You alone?"

"Yassir."

"Come in, Rufe."

Inside, he looked around and said, "Mr. Hardin say come see him. He know somethin' you wants to know."

"He say when?"

"Nassir, jus' come. Didn't tell me no more."

"Thank you, Rufe. Tell him I'll be there. You doing all right?"

"Better since them mens got 'hind bars."

Late the next afternoon I went to Hardin's with one of my headlamps in hand and told the clerk I need to see his boss about the light he'd sold me. No, he couldn't help me. I needed to talk to the man who sold it.

Inside his office, with the door closed again, Rowe Hardin looked tired and thinner than last time but was smiling grimly. "Well, Mr. Ford, I've found out what hold Kidd Saunders and the church folks have on Sheriff Callahan. It's not just liquor running."

"I hope it's something that will make a difference in Cromwell."

"I think it will. He's a bigamist. Seems he forgot a wife back in one of the eastern counties when he married Mona Woods here. I understand they had to get married in a hurry. For that little boy they have. Couldn't afford the scandal last time he ran for reelection."

"How did you find out?"

"Don't ask. More important, Kidd Saunders found out during one of his trips east. Now he's got Callahan in his pocket. Those church folks know too, but can't admit they know."

"Do you think that can be used to turn Callahan against Kidd?"

"That's why I called you. It's a chance. I don't think his wife here knows about the other wife. You might get her to make Callahan turn state's evidence."

"That sounds tricky, but it's worth a try."

"Good luck, then."

∞

It didn't take me long to realize I needed Kate with me when I went to see Mona Callahan. If one woman could talk to another about a bigamist husband, Kate should know how. But would Kate be willing? She had kept her marriage to Walter in the past, untalked about, and let folks say what they wanted. Still, she didn't have to tell Mona about her past. She could just be a sympathetic listener. When I told her about Mona's situation and asked if she would go with me, she agreed readily.

"Of course I will. We women have to stick together against you men."

"That wasn't what I had in mind." She laughed.

"I know. She'd probably shrink from you. You're hurting her husband, she thinks. Besides, she might not believe you. You could be trapping her. But she might listen to me."

"Would you have to tell her about Walter Cornelius?"

"I might. If it would make her believe me, I would."

"That's asking a lot from you. I don't know whether we should."

"Let me decide that."

Sure enough, Mona didn't take to me. When she looked out the window of the little white house and saw the car, she must have heard alarm bells. The woman in the door was blonde, pretty in a country way, and looked scared. She let us in but didn't say a word when I introduced us. I said we'd come to try to help her. She looked like she doubted it. Then I said her husband was in big trouble because of her. That jarred her.

"I done nothin' wrong," she finally said.

Then Kate came into the talk. "Could we go into that room, just you and me, and talk woman to woman?"

"I reckon." She looked relieved to be talking to somebody besides me. "Junior'll wake up from his nap 'fore long."

While Kate was in the other room with Mona, I looked around. The room was neat and clean but worn around the edges. The chairs had seen better days but had been dusted recently. Neater than my rooms, I thought. I've got to get Nellie in there more often. Several tintypes of older folks, probably relatives, were on a table. And a framed photograph of a little boy smiling. Maybe little more than a year or two. I couldn't be sure. Anyway, he was more than a baby. A Bible at the end of the table, but no more books to be seen. The Bible looked old. I wondered if it had births and deaths written in it somewhere but didn't look.

After about half an hour, Kate and Mona came back in. Mona's eyes were red like she'd been crying. Kate's eyes looked teary too, but she nodded.

"Mrs. Callahan understands," Kate said. "She didn't know about the other Mrs. Callahan. I told her about my marriage. But an annulment is out of the question. She's pregnant and needs a husband."

"And I got no family to go back to. They shucked me when I took up with Reuben."

I hated to do it, but I pressed on. "Mrs. Callahan. You know, don't you, that those ministers in town will turn on your husband when the facts of his marriages become public knowledge. They'll shuck him and you. He'll go down and won't be able to help you or the boy."

She started crying again. Kate twisted her handkerchief.

"But if you could see your way clear to have your husband turn state's evidence against Kidd Saunders, he'd get a lighter sentence. He'd still go to jail, but not for as long as he would if he was convicted by a jury all stirred up by that railroad lawyer. The railroad wants to save Kidd Saunders, not your husband. They'll throw your husband to the wolves."

"But what about me? All that ain't gettin' him unmarried to that other woman."

"Let me offer this. I think I can find the other wife. I'll see if she's willing to divorce him. She's got grounds enough, at least under present law. Desertion's enough. No proven adultery required. I don't know what kind of woman she is. Whether she carries a grudge. She might welcome a divorce, again might not. That's a chance we take."

"He left her, didn't he?"

"It appears so. Time is the tricky thing right now. Any session now, the legislature is going to tighten up the divorce laws. They've been building up to it for several years. We need to act before they do."

"I don't want to be mixed up in no adultery."

"No need to. You're not in a valid marriage now, though, and Sheriff Callahan can't legally marry you until he's divorced. He's got big trouble, and you can help him."

"What do you want me to do?"

"When he comes home, tell him I came and told you about the other wife. Tell him soon the whole town's going to know. Ask him what he thinks Kidd Saunders and the church folks and the railroad are going to do to save him when it all comes out. Tell him I said the way to beat them is turn state's evidence and get a lighter sentence. Work with the prosecuting attorney. You can also tell him I'll see the other wife about a divorce."

"All right, I'll see what Reuben says."

Before we left, Kate and Mona hugged like sisters in sorrow. Mona closed the door behind us, and I wondered if she cried again.

On the way back, I could tell that Kate was looking at me a long time.

"All right," I said. "What is it?"

"Will Ford, you really surprised me. I think you're a softie after all. You didn't have to offer to find that other woman. You did it for her. To help her."

"Sorry. I'll try to do better." She laughed and hugged my shoulder.

Late the next day, Reuben Callahan came to the house as I was finishing the soup I'd been eating for three days. He looked shaken. He was a beefy man but looked smaller when he slumped into my other chair. I gave him a cup of strong coffee. He just held it while his hand shook.

"Will, my life has turned to dung. First that arrest over in Brand County. Now this. Mona told me how you and the McCloud woman came. She's been cryin' ever since. You were right, though. Kidd and that railroad lawyer would shuck me. Kidd tried to weasel out on me out in the sticks, you remember?"

"I was there."

"Mona says you told her I could get a lighter sentence if I turned state's evidence against Kidd and those buggers from out in the county. That true?"

"I'm not the prosecutor, but I can talk to Billy Eustis. I reckon he'll see it that way."

"How about talkin' to him for me? If he agrees, I'll come in."

"All right. First thing tomorrow."

"And Mona said you'd see that woman back east, Hettie I mean, about a divorce. That true?"

"I said it. Have to find her first. Can you help?"

"Reckon so. If she still lives with her family." I thought about Walter's wife and got a cold lump inside.

"What's she like? She likely to want a divorce? Or does she want to hold on and see you squirm?"

"It's been a long time since I seen her. I reckon she would give one. Has her own life. Did a long time 'fore I left her."

"She religious?"

"Not 'specially. Not 'less there's good-lookin' young preachers to look at."

"Well, I'll find her and ask her. Here's paper. Will you write down how to find her?"

"Sure." He started to write, then looked up. "Why're you doin' this for me? You don't owe me nothin'."

"Doing it for your wife. We want to make a proud woman of her. Kate, the McCloud woman you called her, has a hand in it."

"Well, you're doin' it for me, too. I never felt for Hettie what I feel for Mona. And the boy."

So he finished writing the directions.

❦

Billy Eustis almost fell out of his chair when I told him what Callahan had agreed to do. Then he jumped up and started shaking my hand, and then my arm. "Damn right I'll work with him and make the best deal I can. This is great! Wonder what Whittington's face looks like when he hears about this." I sent Callahan on to Billy Eustis, and they began huddling. A few days later Billy stopped by the office for a moment. "We struck a gold mine," he said. "Kidd Saunders knew plenty about Callahan, but Cal knows a lot about Kidd, and he's going to tell it all. I think our case is building."

I followed Callahan's directions and found Hettie Callahan in Adamsville without much trouble. It was a good-size town of tall pines and low white houses not far from the coast. Flat land and wide fields all around the town. I saw a lot more blacks than we were used to in Ireland County. Mostly they were in small houses on dirt roads that ran through the big fields. Some places they were in settlements at a crossroad. The Thornton place where Hettie's family lived was one of the larger white houses in town, I saw, as I drove around the town before getting down to business. I had driven through dairy farm country before getting there, but this was cotton and tobacco land and doing well. The town showed a good bit of activity. Stores, gins, and warehouses looked painted recently and had lots of people coming and going. The Eastern and Southern depot had freight cars on the side tracks waiting to be loaded.

I decided to push ahead and do my errand. I doubted I could find out much about Hettie or the Thorntons by asking around. I was too much an outsider to gain many answers. About midmorning I went to the big house and knocked. While I waited, I saw a couple of newer cars in the shell drive. A black woman in a dark dress and frilly apron opened the door. I said I was from Cromwell in Ireland County and would like to speak to Mrs. Hettie Callahan. As I said Callahan, she looked startled, then asked me to wait a minute. I waited and looked at the cars again. A young woman with dark hair, dark eyes, a lively face, and wearing a modish dress came to the door.

"Yes?"

"Mrs. Callahan?"

"Yes. What do you want?" She looked suspicious and amused.

I told her who I was and said I'd come on business from Mr. Callahan. She said I'd better come in and go into that sitting room. She'd be with me in a moment. While I waited, I could hear voices in a room deeper in the house but couldn't hear what they said. She came back with an older man wearing a coat and tie. "This is my father. Mr. Thornton. Mr. Ford." We're on a formal basis, I thought, as we shook hands. "Please sit down, Mr. Ford."

I said I was an attorney in Cromwell, Ireland County, and came on behalf of Mr. Reuben Callahan.

"What is your business with my daughter, Mr. Ford?" Thornton was all business, no talk about the weather or crops.

"Mr. Callahan asks to have your daughter divorce him on grounds of desertion."

I thought Hettie looked amused. Mr. Thornton kept a stern face. "Why does that man want a divorce after such a long time?"

"He wishes to marry in Cromwell. It's a matter of some delicacy."

Hettie gave a low laugh. "I'll bet," she said almost too low to hear. Thornton gave her a sharp side glance.

"What's that man doing now? We've lost track of him."

"He's the sheriff in Ireland County."

"You people in Cromwell don't have much to choose from," he said with a drawl that had something of a sneer in it.

"Elections bring strange results sometimes."

"Divorce is out of the question, Mr. Ford. Divorce is not acceptable in Adamsville. You can tell that man."

"Divorce is going to be more out of the question soon, Mr. Thornton. The legislature is at work now on stricter requirements. It soon may be all but impossible."

"That's to the good. We have our people working on it."

"Daddy is a big fan of Martin Maguire," Hettie said. "Guess you've heard of him way out in Cromwell."

"He's in the papers."

Thornton stood up. "I have no more to say, sir. The question is closed." He started to leave. As I was moving to stand up, I saw Hettie give me a hand signal to sit down again.

"I want to stay a minute, Daddy. I want to ask what Reub is doing now."

"I don't see how that could interest you." He went out and closed the door sharply.

Hettie crossed her legs, showing a good bit of stocking in the process. I could tell I was supposed to see it. She still kept her amused smile. "Don't mind Daddy," she said. "He thinks Adamsville is the center of the world."

I nodded.

"You saw those gins and warehouses? They're his."

I nodded. "Owns a good part of his world, I reckon."

"So Reub's got himself in a pickle again. What is it this time?"

"He needs to get married."

"Little one on the way, right?"

"Something like that."

"What's she like? The little woman, I mean."

"Country. Like Cal."

"Peach blossom complexion, right? Runs to flesh after the baby comes, right?" I saw she'd kept a trim figure.

"So what have you been doing, Mrs. Callahan?"

"For Pete's sake, call me Hettie. Nobody around here calls me Callahan anymore. If Daddy had his way, my name would still be Thornton. That's what people around here call me. The Thornton girl."

"So what have you been doing, Hettie?"

She'd been cutting a swath, she said. As far away from Adamsville as she could. She'd just come back from Baltimore, where she had friends who knew how to have a good time. Did I like to have a good time? You couldn't have a good time in Adamsville. She had outgrown the town. You couldn't have a drink here or smoke a cigarette unless you hid behind doors. Big cities were different, and she liked them. She had outgrown Reub, too. They'd had to get married, or thought they had. Maybe she had miscounted. She laughed at that. Anyway, Daddy put Reub to work at one of the warehouses. She knew she'd made a mistake with Reub and couldn't stay home all day. She ran with her friends, and he worked. One day he didn't come home from work, and that was that. She'd been so busy going to Baltimore and Richmond and Charleston she hadn't thought or cared much what Reub did or where he went. Guess she should have. Maybe if her mother had been living, she might have. Might have cleared up both their lives. Daddy didn't like Reub, almost as much for leaving Adamsville as for getting her in trouble. She laughed at that. Adamsville! Maybe she should divorce Reub. She could handle Daddy. He listened to his preacher too much, but he'd listen to her. There was that railroad man in Baltimore who wanted to marry her. She'd laughed at him. But he had money and no wife. Daddy liked that. Besides, she'd found that being married gave you more freedom and made you somebody. Being the Thornton girl in Baltimore didn't mean what it did in Adamsville. She wasn't getting any younger, either. Maybe she'd better settle on something while she still had her looks. Are you married, Mr. Ford?

"I hope to be."

"You don't talk quite the way people here do. Are you from these parts?"

"I lived in Germany some. Maybe that rubbed off."

"I'd like to go to Germany sometime. I'd love to waltz."

"That's Austria, isn't it? Germany marches."

"Come to think of it, I know somebody from Cromwell. What was his name? Kit? Chris?"

"Kidd."

"That's it. He came home with Daddy once. He was nice. Do you know him?"

"Some."

"He was a good dresser. And could talk. I bet he could waltz."

"So what do you want to do about that divorce? You want your freedom? You want to drop Reuben?"

"I say yes. But I'll have to swing Daddy that way. He pays the bills for my fun."

We agreed she would let me know. I was staying at the Carriage House.

The next afternoon, while I was keeping one of the rockers going in the autumn sun on the Carriage House veranda, an older man in a dark suit came up.

"Mr. Ford?"

I stood up. "Yes sir."

"I'm Reverend Bly. Walnut Street Church. May we talk?"

"Please." I offered the empty chair next to mine.

"The sun's nice," he said as he leaned back in the chair.

"Pleasant out here."

"Mr. Ford, I come on behalf of my friend and a member of my congregation, Mr. Thornton, whom you met yesterday."

"It was a pleasure."

"I'm sure it was. I respect your tact. Mr. Thornton has his abrupt ways. He's a fine man, though, and is much concerned about his daughter, whom, I believe, you also met."

"About the divorce?"

"I'm glad we came right to the point. Mr. Thornton has sought my advice about that. As you might imagine, Hettie has given him no rest. He wants what's best for her. But is a divorce best for her? And is a divorce best for our society? And for our times? Scripture is against it. You must know that Mr. Thornton has been working with those of us who want to bring state law into agreement with Scripture. Mr. Thornton is in a dilemma. He is much concerned."

We rocked and talked. Reverend Bly quoted Scripture denying divorce except for adultery by the wife and no remarriage for her after that. I quoted passages that gave different reasons for divorce. He laughed and said I knew Scripture too, but the devil could quote Scripture. We agreed the devil could quote Scripture out of context but others might, too. I suggested that the Scriptures he quoted were written for particular readers in their own historical times and circumstances, and their application was limited. A matter of limited jurisdiction. He thought their application was unlimited by time or circumstance. We agreed, though, that some laws of other times might have been set aside. He liked his ham.

To get down to cases for Hettie, I said I thought Scripture said somewhere that the law was made for man, not man for the law. That was about the Sabbath, he said, but later views approved changing the Sabbath from the seventh to the first day. I wondered if changing the civil law on divorce would change what had been done earlier by current law. He thought there was something ex post facto about that. I wondered if Mr. Thornton's conscience would be eased by having current law applied to his daughter's case. Desertion by the husband rather than adultery by the wife. He agreed that would be easier on Hettie. She might find a husband who would cherish her properly. We agreed we hadn't quite settled the question, but he'd talk some more with friend Thornton.

I don't know if Reverend Bly settled the question with friend Thornton, but Hettie did. I got a note the next day saying Daddy saw things her way and was telling his lawyer to start a divorce action and work fast. And if I was ever back in Adamsville to come see her. Not likely, I thought.

∞

Back in Cromwell, I told Billy Eustis about my trip. "Great!" he said. "I'll tell Callahan and get him to testify against Kidd. This case is moving along, Will." I reminded him to warn Callahan the preachers would come down on him hard. He said Cal knew that. He just wanted to protect Mona and the boy. He just wished he could get them away from town before everything fell in on him. I wondered if Kidd knew yet that Callahan was going to testify against him or why. The word would get around soon, I knew. Somebody in Billy's office would talk.

Next day I met Kate coming out of the Judge's office. It was one of his days for shuffling papers for his small practice.

"Welcome back, Will. We've been thinking about your travels. How did it go?"

I told her about my meeting with Hettie and her father. And about my long rock with Reverend Bly. Hettie would have her way, I said, and Callahan would get his divorce. I told her how Hettie wanted to keep waltzing but forgot to mention Hettie's invitation to visit.

"Well, I hope you didn't waltz with her."

"Didn't get quite that far."

"Will, you did a good thing for Mona. You're getting better all the time. I've got hopes for you."

"What hopes?"

She smiled. Then seriously, "Hopes you'll think of something to help Mona through the bad time. What's she going to do while Callahan is in jail? She said she has no family to go back to. What's she going to do? Take in washing?"

"I'll think of something."

"Good. Now I'm off to see Geraldine Tyson and her new baby."

As Kate left, I went in to talk with the Judge. "Will, my boy, happy to see you back. How was your trip east?" So I told him about it. He laughed. "I see you haven't forgotten that rule about narrow application of the law. Even preacher Bly's." I told him I still needed another application. I needed to move now on my claim against the railroad for Mama and Papa's deaths. The county boys' confession they had caused it while acting under instruction by the sheriff and Kidd made it timely. The boys pinned down Kidd as an agent of the railroad. He said he thought the claim would stick if Whittington couldn't discredit their testimony. I said they were pretty mad about being dumped by Cal and Kidd.

Next day I caught the train to Richmond. At one of the local stops, I thought I saw a familiar figure stepping up into the car. As he came into the coach I saw it was Simon Dunaway, still in his seedy suit. He must have seen me after a couple of steps and came toward me smiling and holding out his hand.

"Well, I'll be, if it ain't Will Ford. How you doin', Counselor?"

"Not too well. I keep losing customers."

"A shame that was. Ever find out who did it?"

As we sat together and rode to Richmond, I told him what had happened, about catching the county boys and what they'd said. I told him what they'd said about crippling that Bristol train. He said that filled out what he and his friends had learned. Then I told him how the sheriff was going to turn state's evidence and testify against Kidd Saunders. The sheriff was doing it to protect his wife and child. They were the ones I was worried about. I was afraid the railroad crowd had some more rough boys and might threaten to hurt the woman and boy to keep Callahan from testifying. He said that figured.

Then Simon asked, if it wasn't indelicate to ask, why I was going to Richmond. I told him how Mama and Papa had died and how I was going to file a claim against the Eastern and Southern for their deaths, now that the county boys had connected that smashup with the railroad's agents. He wanted to know if his folks couldn't make the same claim. The same agents tried to pile up his friends and him. I said I thought they might. He said he'd better advise the brethren to keep their affairs and wills in order, like Zeke, if they were going to live and maybe die under persecution.

I didn't find out what business Simon had in Richmond. He just said he was doing a regular check with some of his brethren. He didn't say he was going to Richmond, I remembered. For a talkative man, he could keep his secrets. I wondered if I had talked too much.

At the Eastern and Southern main office, I filed the claim for punitive damages for the deaths of Jonathan and Wilma Ford resulting from the intentional actions of agents of the Eastern and Southern Railway, Incorporated. Writing out the claim, I wondered again what Mama and Papa felt when they knew the car wasn't going to stop. The attorney who took my claim denied railroad responsibility and said I would hear the company's reply in due course. I thanked him and sat there.

"Was there something more, Mr. Ford?"

I suggested that before the company put itself in an indefensible position it might wish to consult with local agents in Cromwell and Ireland County. He might not be familiar with recent developments there. He gave me a condescending smile and said the company stayed informed. Would I excuse him, he had an important appointment.

On the way back to Cromwell, I rode alone and wondered what to do about Mona and the boy. I hadn't really thought that through, and talking to Simon had raised fears I hadn't considered. Maybe finding a way to keep her supported while Cal was in jail wasn't enough. She might need protection from the railroad. That was going to be hard. Trouble was, you didn't know where to look for the railroad's hired roughs.

Back at the office, I found a letter waiting for me. Charles Jacobs, attorney for Mr. T. H. Thornton and Mrs. Hettie Thornton Callahan, informed me that he was proceeding directly with a divorce action on behalf of Mrs. Callahan. The action was proceeding as rapidly as possible at Mr. Thornton's insistence, for reasons best known to him. He needed from me evidence of Mr. Reuben Callahan's residence in Ireland County for the period in question. Mrs. Callahan could establish that no communication with Mr. Callahan had occurred. Luckily, I thought, Reuben's residence was a matter of public record. He'd been in Ireland County to get elected.

It took several days to gather the records years back showing that Callahan had filed for election as sheriff of Ireland County. Then I thought I'd better see Mona and warn her to watch out for strangers. Kate had said she had seen Mona several times to make sure she had food and the rent was paid. I wondered if they cried together too.

As I drove up to the little white house, I saw an old car pulled up in back of the house and got a feeling of dread. Not already, I thought. I didn't carry the Smith & Wesson these days and wished I had thought to bring it. Better sidle in the back door and do what I could. The door was half open, and I walked as softly as I could to the jamb of the door leading into the next room and listened.

"Miss Mona, I bring you greetings from your friends in Bristol."

"Simon!" I stepped out into the doorway. She looked around. Simon turned to face me.

"Well, I'll be, Will Ford again." We shook hands.

"Mr. Ford," Mona said. "You know Mr. Dunaway, then?"

"Will, Miss Mona has seen her way clear to become one of us. Fine lady. We been talkin' about her comin' to Bristol to stay with some of our folks while her husband works out his troubles. Her and the boy. She's seen the light of the true way. We protect our own in this time of persecution."

"That all right with you?" I watched for signs of fear.

"I'm right grateful to Mr. Dunaway here," she said. "He's been mighty kind."

Simon explained how he was coming back with a wagon next week to take Mona, the boy, and her things to Bristol. She would stay with his cousins there until Reuben got out of jail. His cousins were fine people and knew how to do for a lady in her condition. I asked her if Reuben knew. She said he was grateful too. I told her about the letter from Thornton's lawyer and said the woman back east was willing and had agreed to the divorce. She said she was grateful to me too.

"Until next week, then," Simon called. "And pray for the faithful."

The more I thought about how Callahan was the key to Billy Eustis' case and how Mona and the boy were the key to Callahan working with Billy, the less easy I felt. Mona and the boy were the weak point. Let somebody hold them hostage and Callahan would balk, or maybe change sides. I thought somebody better keep an eye on them, and that somebody was me. I could use help, I thought, if more than one person came for them. And if they were the shooting or knifing kind. Sure wished Richard was here again. It would be five days before Simon and his friends came with their wagon. Five days to keep watch.

So I went to Billy. He agreed it was smart to protect our witness's interest and spent a couple of nights sitting in the car with me, watching Mona's house. But then he got word C. K. Whittington was in town and said he needed to keep watch on him. Josh Walker said, what the hell, folks knew about his part in the arrest, he'd watch the other three nights with me. I'd told Mona I and some friends would be watching her house so she wouldn't be worried if she saw us or found out we were there. I was carrying the Smith & Wesson regularly now. Josh came with a big navy revolver he said he'd used a bit in his younger days. Didn't think he'd forgot how.

The fourth evening, when we pulled up in the patch of bushes beside the dirt road leading to the house, we saw an old truck pulled up to the side of the house. It was turned to face the road out, probably to make a quick getaway without turning around. Better look into that, we both said and walked in the shadow of the bushes as much as we could. As we got nearer the house we heard a woman scream and then some men's voices.

"They won't go far without the truck," Josh said and shot three times into the radiator and front tires of the truck. For a second, I could imagine what those big revolver slugs did to that motor.

The house was quiet for maybe half a minute. Then two big dark figures came running out of the back door. By then I was coming out of the shadows. "Stop there!" I yelled. They didn't stop, and I shot twice at one and saw him fall. The other turned and fired. I could see the flash of a gun and felt something like a heavy kick in my left side and I was falling. As I fell, I heard Josh's big gun let go again and heard somebody yell.

I must have passed out for a while. Next thing I knew, Mona was holding a lantern over me and Josh was pulling my clothes loose. He felt and probed while the pain began to come.

"Be careful, for God's sake!" I yelled.

"Close, but no cigar," he said. "Couple of inches closer in and you'd've had a hole in your lung."

"How bad is it?" Mona asked.

"Flesh wound. No bones or arteries. Doc Washburn can patch him up. You got something I can use to bandage him? Pillow case? Clean diaper? Something like that."

"Yes. Just a minute." She gave Josh the lantern and went off.

"They get away?" I asked.

"Naw. You got yours in the leg. He's over there trying to hold his leg together. I got mine in the neck. He's over there. Thinks he's dying, but he ain't. I got their guns, and one had a knife."

Mona came back with a folded cloth. "I put some iodine on it," she said. That's when I really yelled, when Josh stuck that iodine cloth on me.

Maybe it was the gunfire, maybe the yelling. Anyway, soon one of Mona's neighbors came running up. "What's goin' on here?" he called as he came up. He had a double-barreled shotgun.

Mona explained to him how those two out there came to kidnap her and the boy and how Josh and I had stopped them and how they needed to get me and them to the doctor. "Ain't much, but I'll get my chicken truck and help carry them in," he said and ran off.

While he was gone, Josh tied up the two men, stuck some iodine bandages on them, and listened to them yell. So they went to town in Luke Joyner's chicken wagon, and Josh drove me to Doc Washburn's. Luke's wife had Mona and the boy come stay with her and her six children.

"We've got to stop meeting this way," Doc Washburn said when Josh helped me into his office. "You going to make this a habit?"

Luke Joyner soon came in with the other two. "Good hunting tonight, looks like," Washburn said as he worked on them. "You want them fixed up like last time?"

"Might as well," I said. "Billy Eustis is going to want to hear their stories."

"You better stay here tonight and let me watch you too," Washburn said. "Hope you don't smell as bad as those galoots in there." In a minute I felt a sting in my arm.

When I woke up, I saw Kate's face looking down into mine. "What angel is this?" I croaked. The drug Doc gave me did funny things to my voice.

She smiled. "Will, are you all right? We were so afraid when we heard you'd been shot."

"We?"

"Papa's here too."

Then the Judge looked down at me. "Will, boy, good to see you come around. Dr. Washburn sent a boy to tell us he had you here. We came soon as we could."

Washburn's voice came in from behind me. "You're going to need to stay quiet for several days. Don't want that wound to break open. These folks have agreed to let you stay with them, though I can't see why. Must have a weakness for night types."

"Right, Will. We want you to come stay with us," the Judge said. "Kate and Miss Maud can bring you soup, and I'll tell you war stories."

"Papa, he's had enough war."

∞

So they took me to their house to stay until I felt stronger. I never knew Kate could be so gentle as when she changed the bandage. "No iodine?" I asked. She said potato soup would help more. Did I want it poured on the bandage or in my ear?

"I think you do need to go to that hospital in Richmond and learn to treat the poor and pitiful like me," I said. A funny look crossed her face. I couldn't tell what she was thinking.

Later that day, Billy Eustis came in. "Big news, Will. Whittington and the railroad have withdrawn from Kidd's defense."

"How come?"

"Those two you and Walker brought in are really singing. The same song the three in Johns County are singing. Guess the railroad wants to get out before its hands get any stickier. Anyway, Kidd's got to go it alone now."

"What about all that town support Kidd has?"

"It's fading. Kidd's too exposed now. Makes them look bad."

I saw what he meant the next day when Mr. Bascomb came to the McClouds' in his dark suit and silver hair to make a pastoral call. He told Kate the library would be ready to open any day and he looked forward to seeing her among the books again. He told Miss Maud he would raise Richard in his prayers for those defending their country. The Judge said Richard was picking up Spanish right well and might be sent to the Panama Canal as soon as it opened. Cromwell was proud of me for exposing the evil in its midst, said the preacher. I thanked him and kept my face straight.

Josh Walker came by too. He asked if I needed any more iodine treatment, then said I needed to get some more practice with that Smith & Wesson. I had almost hit him in all that shooting. Soon as I got better he'd take me out to shoot at some boards. We agreed that for a lawyer, the pen was safer than the gun. Before he left, he told me that Simon and some folks from Bristol had come for Mona and the boy. She was all right now. They'd take care of her.

The next time Kate changed my bandage, she got to talking about Kidd Saunders. "Think how lonely he is, Will. All his friends have abandoned him. So has the railroad. And he knows by now Callahan is going to testify and tell all their dirty secrets. Any political hopes he had must be gone too. He's likely to get a term in jail instead of a term in the legislature."

"Maybe," was the best I could answer.

"Do you remember how he was that Sunday he came to the house? I thought he was lonely then, too. Mary Louise gone and all that."

She must have pressed too hard on the bandage. "Ouch!"

"Sorry."

"I'll be all right," I said with a mock groan.

"You're such a wonderful martyr."

"I suffer a lot," I said. "The woman I want to marry has wounded me more than Mona's friends did."

"I suppose you're lonely too. Poor you."

She laughed and went back into the house to help Miss Maud. I lay in the day bed in the sun parlor and thought what a long way we had come since I had returned from Germany. She was right. I was lonely, but in a different way. I was in Cromwell, probably to stay. But I couldn't feel at home with the church folks in town or with the Amosites. Folks could change, I knew, but it took such a long time they didn't know they were changing. Maybe the thing to do was take the long view of history and see things the way they are now as part of something that's been happening a long time. Cromwell may be just a dot in history. Just a small event in a long story. But you couldn't live outside history. You had to live somewhere. Cromwell now was our time and place in history. Maybe the thing to do was to live with the churches and Amosites, the town and the railroad, as forms for living your life, but see them only as historical circumstances, not real answers. Somehow you had to believe and not believe at the same time.

The peaceful time in the sun didn't last long. Next morning Billy Eustis came running into the house. "Will, Kidd Saunders killed himself last night or maybe this morning. Shot himself in the heart."

"What?"

"That's right. They found him at home when he didn't come to the office. And guess what else?"

"Tell me."

"He had a letter on his table, right in front of his chair. Letter was to Zeke Morgan from Julius Meadows. Said he agreed to extend Zeke's note."

"How'd he get it? Did the thugs who shot Julius get it when they shot him?"

"Don't know for sure, but that figures. Don't know how long he had it."

"Wonder why he sent those thugs to my place if he had the letter."

"Maybe he thought there was more than one paper. The letter said something about 'per our agreement.' Maybe he thought the agreement was in writing."

"Poor Kidd. That's a blow."

"You're telling me! The town fathers are in shock."

"And the railroad?"

"They never knew him."

Billy tried to be mournful, but he knew he had a solid case now and couldn't help showing his relief. Kate and Miss Maud and the Judge had come in by then, and Billy told them the news. "Oh my," breathed Miss Maud.

"So that's the way it ends," the Judge said.

I thought Kate's eyes had real tears, but she said nothing.

Billy was right. As soon as the circuit judge got back to town, he tried the three Ireland County thugs and the two from the railroad and sent them to prison for long terms. He accepted Billy's plea for Reuben Callahan and sent him up for two years. Then the judge made a speech about how Cromwell needed to return to decent order and adjourned the court.

The county magistrates said we needed to get busy and elect a new sheriff. Johnny Patterson, the deputy who had taken the thugs off Doc Washburn's hands, was elected. Sheriff Burton over in Brand County complained he'd been cheated of his rightful prisoners.

During that winter I got back on my feet, and after many thanks to Kate and Miss Maud and the Judge, got back to my practice. I was mildly surprised at how many folks in Cromwell needed me to do their legal chores. Day after day the office door opened, and in they came. One day in early spring the door opened, and there stood Simon Dunaway, rumpled suit and all.

"Will Ford, I bring you greetings from your friends in Bristol."

"Simon! Wondered if I'd see you again."

"Back in town on business, Will. Thought you might like to know I just paid off Zeke's note, thanks to his friends in Bristol. He willed both the Ireland and Brand County plots to the brethren, you know. Title's clear. Land's safe now with the true believers."

"What about that hold Walter Cornelius has on the place in Brand?"

"He says he'll sign it over if he can be buried there with Amos. Seems he thinks he ought to stay in Mexico some longer. Don't know why, but that's what he said."

"He must have a reason."

"Mona's comin' along fine. She sends her thanks. That boy of hers, now he is somethin'. Smart, I mean smart. Reckon he might be one of our best soon as he grows up. And we're growin', Will. Gettin' stronger all the time. Persecution's still powerful, but it makes us strong."

I asked about the others in Bristol, and he allowed they were mighty active and still arguing, trying to decide on the true and faithful writings. Then he had to go.

I didn't wait until evening to go tell the McClouds. After we sat with Miss Maud and the Judge, Kate and I walked out into the garden to see the spring blossoms. I could tell she was in one of her droll moods.

"Will, I think it's time I made an honest man of you. If your offer's still open, I'll marry you even if you don't know how to say you love me. You do, don't you?"

"How would 'my favorite friend' do?"

"It's a start. Now that you're a man of ardor, tell me how you're a man of fortune."

"I thought maybe you could support me with all those earnings as a nurse you're going to have."

"I seem to have lost my map of the road to Richmond."

"Maybe there's no need. Richmond sometimes comes to Cromwell. One of my visitors to the office the other day was C. K. Whittington."

"Oh my! What did he want this time?"

"Wants to give away money. He said that, in light of recent developments, the Eastern and Southern has realized it needs to clear accounts on Mama and Papa's deaths. Since Papa was on railroad business, his estate is due compensation for his quote 'accident.' They want to pay a year's retainer to the estate in return for no claims of responsibility for their deaths. And they want to close permanently the approach to Dawson's Crossing and build an overpass for the road. He also let me know the railroad would fight any criminal charges and could get witnesses to rebut the county boys' testimonies."

"So what did you do?"

"I remembered how to spell my name."

"That's probably better. They can play rough."

We walked on. After a few steps, we both turned, and she was in my arms. I whispered three words in her ear. She laughed and put her face up to mine, blue eyes close to mine. With her close to me from face to toe, it was a kiss to remember when you're ninety.

"Sorry I don't have anything to pour in your ear," she whispered. "Will words do?" Then she whispered some more.

When we told the Judge and Miss Maud and I made a proper plea for their blessing, the Judge pronounced the motion sustained. Miss Maud beamed. "Kate and Will, we're so pleased. It's like a good wish come true. Years ago, Mr. McCloud and I and John and Wilma said what a good match you'd make. Now it's come true."

Kate and I talked during the next several days about how we could open Mama and Papa's house to full living, and I could quit my bachelor wing. She agreed she'd see I wasn't lonely like Kidd Saunders, even if she couldn't accompany me in those lonesome stretches of questioning about religion in Cromwell. She needed people and music and bright visions of hope. We'd live in Cromwell and be part of the life there, even when we sometimes had to stand at the edge of things and look in. I even agreed to go to her church and try to stay awake.

So I went to her church, and there was Kate, blue eyes shining and lips smiling, singing in the choir:

> *Shall we gather at the river*
> *Where bright angel feet have trod*
> *With its crystal tide forever*
> *Flowing by the throne of God?*

Such Were for the Saints

SUCH WERE FOR THE SAINTS

There came a Day at Summer's full,
Entirely for me—
I thought that such were for the Saints,
Where Resurrections—be—

Emily Dickinson

Chapter 1

"Roy, we've come on a sensitive and embarrassing matter and don't really know how to talk about it, but we hope you can help us."

"Be glad to do what I can. Can you tell me about it?"

They sat there in my office at the funeral home and tried to gather their words while I waited. Titus and Joanna Bruce. Older, of the generation of my parents. Among the first families of Cromwell. Well fixed, I thought, but not among the richest. Both still dressed in dark clothes for mourning. Titus a quick-moving man of middle height. Joanna a taller woman with a soft, pleasant face. I had seen them often in happier times at their house. They had three attractive and unmarried daughters, and I had been one of several town bachelors who spent pleasant evenings there talking and sometimes dancing to the new tunes on the phonograph with the daughters. Titus and Miss Joanna indulged their daughters. Looked in from time to time on the fun but mostly kept to their sitting room in the back of the house.

Finally Miss Joanna spoke. "What we want to know, Roy, is whether you found any letter on Titus's sister Greneda when she was being prepared for the funeral."

I had been in charge of the funeral and burial of Greneda Bruce a week before.

"What sort of letter, Mrs. Bruce?"

Another silence. Then Miss Joanna spoke again. "To put it plainly, it was a blackmail letter to Greneda. It threatened to destroy her reputation if she didn't sell her property down by the railroad."

"Well, who wrote it?"

"We don't know. It said 'An Old Friend.' We think Greneda knew, but she wouldn't tell."

Then Titus added, "We think that letter is what brought on the stroke that killed her."

I thought of the highly respectable maiden lady Greneda Bruce, owner of valuable property in town and benefactor of the poor, and wondered what scandal could threaten her reputation. She's in the ground now, I thought, and safe from scandal.

"I blame myself, partly at least, for losing track of that letter," Miss Joanna said. "I get flustered sometimes and leave things lying where I put them down. With all the upset at Greneda's collapse, I plain forgot that letter, and now I can't find it. I've looked and looked. Now I wonder if Greneda picked it up and maybe put it in a pocket in her dress. Or maybe inside her shirtwaist. That's why we've come to ask if you found it."

"Well, you know, I don't prepare the women for burial. We have a woman, Mrs. Mabel Donahue, to do that. I can ask her. But if Miss Greneda took it with her, isn't that the end of the threat?"

"May not be," Titus said. "That letter might still be used to threaten the reputation of the whole family. We have three girls' reputations to look out for. You know how people say young folks repeat the sins of their elders. That letter might be used to blackmail the family into selling that property. Rents from it were a big part of her income. That income goes into her estate, which our girls will inherit."

I looked the question what did that letter say, but didn't put it into words. They read my thoughts, though.

"We're not prepared just yet to talk about the contents of that letter," Titus said, "but it could hurt a lot of people."

"Yes?"

"The Eastern and Southern Railroad wants that property to build a switching yard and will one day pay a stout price for it. Greneda has warehouses on it right now, mostly used by the railroad, and gets a nice income from the rents. C. K. Whittington, that railroad lawyer, talked with her several times about selling the property to the railroad. But we're pretty sure he's not the 'old friend' who wrote the letter. He must have talked to somebody else, and that somebody, whoever he is, must want to get in on the increased value of the property and must have written the letter."

"It's not just the money I worry about," Miss Joanna said. "It's the reputation, too. Family pride, I guess you'd call it. We seem to have our share. Sometimes I feel real bad when I think how Greneda's life was ruined by family pride. She could have married when she was young and had a nice family, children and all, but Papa Bruce, that's old Ferguson Bruce you may remember, wouldn't hear of it. Said the young man wasn't good enough for her. Lived over his store, and no daughter of his was going to live like that. Makes me feel real bad when I think about that."

"Now, Miss Joanna." Titus patted her hand.

Listening to them, I thought again how we funeral directors see guilts and angers come out when a family member dies. It was one of the things we had to deal with, to smooth over if we could and get the funeral done without undignified displays, but it was a delicate act. Things get real when death comes, and sometimes folks don't postpone reckonings as they've done for years. I've seen a couple of good fights within the family around a funeral, and it isn't pretty. Somehow I could feel sympathy for them. But a funeral director's job is to keep things moving smoothly. So I got back to practical matters.

"I'll talk with Mrs. Donahue and see if she found the letter. I'll let you know one way or the other."

"Good. Thank you, Roy. We'll be waiting. Oh, I almost forgot. Mollie said to tell you hello. She wants to show you some more of what she's written."

Mollie was their oldest daughter. She taught school in town and did some writing when she had time. She was not a bad writer—pretty good, in fact. Maybe I was biased, as she looked pretty good, too. She had shown me some of her writing and wanted my criticism because, she said, I had been out in the world more than she had and could tell her when she hit a false note. I wasn't too sure about that.

When I asked Mabel if she had seen a letter while she was preparing Miss Greneda for the casket, Mabel said she hadn't but couldn't be sure there wasn't one. She hadn't been looking for one.

"But I will tell you, Mr. Roy, what I seen. As I was rearrangin' her clothes to put on her funeral dress, I seen her belly." Mabel used plain talk, and I was glad she didn't deal with the clients. "She had stretch marks on her belly. Them's from havin' a child, I said to myself. What's a fine upstandin' maiden lady doin' with stretch marks on her belly? I'm glad you asked."

That wasn't quite what I'd asked, but I thought fast. "Let's keep that between us. Don't tell anyone else."

"Don't worry. I know my place. Ain't the worst thing I seen doin' this work."

When I told Titus and Miss Joanna that Mabel hadn't found the letter but couldn't be sure it wasn't on Miss Greneda, their unease got worse.

"So we don't know where that letter is yet," Miss Joanna said. "If it's still around, it's dangerous and waiting to be used. It'll be our reputation at stake."

By now I didn't need them to tell me the contents of the letter. "Blackmail is a crime," I reminded them, "and I think the blackmailer would be more at risk than you are."

"I reckon he, or she, has already thought of that and is willing to take the risk to make some good money," Titus said.

"I still think the letter was somewhere on Greneda," Miss Joanna said with a frown, "and we've just got to know. If it's with her, that's fine, but we have to know."

Titus thought a minute. "Could we get a court order to open her grave? That way we'd know."

"Opening graves is pretty messy," I said. "Not a pleasant sight for anybody concerned. And it's true, once a person is in the ground, the burial becomes part of the public record, and you have to have the court's permission to change the record." I could see what was coming and didn't like it.

"What reason could we give for opening that grave?" Miss Joanna wanted to know. "We can't tell Judge Harrison about a threat of scandal and blackmail."

"We could give another reason and look for the letter while we're doing whatever we said was the reason." Titus again.

"Well, I just don't know," Miss Joanna worried.

I thought I'd better let them know some of the complications. "You know, Dr. Brandon, the coroner, would have to be present at the opening. He'd soon realize something was going on."

"I know Jack," Titus said. "We're poker friends. He'd look the other way."

"Well, I just don't know what in the world we could say." Miss Joanna again.

Titus, I could tell, was beginning to feel stronger about his idea. "We could say a valuable family heirloom was left on Greneda's body, and we need to get it back. Tom Harrison might be sympathetic, even if he is from out of town."

"If it was Lawton Harvey holding court, I'd feel better about it," Miss Joanna said. "He's almost family. He'd understand." I saw her look slantwise at Titus and wondered what that look meant.

"I'd say it's worth a try. Will you support our petition, Roy? They'd want to know how you stand, since you did the burial."

I nodded a reluctant yes.

"Good. We can get Will Ford to present the petition. He knew Greneda some these last years."

When their lawyer, Will Ford, presented the petition, Judge Harvey was holding court. Gray and handsome, maybe mid-fifties. About as much an aristocrat as Cromwell could produce. Titus and Miss Joanna looked relieved and confident while Will described a pendant necklace that had been Miss Greneda's since the beginning of the century. The Judge asked a few more questions, mainly about disturbing the body during the search, then gave his verdict.

"Petition denied. Let the pendant stay with the deceased."

Titus and Miss Joanna were so stunned they could hardly speak. Will Ford offered his regrets and said he could try again when Judge Harrison came up on the circuit.

Outside the courthouse, Titus and Miss Joanna finally found their voices. Miss Joanna said she just couldn't understand that verdict. Harvey was practically family and owed a debt to the family.

Titus thought different. "I reckon Lawton is in the pay of the railroad and don't care about family no more. He must know how the railroad wants that property and ain't about to help the family."

When Will asked again if they wanted to try the petition another time, Titus said, "No. That's it."

I wondered why they had lost steam so suddenly but couldn't think of a good answer. So I asked a question they could answer.

"How did Miss Greneda come by that property? It sure seems to be at the center of things."

"She come by it twenty-five years ago," Titus said. "Bought it with her inheritance from my granddaddy, Silas Bruce."

"Nice inheritance," I said.

When I got back to my office, though, I began to think things didn't add up. As I remembered Mama and Papa talking about Silas Bruce, he didn't have a lot to give. Small-time farmer with a houseful of children. It was Ferguson Bruce, Titus's father, who made the money in the family, they said. Cotton trading. And that property beside the railroad was valuable even twenty-five years ago. Maybe not as much as now, but still worth more than a small inheritance. Maybe the real answer was in the property records. Find out who owned the property before it was sold to Miss Greneda. Need to check into that one of these days.

And then there was Miss Greneda. Even while I was growing up in town before the war, she had a reputation for doing good works in Cromwell. Ran a school for children of the mill workers so they could learn to read, write, and figure, even if they had to miss public school to work and help support their families or help keep the younger kids when both parents had to work. And with the help of Dr. Washburn and later Dr. Kathleen Sullivan, she ran a clinic for those kids to dose their earaches and fevers and vaccinate them against smallpox. And check them for signs of tuberculosis. More than Ireland County or Cromwell did for them. Mama and Papa also thought she was said to have worked with Jane Addams at Hull-House in Chicago, doing some kind of social work, before coming back to Cromwell.

While I was thinking over those puzzles for a couple of days, I had a call from Sheriff Patterson to come out in the county, where they'd had a bad automobile accident. Where the Danville Road crosses the Davis Mill Road.

"Do I need to fetch a doctor, Johnny?"

"Naw. One's all right, just shook some. The other's past doctorin'."

"What about Jack Brandon? Will you need a coroner's report?"

"He can do it when we get the body to town. Nothin' complicated here. He just went off the road. No collision."

"I'll be there soon as I can."

"I got to get back to the wreck. It's a long way between phones out here. See you there."

So I told Johnny Dayton where I'd be and went out to the big garage behind the trees, where we keep our service cars. Johnny is my assistant, doing his practical training with me. He's already been to mortuary school but needs the practical experience and the money before he sets up on his own. Been saving up for a couple of years and, with help from his wife's father, should soon have enough to go into business in his hometown.

I got in our second truck—not the hearse, but the older one with the covered sides and top. Save the hearse for funerals. The older one Johnny calls the meat wagon, but I told him to be careful who hears him say that. We keep the jokes going when we work in the back room, but you have to keep things solemn when you're with the bereaved family and their friends. I guess we live a double life of sorts, but it's part of the work. I went around to the side workroom and told Jess, our do-it-all, to come with me on a call. We had a body to collect.

"Hope it ain't bloody, Mr. Roy. That gets me some time."

It was bloody some but not bad. The well-dressed young man's head was bashed pretty bad, and I guessed he died from a skull fracture. Jack Brandon would say soon enough. Johnny Patterson and his deputy had already pulled the man out of the ditch and had him at the edge of the road. They had the young woman sitting in the sheriff's car. She looked dazed but all right.

"This is Miss Jackie Carter, from Richmond," Patterson said when I went up to the car. "She says the young man is Henry Stutts, also out of Richmond." He introduced me as the man from the funeral home in Cromwell.

"Ma'am," I said and nodded.

She just nodded. I looked at her again. She was youngish, maybe in her twenties, blonde, had on stylish clothes, and had bobbed hair like what the papers said party girls wore these days. Her dress was pretty short, and she showed a good bit of leg but didn't seem to care if the deputy was sneaking looks. Different from what he was used to with most Ireland County girls, I'd think. Her dress was rumpled some and had a couple of dirt spots but didn't show any tears. Her eyes were teary but not red from lots of crying the way I'd seen some folks. She had a smudge spot on her nose and another on her forehead but no bruises or cuts that I could see. Still in shock, I thought.

"You all right, Miss Carter?" I asked. "We can get you to a doctor if you need one."

"I'm okay. Is Henry really dead?"

"Afraid so. We'll take him into town. You can see him there after we get him cleaned up."

"I want to take him back to Richmond. Can you arrange that?"

"Yes, ma'am. We'll arrange that when you get to town. Do you know anyone in Cromwell? We can have them meet you."

"The Bruces. We were going to visit them before this happened. They're cousins. Do you know them?"

"Yes, quite well. I'll let them know."

Then I decided to do something about those smudges. "Do you have a mirror, Miss Carter? Might want to check your face before you see your cousins."

"Oh!" she said and grabbed a compact mirror out of her purse.

While she was repairing her face, Jess and I loaded the young man into the back of the wagon. I figured it would be good to have her look at something else while we did that.

"All right, Sheriff?" I asked.

"Take him away," Patterson said. "I'll get her to town."

Back in town, Jack Brandon examined the body and filled out the death certificate saying Henry J. Stutts died of a skull fracture, then said, "I also found plenty of evidence of alcohol in his body. Didn't put that on the death certificate, though."

I looked at him. He was beginning to age. Looked older than I thought a man in his fifties should look. Hair was almost all gray, his face lined, his suit in need of a good pressing. I remembered his wife had died a few years before. He had a woman come in to look after his house but no one to look after him. Keeping a practice going in town and acting as county coroner probably drained him.

"What do you make of that?" I asked.

"Hard to tell. That is, if he was driving. Was he?"

"Didn't hear anybody say. He was in the ditch outside the driver's side of the car. The woman was in the sheriff's car when I got there. Don't know how she got out of the car in the ditch. Her clothes didn't look like she'd rolled in the grass. Had smudges on her face like she'd hit something inside the car."

"Hmm."

"You think he lost control and she grabbed at the wheel?"

"Might be. She smell like alcohol?"

"Not so I could tell. Didn't get real close to her, though."

"No bottles in the car?"

"Didn't see any. Haven't gone through his pockets to see if he had a flask. Reckon Johnny Patterson will check over the car."

"Don't you funeral types have to check bodies for identifications and valuables before you bury them?"

"The young woman says we'll be sending him off to be buried in Richmond." I wondered if he'd been talking with Titus and Miss Joanna.

"Well, he's yours now. Good luck."

Meanwhile, I knew the Bruces were consoling and pampering the Carter girl. The Bruce girls—Mollie, Livie, and Sally—would know how to comfort her and sympathize with her. Their house usually sounded with laughter and chatter, and no matter how sad she was, the cousin would feel their spirits.

Next day, with Titus Bruce along to brace her up, Jackie Carter came to the office to arrange for Henry Stutts to be sent home. I told her it was a fairly routine procedure, and without going into details about embalming, told her he would have to be prepared to be sent home. I had to ask her if she knew of a mortician to be notified, and she said have Richard Lee Brooks meet the train. He was a family friend of the Stuttses. I said I would look him up in the directory and give him a call.

Then I had to ask her if she had notified Henry's family yet. She said no, she had cringed at the thought, and the Bruces had deferred to her feelings. I said we needed to do that right away, did she have a clergyman who could inform the family? She looked relieved and asked if I could call Reverend Hugh B. N. Martinson and have him tell Henry's family and hers. She had his number in her purse. He had been going to marry them, and she had talked with him several times.

I told her I would have to ask her some questions about her family and Henry's so I could fill out the forms for the records funeral homes had to keep. Usually, if the death occurred after an illness, you had to ask how long the illness had been known, who had been told and when, whether those who knew expected the death, and who else should be told of the death. Since in this case no expectations had been held, could she tell about the circumstances surrounding the accident? It's at times of these interviews that you learn much of the sadness and subdued lives of the families.

Henry's family was in banking in Richmond, she said. Henry was a stockbroker and had a good future. She and Henry were engaged and were to be married soon. She was bringing him to Cromwell to meet her cousins. This was to be their pleasure trip before getting into all the social rounds that went with a wedding.

To that point, she had kept her poise. Finally she began to break down. For a few moments she seemed almost paralyzed with grief and regret, I thought. Through tears, she said they were too happy, she should have known they would crash from floating free. She regretted their flings, their heavy drinking and late dancing, their taking advantage of their indulgent parents. Now she had a dark time ahead. She knew Henry's parents would blame her for his death. She didn't know how she could face them.

Who were her parents? Jackson and Elizabeth Carter of Richmond. That's where she got the name Jackie, I thought. No brothers or sisters, she said.

As they got ready to leave, Titus said, "Will you take care of all these arrangements, Roy? I'll see you next week about the expenses." We shook hands all around, and they went out.

While I made notes on actions to take and filed the interview notes, I thought how those files held the secret history of Cromwell and Ireland County. Lots of things that never got into the public record or into records of families unless they were careful keepers of letters and diaries. I'd heard too often at times like this how sons and daughters and grandchildren couldn't find the letter that told how Mama wanted her funeral done or where she wanted to be buried.

But a file like this and work like this gave insight into lives in the community, held hints of secrets that come out when citizens die, of family disputes, rivalries, jealousies, and unacknowledged loves. You come to see the time of death and grief as the frontier between the frets of living and the long view of loss, between the hopes for change and the judgment of lives finally finished. In this work, you help families and individuals deal with their grief while you take care of the practical cleanup of the details left over after lives are used up. Somebody has to clean up, and most don't know how.

Sometimes you're caught up in the conflicts of living that carry over into death, and whether you want to or not, you have to decide. It's happened to me. I was caught between the family pride of the Vances and McMillans when my mother, Martha McMillan

Vance, died. Was she to be buried with the Vances or McMillans? Uncle Jeremy McMillan let me know that the McMillans expected her to be buried as a McMillan. They were a longer-standing family in Cromwell than were the late-arriving Vances. There was already a plot waiting for her in the McMillan area. He knew I would want to honor the McMillan part of my name by putting my mama with her people. But I remembered how Mama had said she chose Papa over the reservations of her family and told Uncle Jeremy she'd made her choice thirty years ago. I missed being invited to several McMillan reunions after that.

Chapter 2

As I thought how folks continued to keep a hold on me because I knew some of their secrets and maybe had helped, I began to remember how I'd come to be an undertaker in Cromwell. Not exactly a straight track.

I started here in Cromwell, born in 1895 to Vernon and Martha McMillan Vance. Papa was a tobacco buyer, came in with the tobacco market from the eastern part of the state. A late but welcome addition, Cromwellians said as they struggled to get over the effects of the war. Mama was from a longtime Ireland County family that had branches all over the county. Some had moved to town, some stayed on the farm. But they were all one clan, family they called it, and were ready to tell how they had been here for six generations. That's why they looked askance at Papa. To them, he had no family.

My brother Roger was born late the next year, barely nineteen months after I was. We were close enough together to spend our childhood and youth years hearing from grandparents, uncles, aunts, and cousins how McMillans and Ireland County were practically the same. While Mama could take up for the Vances, she shared the McMillan hold for strict religion, and when it came time for us to go to college, she insisted on a church school, though Papa went on record that one of the public colleges would be just as good.

I went off to Zion College one year, and Roger went the next. With much McMillan encouragement, I said I would study to become a doctor and spent four years mostly in physiology and chemistry labs. Roger thought engineering was more his style, spent much of his time in physics labs and all his time arguing with Mama and trying to get transferred to a state engineering school. But after college I decided to spend a year traveling before going to med school. The McMillan elders pulled their gray beards and gray faces and wanted to know why waste a year. Partly their reluctance came because I wanted to go to Washington state to visit some of the Vances who had moved there. But they finally said go.

I went to Washington all right and saw the Pacific, but I spent a good part of the trip in the Rocky Mountain states, Idaho and Montana in particular. I really liked the openness of the big country, bright green in summer, cold gray and green most of the rest of the year. That was when the Montana copper miners were fighting the mining syndicates. Tension was in the air, and guns sounded on the streets. I never was in the battle line during the strikes and lockouts and shootings, but I was there to help carry out the casualties, and I saw what men did to men. No family or religion there. I began to lose my belief in social progress when I saw miners clubbed and shot and the IWW labor union, broken by the mining syndicate's toughs and the government's lawyers and judges.

I remember at one of the gatherings around the fires before a big fight to come the next day, old Bill Haywood told me, "Roy, we've got plenty of men mad enough to fight. We need folks like you to clean up after the fight." I didn't know it then, but that was setting my pattern.

About that time the country was ready to go to war again, this time with Germany, and since I didn't have the McMillans to hold me back, I answered the call. I was among the earliest to volunteer, and they sent me to the 120-day training school for reserve officers at Fort Myers, Virginia. I expected to get a rush through infantry school and be sent to France first thing, as the papers kept saying how we needed to get the American Expeditionary Force into the line quick to stop the Germans. They had other plans for me, though. When they handed out assignments, Second Lieutenant Roy McMillan Vance was sent to the Communications Corps, later called the Service of Supply, and I got put in the Graves Registration Division. Roger had volunteered for the Marines, and they were pushing hard to get him and his unit into the fighting to prop up the French. Good thing they did, as we know now the big German push in spring 1918 was building up.

My unit of service troops was all black. Mostly from southern and Midwest states. The AEF was not very concerned about amenities for colored troops during the buildup, and my job was to protect, scrounge, borrow, steal, and sneak what I could to provide for my men. According to the AEF in France, they were supposed to be happy with unheated and unfloored canvas tents and stay out of the soldiers' canteens. But with the talents I found in the unit, they soon had winter-tight huts with plank floors and stoves and a canteen of their own furnished from the backs of trucks during the night. They were cagey too, and kept the outside of their area looking ramshackle outside but neat inside. They didn't tempt commanding officers to inspect them. Corporal Dan Blue was their working boss, and we kept a silent but congenial arrangement going within the army, both stateside and in France.

We got to France before most of the big fighting units did and were sent to the St. Mihiel sector to learn from the French how to handle our casualties. What we learned wasn't pretty. Most of the dead were so smashed up that identification was a bigger problem than burying the remains. The French infantry, and later the

American infantry, were pretty casual about keeping their official identifications on them and lots of times would leave behind their discs with a buddy or friend who wasn't going into the line or over the top or on a trench raid. They said it was to keep the Germans from knowing their units in case they were captured, but my view was they wanted to make it hard for units like ours. I had to become a detective of sorts to establish the identities of casualties. The question was not Who Done It? but Who Was It?

Examination of the bodies wasn't enough. You had to check with unit commanders after an action and count noses to see who didn't come back. Or check with others in the unit to see if they knew what happened to their buddies. Or check with the medical dressing stations to see who didn't make the triage, where they sort out the wounded into those who can make it back to the base hospitals, those who might, and those who can't. Sometimes the padres could help, since they were supposed to know whose remains they had said burial prayers over. And you had to make sure that some hadn't been sent to the rear. Getting the death reports right was the big job. Actual burial was more casual.

For those certifiably dead, you wrapped them in their blankets or any decent covering and put them in the ground behind the front, with a chaplain there to do burial rites. One of the sad secrets of the war was that those neat military cemeteries they would build later would be filled with death markers, not grave markers. The bodies were back there near the front, sometimes on the wrong side of the trench line if the front had shifted, and nobody wanted to dig up bodies in an area filled with unexploded shells.

The need to get the records right came home to me one evening when Corporal Blue called from an airfield where he'd gone to pick up bodies after an air raid.

"Lootenant, you remember the fly boy you did the report on, the one that crashed but didn't burn?"

"Yes. Have it on my table right here."

"Don't send it."

"How come?"

"Wrong man."

"How's that?"

"Tell you later. Cap'n here don't like body-snatchers usin' his phone, but one of the fly boys let me use it anyway. Got to get off this talkin' box."

When he got back, Blue said the man we thought had been in the crashed plane was at the airfield. His buddy's plane had been in the bunker for repairs. When the alert came, the buddy had grabbed our man's jacket and plane, took off, later came down shot up, and crashed. We had gone by the plane's numbers and the name on the jacket. Our man's squadron didn't know where he was and said we must have their man. So with the casual ways of the fly boys, we were about to make a big mistake. To make matters worse, the flyer we were about to report as a casualty was the nephew of a Midwest politician with influence in Washington. I hated to think of the screams from Washington and AEF headquarters when we sent in a wrong death report.

A blunder like that, I thought, would stop any chance for promotion and better pay. But as it turned out, I came out of the war at the same rank I went in. They tried to ignore the need for units like ours and forgot us when awards were handed out. We did more and more business as the Argonne push got going in early October 1918. Those German machine guns must have been hell to face. We had a lot of cleanup to do after the "Lost Battalion" of the 77th Division was surrounded by Germans and held them off for six days. They paid the price for their position, and we helped bury it. They had buried some of their dead within the position even while the fighting went on, and we had to find the shallow graves, get the identifications, and help the heroes get their rightful recognitions.

Near the end of the war, we were burying almost as many victims of the Spanish influenza as we were casualties of bullets and shrapnel. They said the German army was weakening because of the flu, but we were hurting too. One of the doctors recently over from the States said it was wrong to call the influenza Spanish. The Allied and German presses were so censored that almost no one on our side knew the extent of the epidemic. The Spaniards weren't in the war, though, and their press published uncensored accounts of victims in Spain. The American and British presses picked up on those reports and said the influenza was coming out of Spain. Somehow the influenza didn't pay attention to the armistice and kept going right on through 1918 and into 1919. They kept us burial details busy in France, even during embarkation at Le Havre, after most of the fighting units had gone home to be demobbed and maybe carried the infection with them. We didn't have the problems of identification we'd had earlier, though. These victims knew well before their last breath that they were in for a fevered hell and had us and the padres send last messages to the folks back home. When I got back to the States and followed up on some of those messages, I learned how some families dealt with their griefs, endurances, desperations, and quiet heroisms. Some cried at the cruel fate that let their men escape the bullets and then get hit with the flu. Maybe that was part of my preparation for what came next.

After I was demobbed, I thought medical school had been put off too long, and I was ready to do better what I had been doing the last two years. So I went to mortuary school in Richmond, did my practical year at Mechanicsville, and began looking for a place to start my own funeral home. The unspent pay from my time in France helped pay for school. Still had some left to put into the business. At that time, I had no plans to come back to Cromwell, but I heard through my McMillan connections that Clyde Rogers wanted to sell his funeral home and retire. About that time, Papa died and left me a small inheritance, though, of course, most of his estate went to Mama. I offered Mama my part, but she said to put it in the business. She was feeling right blue at the time, not only because of Papa's death but because Roger was failing. He'd made captain in the Marines during the war but had been wounded and gassed. He'd been in navy and veterans' hospitals, and it was clear he wasn't going to get better. He died shortly after I set up business and went to his plot at Arlington.

Clyde Rogers' place was an old-style funeral home, at one time a good-size mansion not far from the center of town, with big porches on the front and one side and wide roof overhangs all around. Clyde had reshaped the downstairs to make an office, viewing rooms, and a chapel for funerals. He'd added a wing out back to do the embalming, and he lived upstairs. The approach from the street was through a nice arrangement of tall trees in the front and on the sides and shrubs that helped give the feeling of home to the funeral home. I could see, though, I'd have to add more parking area as more people bought autos and rode them in processions out to the cemeteries. Garages for the hearse, trucks, and limousine were way to the back of the area and were masked by evergreens that kept them out of sight and mind all seasons. There was room for additional wings if the business did well. So I made the plunge, used my leftover army pay and Papa's money to make the down payment, and borrowed the rest. At the bank, John Gentry said the loan was good—I'd always have a demand in Cromwell, and he was glad a hometown boy would keep the tradition going. A new man in town might have trouble gaining the confidence of the folks in the town and county. So he agreed to hold my mortgage until I paid it off.

On the day I signed my mortgage, I went back to the place, walked the grounds, and looked around the neighborhood. The street was paved and wide as neighborhood streets went, but not so wide as to keep the big trees from forming a tall green archway over the road. Sidewalks on the other side and big two-story houses much like mine set back from the sidewalks. Houses with wide porches and several with wings added to accommodate growing families over two or three generations. I knew most of the houses and families from my time growing up in Cromwell. The Ellises and Barnwells still lived there. So did the Ramsays. Some had different families from the original owners, but in good Cromwell usage, the houses continued to be called after the original owners. The Matthews lived in the Saunders place, and I wondered how long they would have to live there for it to be called the Matthews place. Old-timers still called it the Saunders place and shook their heads. Kidd Saunders' wife had died there, and Kidd had killed himself there. But that happened while I was away at college.

Clyde stayed on a couple of months after he sold out, to show me the local tricks of the trade and tell me about quirks of folks in town, he said. I guessed he had a hard time letting go. His wife had died while I was away from Cromwell, and his children had moved out of town. He was supposed to go live with his daughter and her family in Johns County but was in no hurry, even if he had moved out. He had called the place the Community Funeral Home, and since he hadn't named it for himself, I kept the name. I knew I had not learned all about dealing with death and loss, but I was learning fast.

I soon found I needed help to keep a business and a place that big going. I hired Auntie Flo Bessemer to cook meals and keep my living quarters decent. She soon let me know her nephew Jess could use some work too, and I hired him to help keep the funeral home dusted and shined and before long to help Johnny Dayton or me bring in the deceased. After a couple of weeks of funerals, I realized I needed more help directing the mourners and hired Reverend Cyrus Benton part time to assist in keeping funerals moving along smoothly. He had a dark suit and dignified gray hair, was formal but easy with folks, and was retired. He could use the money. After some uneasy questions from families of women who'd died about the propriety of dressing their bodies for burial, I hired Mabel part time to do that job. She had a natural touch for doing that kind of work and a salty tongue for talking about it.

I started courting Mollie Bruce not long after I came back to town but was not making much progress. I'd had the usual round of casual girlfriends during college and a couple during my trip west but had missed meeting any of those French women they talked about in the army. Maybe my courting manners were rusty, or just out-of-date. In any case, Mollie was the first woman I'd met I'd want to take home to meet the family, if I had a family. But I suspected Mollie didn't see herself married to a funeral home. Her writing was my rival. We could talk politics and the new kind of writing all day, but she shied away from intimate talk and turned it into humor. She was domestic enough. I knew she could run the Bruce household with a sure hand when Miss Joanna sometimes lost track of where things had been put. Like most young women of the day, she'd had her dark hair cut but not bobbed. Probably a concession to teaching in the classroom at the elementary school. She was medium height as I was, quick to move, and light on her feet. She liked dancing the reels more than the Charleston and wanted to get everyone moving across the floor.

Her next younger sister Livie was taller and blonder and wore her hair and skirts short. She worked in Titus's office but really wanted to move to a larger city and swing with the moderns. She attracted a lot of suitors but seemed unable or unwilling to choose any particular one. Not very domestic either. Miss Joanna referred to her more than once as "our flighty child." Titus seemed to dote on her, though. She probably brought sparks to his life.

Youngest sister Sally was tall, blonde, leggy, and moved like a colt. Which was fitting, I guess, because she liked horses and wanted to train them. She rode every chance she could get and shared her enthusiasm for horses with William Walker. William ran the lumber company after his father Josh had a stroke and retired from the business. I thought they had some sort of unannounced understanding, even though she did her share of dancing with the young men who came to the house. They were mostly Episcopalians and didn't mind a drink with their dances, but you didn't ask where the drinking stuff came from. Unlike the dour Presbyterian McMillans, who had voted for Prohibition.

Meanwhile, I was learning how to run a funeral home in Cromwell. Most calls were routine, but the complications could set in after that. Sometimes folks balked at the cost of a funeral, but they usually talked about something else. The two daughters of Mrs. Julia Haskins came to complain that we failed to make their mother look dignified in the casket. I asked them what they wanted different, even though the funeral was the next day. They said the mouth wasn't Mama's and something was wrong with the hair. I said we'd take care of it, though we couldn't do much but put some more makeup on the face. I knew the mother had had an autopsy because of the peculiar manner of her death, and we had to do some remolding of her head to cover evidence of the autopsy. They grudgingly said Mama looked better.

I didn't tell them we couldn't make a body look like she'd just stepped from the land of the living. "She looks so natural" was a fiction. The best you could do was give the deceased the austere dignity of someone about to go on a long journey. I thought the old Egyptians had the idea of death about right. Maybe our embalming wasn't as thorough as their mummification, but it helped give the same effect.

Another problem was the difference between the wishes of the family and the customs of the clergy. Mrs. Harry Holcomb and Reverend Magnus Kane were the case in point. The funeral was to be at Kane's church. Harry was a veteran of the war, and Mrs. Holcomb wanted his casket covered by the flag during the funeral. With his gray hair, dark suit, and square face, Reverend Kane said funerals at his church had the casket covered by the same pall that all funerals there had—it had been that way for years and years. We were at an impasse for a while. Finally we all agreed. The pall was on the casket during the funeral, and at the church door we whipped off the pall and put on the flag for Harry's trip to the cemetery.

The other case was that of the two men, longtime fishing friends, who drowned when their boat swamped in a sudden storm on the lake. Jack Maples was a Baptist, Ron Goodspeed a Methodist, and their families scheduled their funerals at their own churches only a couple of hours apart. Even if the men were friends, I doubt their ministers were. I'd heard their differences went beyond theological. Jack's funeral was first, and Brother Makin's idea of a funeral service was to "preach a funeral." So he preached on while we looked at our watches and fanned. I had had Johnny Dayton posted at the Methodist church funeral so he could get guests met and registered and if necessary extend the preliminaries while we got Maples buried and sped back to the church with the hearse and limousine. At the graveside, I made sure Brother Makin faced the summer sun while he said last prayers. The sun was hot enough to keep folks from lingering, and along with Ron's friends, led by a deputy I'd hired to clear the way, we got to the Methodist church after only two extra numbers by the organist.

One afternoon Mr. Horace Bogart came to the office to ask for advice. As he settled into the chair, I tried to put together what I could see and what I remembered about him. Dark hair tinged with gray, dark face, dark suit, dark eyes that looked straight into mine. He moved with a sense of authority. He had a string of stores throughout the county that were doing well, and he was moving up in Cromwell society, such as it was. To show it, he had built an imposing house on one of the hills overlooking the town. Red brick, tall white columns, formal proportions. It looked like a house built to show position, not to provide ease of living. He wanted to talk about moving the graves of his daughter and son-in-law away from the little Lutheran cemetery near the railroad tracks to Cedar Hill Cemetery, where most of the Episcopalians, Methodists, and Presbyterians were buried. His daughter and son-in-law had died of the influenza back in '19, and Horace and his wife had taken the grandchildren to raise. He knew that most of the plots in old Cedar Hill were taken or spoken for, and he wanted me to speak to Robert Watts, who ran Cedar Hill, to see if some of the plots could be bought for his family. He was ready to pay good money, and maybe some families who had bought plots years ago would rather have the money than the plots. He knew some folks' expectations and circumstances had changed. He thought his grandchildren would be proud to know their parents were resting at Cedar Hill.

I told him I didn't know of any plots available, but I'd be glad to look around and talk to Bob Watts.

Chapter 3

A couple of weeks later, I went out to Cedar Hill to see Watts about Bogart's plan. His assistant at the little gatehouse they used for an office said Watts had gone into town on some personal business. Could he help? I told him what I wanted. He said Mr. Watts had those records in his office in town, but I was welcome to walk around the area to find any untaken plots.

Cedar Hill does indeed have cedars, lots of tall, dark green trees reaching high, some at the crest of the main hill. You get a dark green feeling when you walk around in the older areas. I thought I might as well stop by Papa's and Mama's graves while I was near and walked among the shoulder-high markers, many of them McMillans, past the crest of the hill to a less shadowed area, where the cedars were younger and thinner. There they were:

That Time of Year

Vernon Baylor Vance *Martha McMillan Vance*
1870–1919 *1872–1922*
Good Night, Sweet Prince *She Always Appreciated*

I said hello to them and wished them peace and remembered how Mama loved her Shakespeare. She, I thought, was better than rubies.

About that time, I heard a car on the road on the other side of the crest and then voices. When the voices came again, this time clearer, I realized it was the Bruce girls talking and then another voice, at first unfamiliar. Then I thought—the Carter girl.

I'd heard from Mollie and Livie that Jackie Carter was coming back for another visit. She'd had a bad time with Henry Stutts's family in Richmond. They had blamed her for Henry's death, as she'd expected. The funeral had been an unusually emotional one, with his father's business friends and his mother's social friends wearing long faces and talking about the great loss of family expectations. They had let her know by silences and exclusions she had no place in their grief or sympathies. She hadn't been seated with the family at the funeral. Mollie had said too that Jackie had become religious and had become a regular at the Episcopal church. She wasn't the bright party girl she'd been before. Now she had come to visit her cousins and get away from Henry's family. They hoped they could cheer her up.

They got out of the open-top car and came over in their pale yellow, green, and pink summer dresses and wide-brim hats.

"Roy, surprised to see you here!" Mollie called as I walked over the crest. They were walking around the grave markers, looking at names and dates.

"We've been riding the country roads," she said in a low voice, "trying to get Jackie to brighten up. She's still awfully droopy. Thought we'd come by here and see Aunt Greneda's grave. Not that I'd call seeing graves a cheery thing to do. But Jackie said, 'Let's go in here.' So we decided to find Aunt Greneda. I know they don't have the marker up yet. Do you remember which way it is?"

"Down a little farther," I said. "You can barely see the mound between those markers."

I went with them to the Bruce area. It was almost filled with markers from pretty far back, and not far from the McMillans. The cedars stood tall around. Through the green light, we could see the inscriptions.

"Look at this one," Livie called. "Hello Great-Grandpa and Great-Grandma."

> *Silas Bruce   Annie Lee Cox Bruce*
> *1815–1900   1819–1895*

"I found one too," Sally said.

> *Ferguson Bruce   Amanda Stevenson McDonald Bruce*
> *1840–1905   1850–1898*

"That's Grandpa and Grandma," said Livie.

"But look at this string of other Bruce tombstones. I'd forgotten there were so many. Papa Bruce had a bunch." Livie read them out: "Louisa 1845–1915, Deborah 1843–1909, Boyd 1841–1862. He's the one got killed at Second Manassas, wasn't he?"

I wondered if he really made it back to Cedar Hill.

"Didn't they have any husbands or wives?" Mollie asked.

"Yes, but I'm just looking at Bruces."

"Hmm. Just the real people."

"Roy, look over here at all the McMillans. They go on for acres," Livie said down the line. "Some of them I can't read, but here's David Hume McMillan 1822–1899, Sarah Stevenson McMillan 1830–1895, and their children, I guess. Andrew. Angus. Mollie."

"Mollie, I didn't know you're a Scot," Sally called.

"So are you. Sally is short for Sarah."

"Hey, here's the one. Look at this," Livie called. "I've found my namesake. Olivia Donaldson Harvey Millard 1847–1905."

"Sounds like she went through a lot of husbands," Mollie said. "She was Mama's mama."

"I want to see," Jackie called. I thought she'd been hanging back from the fun up to then.

"There's Papa Millard right next to her. See? 1845–1904. She outlived him, too," Sally said.

"Well, where's the Harvey in that lineup?" Livie wanted to know.

"Harveys are up the hill to the right," I said.

"Let's go see. But which Harvey will it be?"

"Probably one without a wife beside him," I guessed. "She was put beside her last husband."

"So let's look. But what are we looking for besides a single Harvey?" Sally wanted to know.

"Dates," Mollie said. "He'd better be dead before Olivia and Papa Millard got married. Mama was born in 1880. They must have married in the late seventies. If not, we've got a scandal on our hands."

"This is getting interesting," Jackie said. "I've never gone to the Carter cemetery in Richmond. Didn't want to."

"Well, cross your fingers and let's look," Sally called as she started up the hill.

It didn't take long for us to find Gerald Harvey 1840–1878, with no wife beside him.

"That's him," Sally said. "Thank goodness he died before 1880."

"What's missing is wedding dates," Mollie said. "They don't put those on grave markers."

"How do you find them?" Jackie asked.

"Parish register if they're local and you're lucky. It should have wedding and baptismal dates. And funeral dates. If they kept careful records." Mollie was thinking like a detective.

"Can we see them?" Jackie wanted to know.

"Have to ask Mr. Whitfield at St. Barnabas," I said. "He wouldn't want to pull out the old records just for the sake of curiosity. But if you could think up a good reason, he might." Good luck, I thought.

The Reverend Paul B. Whitfield, rector at St. Barnabas Episcopal, was an officious little man but basically decent. We'd worked well together. He could give a personal touch to the formal service if you approached him right.

Before we left, we wandered around other graves. There were several infants' and children's graves for 1900. I remembered Mama and Papa talking about how so many came down with scarlet fever around that time, and they worried about Roger and me. I wondered if Bogart might find a place among families who lost heavily around then.

Jackie must have picked up on what I said about courting Reverend Whitfield. In a couple of weeks, she and Mollie came to the office, and after Jackie made a hesitant tour through the home, embalming room and all, said they wanted to tell what they had learned. Jackie was looking much better. Her complexion was kind of ivory pink, and she had an impish smile, her eyes amused. Mollie was smiling too at the corners of her mouth, and her eyes gave away whatever secret they were keeping.

Jackie had gone to Mr. Whitfield about her spiritual problems—and they were real—and he had sat with her through several sessions of counsel. She was beginning to get over her anguish at the way the Stuttses had treated her. But she found the reverend had his own anguish. He was an amateur historian and regretted the past when Episcopalians were buried in a cemetery named Cromwell. That was before they changed the name to Cedar Hill. He wondered about the propriety of changing parish records to show that Episcopalians buried before the change were buried at Cedar Hill.

The talk about parish records led to her innocent request to see some of the records, and Reverend Paul began pulling them out of the old cabinets. Before long, Jackie was looking at the wedding register and found that Olivia Donaldson had been married three times. First, to Edward Carter, then to Gerald Harvey, then to Moses Millard. Then she got her hands on the baptismal register and found

Olivia recorded as the birth mother of Jackson Lidell Carter, of Lawton Peter Harvey, and of Joanna Marie Millard.

"Jackson Carter! That's my papa!" she said.

"What about wedding dates and baptismal dates?" I asked.

"I got them too." She fished in her handbag. "Olivia Donaldson and Edward Carter married June 16, 1866. Olivia Carter and Gerald Harvey married November 2, 1869. Olivia Harvey and Moses Millard married July 22, 1879."

"What about baptisms?"

"Jackson Lidell Carter baptized July 27, 1867. Lawton Harvey baptized September 10, 1870. Joanna Millard baptized October 10, 1880."

"Whew!" Mollie said, smiling. "They all came in under the wire. No skeletons there."

"What about burials?"

"Got them too, but not all. No burial for Edward Carter. Gerald Harvey buried February 2, 1878. Moses Millard buried February 10, 1904."

"And Olivia was buried in 1905?"

"Yes. August 20, 1905."

"Good work," I said. Jackie grinned smugly.

"Mr. Whitfield was an old softie."

Mollie had a puzzled look. "I wonder why they didn't put Carter's name on that tombstone along with Harvey and Millard. Something funny there. His name's not in the burial record, either."

"That's right," Jackie said. "I wondered why there wasn't a burial date for him. Did he leave town? Or change churches?"

"Well, your father's in Richmond," I said. "Why don't you ask him?"

"I will. I'm going back next week. Got to give Mollie and Livie and Sally a rest."

Before she left, the Bruce girls gave Jackie a going-away party. I had begun to like the changes I'd seen in her and enjoyed hearing her talk about how she was beginning to feel again. She seemed at home in the white rooms with doors and windows open to the summer weather, bright flowers on the tables, and the lacy green trees and shrubs showing outside. Now that she was dancing again, I faked a Charleston once or twice to be with her and liked to hear her laugh at my attempts. All that, of course, was to help cheer her up. But before long I became aware there was another figure in the picture. Early in the party, I'd seen him standing near the punch bowl talking to Titus and Miss Joanna. He was tall, well tailored in a gray suit, cleanly shaved, and looked both elegant and athletic. He looked about my age, maybe a year or two older. Worst of all, he could dance the Charleston without faking the steps.

"Who's he?" I asked Mollie.

"Landry."

"Where's he from?"

"Philadelphia."

"What's he do?"

"Lawyer."

"How'd he get here?"

"Invited."

After she swished away with her short answers, I began to realize my attempts to help Jackie had not been appreciated by everyone. I decided Titus or Miss Joanna might be less terse informants and went to the punch table for a drink and a talk.

"Oh, he's visiting Dr. Sullivan. Don't you like him?" Miss Joanna said.

"Well, yes, all right, I guess. Is he new in town?"

"No. He's been to Cromwell lots of times."

"Visiting Dr. Sullivan?"

"Yes, always."

"Does she have legal business in Philadelphia?"

"She might. I don't think that's why he comes, though."

"So?"

"He's her son. Name's George Landry."

"With a different name from hers?"

"She's divorced from his father. Took back her maiden name."

"What's the story there?"

"She'll have to tell you. She and Greneda worked together a lot. That's how we know her."

I made a point of meeting George during a pause between dances and was surprised to find I liked him. He talked easily. He had been in the war too, in the legal department as a young lawyer, and we found we'd had common problems dealing with the aftereffects of battles. He'd had to help straighten out legal tangles of soldiers who had property at home and went off to war without making proper wills. Last-minute bequests written on the backs of envelopes were just one of his problems. Sometimes the envelopes belonged to somebody else, and the signatures were nearly impossible to read.

Later in the party, I managed to get Mollie to do some of the slow dances with me. Her talk was less terse than before. I saw George and Jackie sitting together on one of the porch swings, deep in talk. He'll be back, I thought, and not just to see Dr. Kathleen Sullivan. Wonder if he's getting her Richmond address.

About that time Titus came up, touched me on the elbow, and said my man Jess was at the back door. I guessed he must have word of a call to some family, and my guess was right. I told him to let Johnny know I'd be right there. While I was making my manners to Titus and Miss Joanna, a young woman and young man came to the front door. The man was Gib Porter. I knew him in passing but not well. The dark-haired girl looked faintly familiar, but no name came. I looked a question at Titus.

"That's Amanda Lee Harvey. Lawton and Mary Lee's daughter."

"Thought you were at odds with the Judge after the hearing."

"We got over it. He's kin, after all. Distant, but still kin."

"Why haven't I seen her before?"

"You probably did when she was younger. Been away to school several years."

"Glad to hear you all patched things up. Doesn't she have a brother?"

"Yes. Howard Lee. Lawyer, I think. Up in Richmond. Guess he's expected to follow Lawton's steps. I hear he's not as sharp as his daddy, though."

I went to find Mollie, thank her for the party, and tell her I had to leave on business. I could see Livie, Sally, and Jackie all busy with partners about to dance. Mollie was moving to the front door. She stopped briefly, gave me a mischievous smile, said come back soon, and said she had to greet Cousin Amanda and meet her new friend. Quick getaway, quick dismissal.

The call was for Mrs. Elsa Blasingame, one of Dr. Sullivan's patients who died unexpectedly. Dr. Sullivan had called for the hospital ambulance, but the woman died before the ambulance got there. Things had been hectic at the last moment, and Dr. Sullivan hadn't filled out the death certificate. I went to her office the next day to get the certificate signed so I could get the formalities started.

"Oh, yes, Roy. Thank you for bringing it. Have a seat while I fill it out."

I could see she looked tired and maybe perplexed while she wrote on the form. She was a handsome woman with a fair Irish complexion and light brown hair just beginning to show touches of gray. In her fifties, I'd reckon. Probably had been a beauty in her younger days. The way she sat in her desk chair, attentive and erect, said here is a woman of discipline. We had met several times before, but then she had been on the move.

She finished the form and passed it to me. "There you are. Sorry for the delay."

"No problem. I understand you had a tough time before I got there."

"Yes, it was bad. I'd rather not talk about it, though. I still haven't figured out what went wrong."

I'd heard in mortuary school that doctors didn't like to talk about their losses. So I tried a more cheerful subject.

"I met your son yesterday. At the Bruces'. We had a good talk. About the war and what we did."

She brightened, smiled, and relaxed. "Good old George. You'll never know how glad I was he came back without injuries. So what did you do?"

I told her about my work with the graves registration, both near the battle line and with the flu victims.

"So you worked with the epidemic. So did I, but with people in the hospitals. Trying to take business away from you." She laughed ruefully.

We sat a moment, remembering. Then I said, "Miss Joanna had to tell me who George was. The different name threw me."

"Yes. George has his own life now."

"In Philadelphia."

"Yes."

"The Philadelphia connection puzzled me. I'd understood you were from Cromwell."

"If you have a few minutes, I'll tell you about him. I have a daughter, too. Name's Rachel. I expect she'll visit soon. I hope you'll meet her, too."

Then she told me about the life of Kathleen Sullivan. She did indeed come from Cromwell, or near Cromwell. Her father was Frank Sullivan, who owned a prosperous textile mill just outside of town. She was a feisty only child who early saw the drudgery of children working in her father's mill and badgered him about getting the children out of the mill and into school. He was annoyed but indulgent with her. The families needed the money the children brought home, he told her. Then she started in on getting doctoring for the children. Some were becoming deaf from the noise of the machines. Some had lost their hearing from untreated ear infections. Some were so dirty and weak they could get smallpox if anyone brought it to the mill.

The threat of smallpox brought Sullivan to action. One summer while she was home after college, he brought in young Dr. Ross Landry to vaccinate the children and treat their ailments. She helped him with the vaccinations and later helped teach them elementary hygiene. He was from a well-to-do Pennsylvania family, and though he had seen his share of the down-and-out in Philadelphia during his intern days, he was aghast at the poor conditions some mill families lived in. He stayed longer than he was contracted for to help the families, but Kathleen was a major reason for the longer stay.

Working together led to personal interest between them, and before he left, Ross let her know he'd be coming back to see her. They had a brief courtship, got married, and went back to Philadelphia so he could specialize in immunology. In due time, George was born. Ross was doing well enough that they could have a nanny for him while Kathleen got away from the house a couple of days a week. She worked as a volunteer nurse at the hospital, and it was there she met Greneda.

At that point, Dr. Sullivan began to look uncertain about whether to continue. I thought her hesitation came from speaking about Miss Greneda's baby, so I told her, speaking on the basis of professional confidentiality, about what Mrs. Donahue had discovered.

"Then you know about her baby?"

"Some," I said.

She told how she had met Greneda when she was supposedly studying art in Philadelphia but was really there to have the baby away from Cromwell. They had gotten to know each other because of their Cromwell days. But she didn't know what happened to the baby or if it lived. She later heard Greneda had gone to Chicago.

When the war with Spain broke out, Ross went to Florida, and later to Cuba, to treat soldiers' fevers. They had more casualties from fevers than they did from Spanish bullets. When the war was over, Ross came back ready to specialize in tropical medicine. With Americans spread all over the tropics in the newly acquired territories, tropical medicine would be a necessity. While he was doing further study, their second child Rachel was born. And when Ross got an appointment at Johns Hopkins in Baltimore to teach and practice tropical medicine, she thought the shape of her life had been set. She would be the doctor's wife and raise his children.

She got her jolt one day when the children were just ready to enter their teens. Ross came home one day, told her he had fallen in love with a younger woman, a nurse at the hospital, had an affair with her, and gotten her pregnant. Now he wanted to marry her. Although she was hurt and disappointed, they tried to be amicable and reasonable with each other about the situation. In fact, Kathleen met the other woman, Emilia Calvert, and liked her. She and Ross agreed to an amicable divorce, and he had settled valuable property in Philadelphia on her to support her and George and Rachel. She would have no money worries. Another concession she got from Ross was the use of his influence at the medical school in Philadelphia to get her admitted to the physician program. The medical school faculty thought she might be too old to hold up under the demands of medical study, but she proved she could do it. She then went on to special study of women's and children's illnesses. When she was ready to start practice, she took back her maiden name of Sullivan so she could be her own person, not Ross's shadow.

The odd thing, she said, was that she stayed in touch with Ross and Emilia's children, two by now, and was fond of them and on good terms with Emilia. (I wondered then if she was still in love with Ross.) Ross and Emilia had named the first child, a boy, Walter Reed, after one of his medical idols. The girl was named Natalie after Emilia's mother.

Even though she intended her practice to focus on women and children, she worked in the army hospitals treating wounded soldiers and, during the epidemic, treating those with influenza. She knew she had been in a risky situation when she helped with the flu victims, but she had escaped the infection.

Kathleen came back to Cromwell after the war when her father set up a clinic at the mill for the workers. She would work part time at the clinic and start a practice in town. Frank Sullivan was still an old-style mill owner, anti-union and paternalistic, but by now he had seen it was in his own interest to keep his workers healthy and keep away the unions.

That was when she met Greneda again. Greneda was trying to set up a school for the mill children and farm children who missed much of their public school terms because they had to work to help support their families. It was a struggle, and Greneda got little support from the town leaders. Kathleen sometimes extended the clinic from the mill to the school so she could reach the children.

She and Greneda acknowledged that they had met before but respected their pasts by mutual silence. So she never asked Greneda what happened to the baby, and Greneda never asked about Kathleen's marriage. In particular, Greneda never hinted who was the baby's father.

Her practice had prospered. She had seen George through law school and Rachel through college. She had not wanted to marry again, even though Jack Brandon had asked her several times. She wanted her freedom. They had talked often about strange cases they had run across in Cromwell and Ireland County. And she had enjoyed hearing old Dr. Washburn's stories about Cromwell people, some of which would raise your eyebrows if you knew.

"So you never learned about Greneda's baby," I said. "Somebody in Cromwell knows." And I told her about the letter the Bruces were looking for and the threat of blackmail they dreaded.

"So that's what's bothering them," she said. "Sure, I knew something was amiss. They're not their usual easy selves."

She sat silent and thoughtful a minute. "George might help. He knows his way around Philadelphia. I'll speak to him and see if he can find out what happened to Greneda's baby. I'd really like to know. And I liked Greneda. I'd not want something bad to happen to her family or her memory."

So we left the mystery hanging. Maybe George would find out.

Chapter 4

So it was back to taking calls and arranging funerals and helping families decide on gravestones. The names and dates they put on the stones were not so much brief biographies as markers that a person had existed a few years in the long stretch of history. Maybe the stone would outlast living memory. Sometimes the families would add inscriptions that tried to carry over into death the ranks or status the dead had in life, or the families believed or wanted to believe they had. Sometimes the families put sentiments on the stones to tell the feelings they had about the dead, or believed they had. But I have seen enough differences between the inscriptions and the quarrels of the survivors to suspect that the inscriptions reflected feelings expressed too late for the dead.

I continued to see Mollie on the street or at the Bruces', but she seldom came by my office. Too morbid, she said, all those caskets in the back room and those files full of details about death and those machines for pumping embalming fluid into bodies. She wanted to write about the joys of living.

She said Jackie had gone back to Richmond to be with her parents but thought she might come back to Cromwell one of these days. Jackie wrote she now found her Bruce cousins more comfortable to be with than the friends she and Henry had known in Richmond. She had also asked when George Landry would be coming back to visit Dr. Sullivan.

"I think she and George have a spark going, don't you?" Mollie asked with a mischievous smile. "Something going on there."

"Could be. Anything going on with the Bruce ladies?"

"I'm writing. Livie's dancing. Sally's riding. What about you?"

"I'm thinking about writing a history of the joys of living in Cromwell."

She laughed. "That might be a short history. I want to write a long story about the fun of living in New York or Paris. That's where people know how to live."

"I hear the wine flows free in Paris, anyway. I keep wondering how I missed out on that when I was over there."

"That's your story. Someday I may believe it."

"Guess I'll have to suffer in silence."

"Poor you," she said, waved, and walked on down the sidewalk, her trim figure moving nicely.

Three weeks later, Jackie came back to town. Mollie called on the phone to invite me to the house. Jackie had some interesting news to tell, she said. Follow-up to our talks about the gravestones and parish records.

"Is this a tea meeting or drinks time?" I asked.

"You decide after you've heard what she has to tell."

"Is that a threat?"

"Come and hear."

So I went to the Bruces' late that afternoon. Livie and Sally were there with Jackie and Mollie.

Jackie's story was an eye-opener, all right. She'd asked her mother about Olivia and her husbands, and Mama Elizabeth had delivered the goods with a certain bitter satisfaction, Jackie said. Her tone was It's Time You Knew the Truth. Seems Olivia had a talent for infidelity and kept all three husbands worried. Edward Carter had committed suicide in Richmond when he found out she was having an affair with Gerald Harvey. That was two years after Jackson was born, so there wasn't much doubt about his paternity. But she had sent young Jack to be raised by his Richmond relatives and blotted out of her life the three years she'd been married to Edward. Jack grew up thinking of himself as a Richmonder with only remote links to Cromwell. After she got rid of Jack, Olivia married Gerald and had Lawton, now the Judge, the next year. Olivia and Gerald said later Edward had died of a fever and had been buried there in the Confederate veterans' cemetery. After she kept Gerald worried until he died eight years later, she married Moses Millard the next year and had Miss Joanna the following year. So that's why there was no Carter name on her gravestone. Her marriage to Edward was a part of her life she didn't acknowledge.

"Whew!" said Mollie. "That's a corker. Things you learn about your ancestors!"

"I guess it explains why Papa wasn't very happy about me coming to Cromwell several years ago," Jackie said. "He's mellowed now. I think, from what Mama says, he began to change his mind after the war."

"I think I'll have that drink," I said.

"Me too," Livie called. "Is that what I have to live up to?"

I looked at Livie. She might be shocked, but she also looked amused. Her eyes were bright.

"Dr. Sullivan said the other day George is coming next week," Sally said and lifted her eyebrows. "Does that interest you, Jackie?"

"It would be nice to see him again." This time Jackie kept a straight face, but the others smiled knowingly. "What's new with you and William?"

"He has a Tennessee walker coming before long. I'm anxious to try her out, see how she performs."

"Horses and ancestors," Mollie said with a wry smile. "What a life!"

I missed seeing George during his visit, but shortly after he had left, Dr. Kathleen called and said come by, she had some interesting information George had brought. We set a time when she was not likely to have a waiting room full of patients.

"Come in, Roy," she said. "Sit there and I'll tell you a story. Not a surprising one, as I think about it."

She had told George about the blackmail attempt on Greneda, she said, and had told him about her meeting years before with Greneda and that she knew she had a child in Philadelphia but didn't know what happened to the child. That much was old news to me, and I noted she hadn't said anything about what Mabel Donahue had seen of the stretch marks and hadn't mentioned me as one of her informants. So George checked the records in Philadelphia, saw that a girl had been born to one Greneda Bruce, and found that the girl child had been adopted by Jackson and Elizabeth Carter of Richmond. The record did not indicate who was the father.

"So Jackie is Miss Greneda's daughter, not niece," I said.

"You're right there," she said. "But until we know who was the father, blackmail is still a possibility."

She sat there a minute, a faraway look on her face. "Another thing. If Jackson and Elizabeth aren't her blood parents, we know only half her genetic background." She smiled. "I gave myself away, didn't I? I'm thinking like a grandmother now. George is still interested in Jackie. Very interested. He wants her. If that develops into a marriage, I'd like to know what kind of blood my grandchildren would have."

"Are you going to tell Jackie who her mother was? Or will George?"

"No. We agreed it's best to keep silent about it for now. Maybe forever. Seems Jackie's happy with the Carters for parents. We'd be breaking faith with them if we told."

"I agree. No good changing her feelings for them."

"Still, we need to find out who her father was. How can we do that?"

I told her how the question of Miss Greneda's inheritance still puzzled me. That was a lot of property to buy with a small inheritance. Maybe finding out who owned the property before she bought it would provide a clue. Maybe the property was a settlement, a gift of conscience, from the unknown father.

"That would mean the father was somebody big in town, wouldn't it?" she said. "Good Lord! What are we getting into?"

"The hidden life of Cromwell, I reckon. Guess we'd better tread softly. Don't want somebody powerful coming down on us."

"But some 'old friend' out there knows and must be ready to tell his dirty tale. That's what Titus and Joanna are afraid of, you said."

"They haven't said much about it since that court hearing. Reckon they might be waiting and hoping nothing comes of the threat. And it may depend on what move the Eastern and Southern makes. Maybe everybody's waiting on somebody else." I winced at the thought of such a tangle.

"I don't think we can wait," she said. "Perhaps you'd better look into those land records. That's the best we have to go on now. If we don't do something, George might."

"All right. I'll check them. I have to help clients find out enough to tell their lawyers. Checking land records might not be too noticeable."

But I didn't get to check the records soon. I'd hardly gotten to the office the next morning before I had a phone call.

"Lootenant?"

"Yes?"

"Dan Blue here."

"Great day, Dan! Great to hear from you. Where are you now?"

"Not far. Just over the line in Johns County. Reckon you didn't know I'm in the trade, too. Got me a nice little place here. Doin' good business with the colored folks in the county."

"Sounds good. Wish we'd kept in touch after we got out of that war. Both pretty busy, I'd reckon."

"I hear about you ever once in a while. That's why I call. Got a favor to ask."

"I owe you. What's up?"

"Reckon you ain't seen the papers yet. Or maybe it ain't in your paper yet. We had a big accident here last night. Train hit a truck full of colored folks and knocked 'em all over the place. Got about twenty bodies on my hands. More'n I can handle in my embalmin' room. Can you help me?"

I thought about what screams the white folks in Cromwell would make if they knew colored bodies were on the slabs where their white bodies were put. But what the hell, I owed Dan. And we could manage it.

We talked some more and agreed my truck would come to his place by dark and bring the bodies here after dark. The garage was out behind the trees, and the way to the embalming wing was in the dark. If the white folks in Cromwell would just stay alive long enough, Johnny and I could do a night's work in the lab and get the bodies back out before daylight. Thought we'd better not get Jess involved. He might talk. Johnny, I knew, would like the idea. He would see it as a great joke on Cromwell. Dan said he would do the cosmetics on the faces. He knew what colored folks wanted. I was glad to let him handle that. Hadn't had any drill on working with colored faces at that school in Richmond.

We were lucky. The night's work went off without a hitch. Luckier than the folks on the truck had been. The truck, Dan said, had gotten stuck on a faulty crossing at the railroad, and the train had hit before the folks could scramble out. Looked like when a big shell had hit, Dan said. He knew he wasn't going to get much for the big funeral they were going to have for the victims. Neither they nor their families had much. Mostly field workers. And they knew it wasn't possible for them to sue the railroad. They were colored, after all. But if Nate Greenwald, the farmer who owned the truck, would sue, they might have a chance to collect enough to bury the folks and get through the work season.

I remembered Greenwald from before the war. He had a fair-size farm and, I'd heard, had done well selling his crops to the government during the war. When the postwar slump came, he struggled. He wasn't broke, but he wasn't making it big now. Still, he was respected by most of the farmers and had some standing in the county. He couldn't be ignored if he sued. I thought I'd see if he was willing.

I found Greenwald without much trouble. Folks in his part of Johns County knew where to find him. Even though he was busy getting in his crop, he took time to talk and go with me to the crossing. What was left of his truck was still over beside the ditch. We looked at the crossing. Sure enough, the boards at the crossing had cracks between them big enough to catch a truck wheel.

"Been this way a long time," he said. "Folks around here will tell you how many times they complained to the superintendent. But he don't do nothin'. Says watch how you drive." I thought his eyes and face looked tired, not just from work. His clothes were neat and clean but worn at the edges. It's been a hard couple of years on him, I reckoned.

I asked if he'd be willing to let Will Ford sue in his name to recover damages on his truck and damages for lost wages of his workers. I'd asked Will if I could make the offer, and he'd agreed not to charge unless he won the case. I asked Will because he'd beat the railroad on a couple of cases before, and I reckoned the railroad took him seriously. He'd even beat C. K. Whittington, the railroad's ace lawyer.

Greenwald said he reckoned so, long as it didn't cost him money. He was right spare of cash these days. He thought Will had better get right on the case, though. The railroad might decide to come patch the crossing because of the wreck. They didn't like to damage their trains, whatever they thought about Johns County folks.

So Will got right out there, took camera shots of the faulty crossing and the truck, and collected depositions from the folks who'd complained to the superintendent. Then he filed the suit in Johns County. It looked like he had a solid case, but you never knew when you dealt with the railroad and their slick lawyers. He was depending on anti-railroad sentiment in Johns County if or when the case got to trial. Still, Johns County was a backwater in the Eastern and Southern empire.

I reckon the railroad banked on the insignificance of the plaintiffs and got postponements on the hearing several times. In the meantime, the families of the victims were barely getting by on make-work and charities. Greenwald did what he could for them, but he was getting close to bankruptcy himself. He hadn't been able to replace his truck and had to depend on the goodwill of his neighbors to help him get in his crop. The railroad looked like it planned to wait out the plaintiffs until they withered away. Besides, the victims were only colored. That was when Mollie got into the act.

She was outraged at the railroad's tactics. She might be a genteel southern lady, but she had a sense of fair play. Will Ford had filed motion after motion for an early trial, but the judges saw things the railroad's way and agreed to postponements. The summer was almost gone, with nothing gained.

She came to my office one day and put a stack of papers on my desk. Looked like a manuscript.

"What's that? By the way, good morning!"

"Good morning to you. That's my piece about the railroad wreck. If the courts won't do something for those poor people, maybe public sentiment will. I'm going to see if Ed Braswell will put it in his paper. And I'm going to send it to the Raleigh paper, too. Somebody has got to know what the railroad's doing to them."

"Good luck. But you'd better be prepared for the railroad's wrath."

"It's a chance I have to take."

Ed's paper, *The Cromwellian,* printed a toned-down version of the piece. Don't want to go too strong, he said. We have to live with the railroad in this town. But the Raleigh paper gave it a full spread. The Raleigh paper was supporting the out-of-office wing of the Democrats then and was glad to have something to embarrass the administration, who were cozy with the railroad. Then the Richmond and Baltimore papers picked up the story and spread it throughout the Eastern and Southern empire. We heard the railroad began to get nervous when reporters from New York and Washington called to find out what the outcome of the trial was. Damn outside agitators, Will Ford said he'd heard the railroad lawyers call them. The liberal northern press wanted to write about what was happening to blacks down south, and the trucking interests wanted to make a case against the railroads. So Mollie's protest got better press than we expected. And the postponements stopped.

At the trial in Johns County, the railroad lawyers tried to make a case that Nate Greenwald's truck stopped on the tracks because of mechanical failure. They made sure they scored points about unreliable trucks and had friendly reporters there to publicize their side of the case. But Will Ford had chosen his venue well and played the country lawyer to perfection. The jury of men from Johns County ruled for the plaintiffs. They also called for a substantial award for damages, loss of life, and loss of wages, with interest compounded through all the postponements. As we expected, the railroad appealed the judgment, and we settled back for another long wait. The question now was whether the railroad had as much influence on appeals court judges as they did on trial judges.

I stopped by Will Ford's office to congratulate him on winning the case. He was not as optimistic as I thought he had a right to be.

"It's not finished yet, Roy. We might need another break before Nate and his folks ever see any of the railroad's money. These appeals can drag on, even if we win them."

"At least the Johns County folks came out to the good. I hear they finally fixed that crossing."

"That's right. And at the appeal we can use that as a tacit admission of fault by the railroad. They were in a bind. They either had to repair the crossing or leave it unrepaired for all the newspaper photographers to take pictures of. I reckon they were more afraid of the press than of me."

"We have Mollie to thank for that," I said.

"Reckon so. I sure hope she won't get hurt because of that good work. That was a strong piece, all right."

But Mollie did pay. She had hardly gotten halfway through her first term of teaching when the school board notified her that her contract for the next year would not be renewed. Score one for the railroad. The merchants on the school board knew they had to depend on the railroad for their shipments of goods in and out of town, and they chose their interests over Mollie's job. One of the school board members also told me they didn't want any of their teachers telling the town's children to be friendly to the coloreds.

When I went to see Mollie, though, and console her on that turn of events, she was smiling. She was sitting on the sunny south porch with a writing board and paper on her lap and looking at the yellowing leaves in the trees on the street.

"Don't worry about me, Roy. This just makes things clearer. Now I can spend more time writing. Maybe writing's what I'm meant to do."

"You still have the rest of the year to teach, don't you? Maybe folks' minds will change before next summer."

"Could be, but I don't count on it."

"So what are you writing now?"

"Just jotting down some ideas. Don't know yet what shape they'll take."

"Something new?"

"Maybe. I was thinking about the piece I wrote about the wreck, what I learned doing it."

"What?"

"Not sure. I had to get closer to people's lives while I got ready to write. Some of those people out at Greenwald's lead pretty precarious lives, but they keep getting by. They laugh when I'd cry. How do they do it?"

"Maybe laughing is stronger than crying."

"We'll see."

"Want to take a walk through the leaves?"

"Great! Let me get my coat and hat. You sure you won't be compromised being seen with me? Bad for your business?"

"We're doing all right. Even the railroad can't stop folks dying."

We walked around town, pointing out the yellows and reds in the trees. We began to count the new cars rolling by, the drivers waving to us.

"Isn't that five so far?" I said. "Cromwell seems to be doing well."

"There's money in this town," Mollie said. "Sorry about the country folks."

As another waved by, I told her, "I'll walk on the street side. Protect you from runaway horses."

"You're so good."

Before long we were on the hill overlooking the railroad and Miss Greneda's warehouses close by the tracks.

"That reminds me," Mollie said. "Aunt Greneda's will was read the other day. The one Will Ford wrote for her a couple of years ago."

"How did things go?"

"A few surprises. The nieces were named heirs. That includes Jackie as well as Livie, Sally, and me. But not Howell or Amanda Harvey."

"Did you expect them to be?"

"Well, they're kin too."

"I wonder why they weren't included."

"Maybe she thought they'd have enough from the Judge. She didn't particularly like Harvey either, as I remember."

I filed that away as another question to be answered.

"Had another surprise, too."

"So?"

"Papa and Mr. Ford found there's a lien on the property. Aunt Greneda borrowed money on the property to invest in Roy Willard's truck repair shop. Papa says they have to clear Roy's debt to the estate before it can be given to the heirs."

"Can Roy pay it?"

"Seems there's some complication with that. I wasn't clear from what Papa said what the complication is."

"I thought Roy's shop was doing well. Last time I looked he had lots of trucks there to be worked on."

"There's some kind of holdup. Maybe you can find out. Would you?"

"Can give it a try."

I checked with Will Ford, and he confirmed what Mollie had said. Roy's business had hit a snag. He said I should check with Roy to get particulars. He would tell Roy I might come by so he wouldn't think I was meddling. I would come as an interested party for the Bruces.

Roy looked tired when I went to see him at his shop. His office was orderly and clean, and he had on a coat with a white shirt and dark tie. But I saw there wasn't much business going on in his office, and as I came in I had seen men working in only a couple of bays in the shop. Lots of trucks in the back lot, though.

"Come in, Roy. Will Ford said you'd come by. Just been to the bank. Not much good there."

"Sorry to hear your business has hit a snag. Will said I should see you about details. Anything I can do?"

"Not likely. Unless you speak for the Eastern and Southern."

"What's the setback?"

"The big alignment machine we ordered was damaged in shipment on the railroad. I need it to carry out the contract with Acme Trucks. They're gonna cancel the contract if I can't keep their trucks rolling. I understand that. Probably would do it myself. That's business. New machinery won't arrive in time for me to recoup before the mortgage is due. Including that money Miss Greneda invested with me. Had to use it to order the machine."

"Can't Acme carry you till you get that machine? They ought to see how the railroad wins if the truck lines lose."

"Got another complication there. William Walker—you know him, don't you?—built the big shop for me. He's carrying me on the cost of that construction. But he's stretched too. If I don't make it, he won't either."

And won't be able to marry Sally if he's in financial trouble, I thought.

"I reckon it's not much," I offered, "but I'll give you the maintenance contract on my trucks and cars."

"Thanks. I'll take it and much obliged. But that's not the big money I need. Acme is big-league money. The bank won't lend more or extend my note. Pressure from the railroad, I'd reckon."

I had to sit silent before such a pile of problems. Finally I wished him good luck and told him I'd look around for other small-timers like me who'd give him contracts. We shook hands, and I left angry at the railroad again.

The big ball of bad news kept rolling on. About a week later, Mollie told me Sally was home crying. William had called off that informal engagement because of his money troubles.

I kept thinking about what I'd asked Roy. Couldn't Acme work with him on his delay and keep trucks from losing out to the railroad? I asked Roy if I could talk to the president of Acme about some accommodation. He said I could try, but don't expect much. "His name's Leland Baker if you get that far."

When I was shown into his office, Baker was all cordiality and sympathy. He was sorry Roy had had a setback, but he had to keep his trucks rolling. If Roy couldn't do the job, he'd find somebody down the road who could. He liked having his work done in Ireland County. It was central to his region. I asked him how far down the road he could take his trucks and still keep them rolling. He hoped for something within fifty miles but might have to look farther.

After I got into the car and was driving home, I thought of Lew Helder. He ran a farm machinery repair shop over in Brand County. Now that the farm season was mostly over, his machinery was idle or at least underused. He did some small jobs during the off-season to keep his machines oiled, he'd told me once. But right now he had unused capacity to do heavy work. True, farm machines were different from trucks, but his equipment might be adapted.

Besides, Lew owed me. Back before he'd got his business going well, he'd had his troubles. He was short of money like most beginners in business. During one of his lean times, I'd buried his old daddy for him in Ireland County where most of his kin were. He'd been grateful and said he wouldn't forget. Soon as he got on his feet, he'd pay. But that promise was still hanging. Maybe now was the time to remind him.

I told Roy about Lew's shop and asked him if he thought Lew's machinery for farm equipment could be reworked to fix trucks. I also mentioned what Baker had said about going fifty miles farther. Roy studied a minute, looked out the window a while, and smiled.

"Hell, let's try it. My man Justus is a wonder at making machines do things we didn't know they could do."

So I went to see Lew Helder. He was closing down accounts after his busy season. We drank some coffee together and talked about how business was going. I couldn't tell whether he remembered his old promise and thought I was there to collect or just wondered why I had come.

Then I told him about Roy's problem and asked him if he'd be willing to talk with Roy about renting his shop and machinery during the off-season. We never mentioned his debt, but I sensed it might be hanging in the air. I thought it might be better to let him appear generous than to feel he was being dunned for a debt. I reckoned he was feeling flush after a good season. He hardly hesitated.

"Sure thing, Roy. Tell him to come see me. We can work something out."

"Great!" I said. "He'll be much obliged. I will too." We shook hands and talked about when the weather would change. Soon I was back in the car headed for Cromwell and wondering if we really could bring it off. Lots of pieces would have to fall into place.

It didn't take Roy Willard long to get over to see Lew, and they soon had an agreement worked out. Roy was depending a lot on Clay Justus being able to adapt the machines to work on trucks. And he had to agree to work in a few small jobs Lew had already promised to handle. Lew was even willing to wait on his rent as long as he got his small jobs done. Now what was needed was fast work. Roy got Baker to agree to send his Acme trucks to Brand County to be worked on. He could handle that. That was back when trucks were changing from wooden frames to metal frames so they could handle heavier loads. Roy thought autos would change to metal frames too in another ten years or so.

Chapter 5

For the next couple of months, Roy got his other machinery and men moved over to Lew's, and they got to work. Clay Justus did a good job of adapting Lew's machines. Roy lost a few local truck jobs because of the move but said the big contract would make up for them. In the meantime, he was prodding the manufacturer and the railroad to speed up shipment of his machine, and the railroad was promising delivery but having unavoidable delays. Between funerals, I stayed busy trying to find small-time contracts for Roy, but the distance to Brand County was a problem for several stores and warehouses in Cromwell. I suspected they'd got the word from the railroad not to help Roy or else.

It soon became clear that the adapted machines were working all right but not fast enough. Acme trucks were stacking up on the lot waiting to be repaired, and Baker was getting nervous. He had to keep them rolling, he said. And the bank continued to refuse to extend Roy's note or lend him more to tide him over until the new machine came, if it ever did.

"It looks like we may not make it," Roy told me when I went by to see how things were going. "Stretch it every way we can, we still come up short. You haven't got an extra $10,000 on you, have you?" I told him I wished I did. I still had a good-size mortgage to pay off.

I tried some of my contacts again to see if any could come through with a helpful contract for Roy, but they repeated what they'd said before. "We'd like to help you, Roy, but we already have other arrangements. We can't afford to break those contracts." Sometimes it got pretty discouraging. And I had to keep my business going. I still tried to go by the Bruces' to see Mollie, too. I was afraid that, with her plans for finding more time to write, she'd find that time somewhere besides Cromwell. She was still talking New York. If she went there, she might never come back.

"Did you see the new issue of the Post?" she asked. "I'd really like to get a story in there. I bet I can do what they do. Or even one of those quarterlies like Transatlantic Review. They're doing the modern stuff. Get published there and you have a chance at one of the big pay magazines."

I groaned to myself but wished her luck.

"We have our own story here, too. Have you heard? Livie has a new boyfriend. You'd never guess. Derek Bogart!"

"Where'd he come from?"

"Out of town. But he's back. And he's seeing Livie."

I groaned out loud this time. "Isn't he one of the railroad's lawyers?"

"Yes, and doing well, I hear."

"What happened to those other men she's been collecting?"

"They're hanging on, but he's got ahead of them."

As I trooped back to the house, I wondered why Derek Bogart had come into the picture now. Thought he was off in Richmond or somewhere. Horace Bogart's son. I remembered telling Horace about those unused plots at Cedar Hill. He had been pleased and said he'd see Bob Watts, I didn't need to. I hadn't heard whether he'd got his daughter and son-in-law moved there, but I was sure he would eventually. He generally got what he wanted. Started small and kept gaining. He came to town from out in the county just before the turn of the century, Mama and Papa had said, lived over the little store he began with, made it prosper by bringing lots of new goods from the cities outside, and built more stores. He must have seen how the roads were going to spread throughout the county and built stores at the crossroads. Papa said once that he saw Horace's hawkers on the railroad coaches selling handy foods to the passengers, too. He'd bet on the railroads as well as their competition.

He was the one, I realized then, that Ferguson Bruce had kept Miss Greneda from marrying. Lived over his store, Miss Joanna had said. But he'd married later. A town woman without much background, Mama had said, but good in a plain way. He'd lost a son in the war and a daughter and her husband in the epidemic. Now the younger son Derek was all he had left, and the daughter's children, of course.

I wondered what Titus and Miss Joanna thought of Livie having a suitor like Derek, without social background. Did they feel the cycle of events coming around again? But maybe lots of money was all the background he needed. Times weren't like they were before the war. I wondered what another twenty-five years would tell us about how we lived now. Would the things that matter for us now look different by then?

I came back to present problems the next morning when Judge Harvey called. His Aunt Louella had died in her sleep the night before, and he wanted me to handle her funeral. Yes, he'd already called the kin and had arranged with Reverend Benfield to conduct the funeral. But he had some special requests for the funeral. Would I come by to talk about them?

I stood outside a minute before going to the Judge's door and looked at the house. It was one of those big white houses with lots of gables, porches on two sides, and lots of gingerbread on the porches and eaves. Built by old Gerald Harvey, Papa had said once. Back in high Victorian times when folks with money knew how to show it. Neither Mr. Gerald nor the Judge had added wings the way some folks had done. Didn't need to. The house had been built big from the beginning. So it still had clean lines. Wide lawns, neat gardens, a driveway going through a *porte cochere*. And you could just see towards the back of the big lot, if you stepped over a few paces, a stable that had cars instead of coaches in it, with living quarters above. For servants, I thought, and it still looked used. I opened the gate in the iron grill fence and went up the walk.

"Come in, Roy," the Judge said as he showed me into his study. I saw we were surrounded by dark furniture and shelves of books. He was neatly dressed, coat and tie, as if he were going to court. "I appreciate your coming so soon."

As I sat in the leather chair across from his desk, he went to the door and asked his maid to bring us coffee. We got down to business immediately. After we got through the details of having Dr. Brandon come to sign the death certificate and calling Johnny Dayton to pick up Miss Louella, the Judge leaned back in his big chair, and his face took on a softened look.

"I'm sorry Miss Mary Lee and Amanda aren't here to talk with you too." His wife and daughter, I remembered. "They're in Richmond and left the arrangements to me. They'll be back in time for the funeral."

I asked about his family. They were well, thanks.

"The special request I mentioned—let's get to that. Aunt Louella was special to me. She was a warm, cheerful woman, full of wit and good sense. I think you may have met her in her younger years, but you probably never got to know her as we in the family did. Many people think it a burden to have a widowed relative living with the family, but it was never that way with us. She added something extra to our lives and gave our children a sense that family is more than mother and father, brother and sister. You could say she helped raise them. In some ways, she helped raise me and was the one I could always go to for comfort and good answers. You may not know, my father died early and my mother remarried. But of course you do. She married Miss Joanna Bruce's father, and you're keeping company with one of the Bruce daughters, aren't you?" His eyes smiled.

What he wanted for the funeral, he said, was to keep it personal and cheerful. He had made an appointment with Mr. Benfield to review Aunt Louella's life so the rector could modify the funeral liturgy and the Judge could provide a personal eulogy of her and remind those present of her good life. He hoped I would prepare for a longer service brightened with such flowers as could be found this time of year and with brighter lights. He was also preparing for a gathering after the funeral where her friends and those of the family could drink, eat, and tell each other good stories about Aunt Louella. I was invited, of course. He wanted the mood of the gathering to be as bright as she was. She was irrepressible, he said, and often had startling insights and ideas that people only later came to see as sound.

Then he surprised me. One of those secrets that come out of the hidden world beneath the surface of life-as-usual.

"She even wanted me to marry Greneda Bruce. Called her a sprightly girl too good for most men." He smiled ruefully.

I nodded and thought it best to keep quiet.

We sat silent, but somehow close, for a few minutes. Then I decided if he was going to confide, so would I. I told him how sorry I was to hear that Miss Greneda's estate was in a tangle because of Roy Willard's problems.

He came back from remembrances at that and asked me to explain. I told him about Roy's struggle to pay off his mortgage and clear Miss Greneda's estate while the railroad delayed and the likelihood Roy would go broke if he didn't raise the rest of the money by next month. The Judge was fully interested then and asked probing questions. I began to feel like a man in the dock.

"How much?" he asked.

"Sir?"

"How much does Mr. Willard need?"

I told him ten thousand.

He reached in a desk drawer, pulled out a folder, looked at it, looked over my head a minute, and said, "I'll cover that debt."

"Sir?"

"Tell Mr. Willard I'll invest ten thousand in his business. Stocks are doing well, but it's time to stop investing in paper and start putting money in hard goods. I'll wire my broker to sell."

I said Roy would be relieved to hear it.

We went over a few more details about Miss Louella's funeral, and I left to tell Roy.

As I drove to Roy's, I began to wonder why the Judge was so helpful. Was he just smart about investing, or coming to the aid of the family? Or was there another reason?

After we got Miss Louella celebrated and buried—and it was an occasion several of the older folks said they'd remember—I began to think again about Miss Greneda's property. In the clear now, but still a mystery how she got it. Meanwhile, the railroad people were beginning to see Roy could survive without the lost machine, so they found it. I went down to the shop to watch Roy's men install it. We drank almost a potful of coffee to celebrate as we watched. The men were joking as they worked.

Then I went to the courthouse to look at those property records. Considering all the things I'd seen, maybe I wasn't surprised to find that property had belonged to Judge Lawton Harvey's family before the deed was transferred to Greneda Bruce. Date: May 30, 1900. Price: $250 and other considerations. I began to wonder if I wanted to know what I might soon know.

The records showed that the property had been bought by one Gerald Harvey in 1869 for $100 after the property was seized for unpaid taxes. Gerald Harvey, formerly of Cincinnati, Ohio, formerly captain in the Ohio Volunteers. Not long after, the Eastern and Southern Railroad gained permits to extend the rail system into Cromwell and on over into Johns County and beyond.

A hundred dollars was, I thought, big money in 1869, but by 1900, with a rail line running next to it, the property was worth much more than $250. And by that time Gerald Harvey was dead, and Lawton Harvey owned it. A nice inheritance. I wondered why he sold it so cheaply to Greneda Bruce. What were those "other considerations"?

That was something Dr. Kathleen and I would have to think about. I'd better get back to her before long. The furor over the train wreck in Johns County had come between us and our search for the "old friend" threatening the Bruces and for Jackie's father. I groaned to myself as I put those records back on the shelf.

But I didn't get to see Dr. Kathleen. I saw George Landry instead. He was back in town, supposedly visiting his mother but spending more time with Jackie. I met him when I went by the Bruces' to see Mollie. Mollie was still talking about what she should do when she finished her teaching contract. I groaned inside again. George sidled up to me while Mollie and Jackie were back in the kitchen bringing coffee and said we needed to talk. Could he come by the office the next day?

"I've been poking around the birth records in Philadelphia," George said as he settled into the chair in my office. He went on to tell me he'd found that Jackie was adopted by the Carters and that she was the daughter of Greneda Bruce. I said his mother had told me. He didn't know we had talked. I wondered how much his courting Jackie had interfered with his visiting his mother. Or maybe she was waiting to see what I had found out before she told him about our talks.

I asked him if he had the date of Jackie's birth from the records. He pulled a fold of papers from his coat pocket. I pulled my copies of the courthouse records from my file drawer. We put them side by side on the desk and began to compare dates of Jackie's birth and Miss Greneda's purchase of the railroad property.

"They're linked," George said.
"Conclusion?"
"Harvey is her father."
"Proof?"
"Not conclusive. Strongly circumstantial."
"What circumstances?"
"He settled the property on Miss Greneda, sold it for less than value."
"Why?"
"Conscience? Not child support if she was adopted by the Carters."
"A payoff, then?"
"Maybe. Maybe an inheritance. For a niece? How could he know she wouldn't marry and have other children?"
"He married. And had children."
"That was later, wasn't it?"
"Right."
We sat quiet a minute.
"Let's try conscience again," I said.
"The soft spot in his secret?"
"The thing that might come out sooner or later. That might make him write a letter or tell someone. Tell why he did it."
"Wouldn't he be too smart for that? He's a sharp lawyer."
"He was younger then. We may be talking more about feelings than money. What he gained or lost. Maybe feelings meant more than money then. Not that he's not sharp about money now."
"How's that?"
I told him how the Judge had invested money in Roy's shop.
"And protected the integrity of Miss Greneda's estate. Sounds like a continued interest," George said.
"So what proof required?"
"Letters? Deeds? Confessions? The last not likely."
After the Judge's confidences about Aunt Louella, I wondered.

We sat quiet another minute. Then George slapped his hand on the desk, got up, put on his hat, and said he guessed we'd have to wait and see what time would tell. He didn't think anything more was to be discovered in Philadelphia. Maybe something would turn up in Cromwell.

I knew he meant I had to run with the ball now.

Chapter 6

While I was puzzling how to deal with that problem, I got a call from Mollie. Come by when you can. New problem. She'd give details when I came.

When I saw Mollie at the door, I knew by her face there was trouble. Inside, we sat in the sunroom, porch plants taken inside for the winter sitting all about us, voices sounding from the back of the house. The sound of distress.

"Livie's nearly in hysterics," she said, "and the rest of us are not much better."

"What's up?"

"It's Derek. He says he's heard a scandal that Aunt Greneda had a baby way back when."

"Where'd he hear that?"

"Didn't say. His father, I'd think. Says he wants us to sell that property to Mr. Bogart to avoid scandalizing our reputation."

"Who's us?"

"Livie, Sally, Jackie, me."

"Why would selling it avoid scandal?"

"He says the scandal is linked to the property. If Mr. Bogart owns the property, it won't be associated with us."

"That's big of him. Of course, he'd own a nice property. Why is he willing to be so generous? He's got a reputation too."

"Guess he knows he's not old family like us."

"All the more reason for him to be careful, I'd think."

"He already has a reputation for sharp dealing in business."

"But what about the scandal? Why do you think it's true?"

"We don't know. We're in shock. Nobody ever thought that about Aunt Greneda. Livie and Sally are saying even the rumor will ruin their chances for a good marriage. You know Sally and William broke up not long ago. They're about to get together again, but she's afraid this will run him off. Livie says she put off her other boyfriends after she started going with Derek. Now she's afraid she's lost him, too."

"What about the others?"

"Mama and Papa are quiet—too quiet. They act like they've been hit over the head."

"Jackie?"

"She doesn't know what to think. She didn't know Aunt Greneda."

"You?"

"I'm shocked too. Maybe not as much. I realize there are some blank spots in her past. Philadelphia and Chicago. She could have had a more complicated life than a niece would think. Maybe we knew only part of her life. Maybe that's the writer in me thinking like that."

"What's the family going to do?"

"Nothing right now. Wait, I guess."

"Good. Best not to act when you're upset."

"What would you do?"

"Wait. Somebody needs to talk to Derek. Get some facts straight. Who told him? How do they know? Is it true? I doubt Livie was in the right mind to ask hard questions."

"She's all to pieces."

So we sat there and waited. I looked at Mollie. She smiled a little, but her chin was quivering. I stood, and all of a sudden she was in my arms, her head on my shoulder, and she was crying.

"Oh, Roy. I guess I do believe it. She must have been so unhappy, and we never knew."

I held her as she cried. Out of the corner of my eye, I thought I saw someone get ready to come into the room, then step back. After a minute she stopped crying, but I held her. Thank you, Derek. She'd never come to me this way before. She was so warm and yielding, I held her close.

Then she hugged me and stepped back. "I'm sorry, Roy. It just hit me so hard." She pulled a handkerchief from a pocket and dabbed at her eyes. "I'm all right now."

We walked together to the front door. Miss Joanna came up and thanked me for coming. I said I'd see what could be found out. Miss Joanna looked a question with her eyes. Mollie gave me a wink, and I left more confused than anyone.

As I drove back to the office, I wondered if I was playing fair with Mollie and the family, not telling them what I already knew. Playing the innocent. Still, I'd bet Titus and Miss Joanna had been doing it for twenty-five years. That would have been a lot to carry. No wonder they acted like they'd been hit over the head. That skeleton never had got stuck far enough back in the closet. And, I told myself, George and I had agreed to keep quiet until we knew more. Dr. Kathleen, too.

I wondered how Bogart knew about the link between Miss Greneda's past and her property. That was another question that begged for an answer.

I mulled the problem for several days. One day, I found a blue envelope on my desk and opened it. Inside, a single sheet, no date, two words: "Thanks. Dan." He knew better than to spell out details.

Out of the possibilities George and I had thought of, I began to think that confessions might be more likely than George had reckoned. Besides, it looked like we had exhausted the documents approach. Birth records, property records—what more could we look for? If there were letters, they wouldn't be from a shrewd lawyer. Maybe from Miss Greneda, but I'd bet Titus and Miss Joanna had them stuck away in an iron box in a dark closet in a forgotten attic.

So how to get the Judge to talk? He had talked, hadn't he? When he said Miss Louella had wanted him to marry Miss Greneda. Was he on the threshold of saying more then? And his investment in Roy's business, George thought, was more interest in her estate than in Roy's shop. Maybe he was a distinguished man in his fifties ready to look back in serenity, maybe nostalgia, at his youth. It was worth a try if I could approach it right.

The chance came a week later, when Judge Harvey called and asked me to come by. He wanted my advice on the right people to make a grave marker for Aunt Louella. She had been a pianist of some skill, with warm feeling in her music. She had taught a number of the town's children in their younger days, and many had come as mature adults to her funeral and had told affectionate stories of how she could make them smile while they kept their hands on the keyboard. She'd even made piano practice into a game for them. Now he wanted her remembered that way. He thought a piano carved on her grave marker would tell the good lady's memory. But would a miniature piano attached to the top of her marker be better or one carved into the stone itself? And who would be the best stonecutter to do it? I told him I liked the idea of a piano on top of the marker, but it might be too much of a temptation to some prankster or vandal, and off it would come. He said he hated to think there were people in town who would do such a thing, but he supposed I was right. We thought Newt Gallagher would do a good job on the piano. He'd taken with Aunt Louella way back before he gave up ivories for marble and granite.

I could tell the Judge was in a mellow mood and decided now was the time. We had another cup of coffee, and I asked him if I could talk with him about Miss Greneda. His comment about Aunt Louella's wish had set me thinking. He said go ahead.

Then I told him how the "old friend" had upset Titus and Miss Joanna with his threat of a scandal, how they had lost track of the letter and used the excuse of searching for a family heirloom. He said he remembered that.

I told him how the search for the letter had led to the birth records for Jackie Carter and to the records on Miss Greneda's property. I said the linkage between the two was pretty clear and George Landry and I had drawn certain conclusions, but I didn't say what they were. Just left them hanging in the air. I told how we'd kept our search secret, and only George and I knew what the records said. Dr. Sullivan knew about the birth records. She had known Miss Greneda in Philadelphia.

"Does Jackie know?"

"We haven't seen yet why she should."

"What about the Carters in Richmond?"

"We don't know. We've never talked with them. Wouldn't be surprised if they did know. Miss Greneda may have felt obliged to tell them. So they'd know both bloodlines."

"Possibly."

"But they have no children of their own. I'd reckon they might want to think Jackie is really theirs. No questions asked."

"Is she their heir?"

"Don't know. Trying to find that out might give away the circumstances of her birth. She's one of Miss Greneda's heirs."

"Yes, I remember."

He looked at me several moments. I thought silence was my best argument. It was what I had been tacitly promising all along.

"Roy, I'm going to tell you something in confidence. It should never get out of this room. Agreed?"

"What about George and Dr. Sullivan? They'd need to know. For their peace of mind. Besides, they're already in pretty deep."

"All right. You can tell them, but in confidence. Nobody else. Especially not Jackie."

"Agreed."

"Remember, this is all oral. I'd never put it in writing. And I'd deny it if you let it slip."

"Agreed."

So he told his story, which turned out to be Miss Greneda's story.

"You may not know this, Roy. My mother married three times. My father was her second husband. To tell the truth, she was better at marrying than she was at being a mother. After my father died when I was eight, I spent more time with my father's family than I did with my mother and her third husband. My Aunt Louella and Uncle Wade were the kin I spent most of my younger years with and even when I got older. Uncle Wade taught me the things a father teaches a son, and Aunt Louella taught me my prayers and my manners. She was the one I could turn to for comfort and sympathy, not my mother. But my mother's kin were part of my larger family, and I often spent time with my cousins. That was when I came to know Greneda."

"She was your half-cousin, so to speak?"

"Yes. Let me tell this while I'm remembering."

So I kept quiet and let him talk.

∞

Even as a child, Greneda was a lively, sprightly playmate and didn't defer to him, though he was five years older. She would demand her turn at imagining games they played and laugh at him when he insisted on his rights as an older boy. He didn't take her seriously and, as he got older and turned to hunting and fishing and ball playing and all the things boys got into and kept from their parents, he grew away from her. She was part of his childhood and in his past. They saw each other sometimes on family holidays, and he saw she was growing up too, but they had gone into separate worlds. He was getting ready to go away to school, and she was a young girl, sometimes awkward, sometimes graceful, and might even turn out to be pretty. He'd heard she had an independent mind and sometimes distressed her folks with things she said. In particular, she gave them fits about her views on the family religion and, he heard, wouldn't join the other young women in their religious devotions. He thought that sounded like the Greneda he'd known in their games, all right. That was when Aunt Louella had said Greneda would make a good wife for him sometime. But he had other things to do and think about.

So he went away to college and got ambition instead of religion. Some of his professors and some of his father's old friends urged him to go into law and make a name for himself, and he began to think he could do it. He studied books and men and made friends with classmates who looked like they would rise in the world. They agreed to help each other if they got into positions of power or influence. They thought the coming new century would be their stage, and they would be major players. (The Judge chuckled to himself as he said that.) He realized that his family money gave him advantages. He was just beginning to discover how many properties the family owned and sometimes wondered how they had acquired so many. He wondered briefly at the time of the Spanish war if having a war record would serve his ambitions, but the war was over before he got into it. Just as well, he thought. A couple of his friends had gone in and hadn't come back.

So he passed his law exams and set up his office in Raleigh, where, he thought, he could be close to the men of influence and power. He still kept in touch with the family back in Cromwell, and on visits there heard talk about Greneda. She had been courted by that upstart Horace Bogart, the one who'd started a store in town and lived above the store. Old Ferguson Bruce had scorned the man and said no daughter of his was going to live like that. The family was afraid Greneda would elope with him and sent her off to stay with some cousins in Brand County. They meant to protect the family rebel from her quirky ideas and save her for a respectable marriage, if they could manage one. He remembered how some of the Harvey and Patton aunts pulled their mouths and quietly gloated when they talked about the Bruce troubles. That Greneda was a handful, all right.

The Judge, then young Lawton, happened to be back in Cromwell when old Silas Bruce died. The family thought Greneda ought to come home for the funeral, and since young Lawton was in town, couldn't he drive over to Brand and bring her in? Aunt Louella thought that was a wonderful idea and urged him to go. He said he really needed to get back to Raleigh, but he went.

The Greneda he met at the cousins' door was a lovely young woman. Something happened inside him when he saw her. Who would have thought that hoyden would turn out like this? Her lithe figure and bouncy pulled-back hair, her saucy smile and oval face with perfect nose and cheeks, her shining eyes—he couldn't stop looking.

"So Cousin Lawton, are you going to take me home or just stand there?"

He thought he had polished his manners in parlors and at parties in Raleigh, but he realized he was fumbling as he put her luggage in the back of the car and told the older cousin he would watch out for horses on the road. Yes, he would be careful. On the ride back to Cromwell through the greening countryside of spring, he fell in love. She talked, and he listened, amazed. She hadn't really changed. Just gotten livelier some ways, more serious in others. Then she confessed. She really lived two lives. Outwardly, she laughed at her world. Inwardly, she thought lots of things the family believed, or thought they believed, were just not so. She might be publicly observant about the family religion, but privately she was skeptical. She even wrote poems about her feelings but didn't want to spread them before the family. Certainly not send them to magazines, even with a nom de plume. ("How do you like my French?" she had said with a wry smile.)

"What kind of poems?" he asked. Would he like them?

"Probably not. But you might. They're in my own special language. Do you remember how we used to play word games? How you had to finish the idea I had started? They're like that."

"I remember you won more than I did," he said.

"Naturally."

They sounded like religious poems, she said, but weren't really. She used the rituals and ideas of regular religion as a kind of vocabulary for her nonreligious, even skeptical, views. It wasn't that she meant to deceive. She just saw other meanings for the words that most folks used. She was afraid a lot of the old meanings had worn out. People used the words but didn't feel them any more.

They sounded more truly religious than the regular religion, he said.

"I hope so," she said. Then she stopped talking. They rode in silence. She looked at him. Then looked away. She smiled. "The sky's blue today. I wonder if it will be for Grandpa Bruce's burial. Or is it a deception?"

Before they arrived at the Bruce place, he knew he couldn't stop seeing her. Quirky, funny, serious Greneda. He'd known her most of her life and hadn't known she was like this. Or he'd been blind to what was before him. She was the spirit missing from his proper life. Would she let him see her again?

She looked at him with a level, serious, questioning, then amused appraisal. "I want that too."

During the next two months, he spent more time in Cromwell than in Raleigh. He balanced enough coffee cups on his knee in the Bruce parlor to become a juggler, he thought wryly, and listened to old Ferguson Bruce tell how he had made his money. Titus was courting Joanna at the time, and he and Titus struck up a joking camaraderie when they both arrived at the house at the same time.

"Time for another story," they'd say and march in together. Greneda and sometimes Joanna would sit in the parlor and watch amused as Lawton and Titus suffered. Titus and Joanna were at that stage of understanding that she could visit with his family. After Miss Amanda's death the year before that left old Ferguson a widower, Joanna was almost like an indulgent chaperone while she humored Titus's father.

But when he was alone with Greneda, she was magic. The hours became luminous, and he could tell she felt as he did. "I'll put you in a poem," she said one day, and he knew they had come to a higher communion. The kisses in the hallway and on the porch were never enough, too fleeting, too soon over. He felt her surrender in his arms and knew he had to have more. "I want that too," she whispered.

Then in June, Titus and Joanna got married. He'd come for the wedding and stayed with Aunt Louella and Uncle Wade. Aunt Louella gave him a droll look and asked if there were going to be more wedding bells. Old Ferguson said he had to look into one of his properties downstate and asked him to carry Greneda to stay with her cousins while he was gone and Titus and Joanna were on their wedding trip to Wilmington. Ferguson would pick her up on his way back to Cromwell.

On their way to the cousins', they passed a farmhouse of Ferguson's that had recently been vacated. Great chestnut trees hung over the house. It rested quietly in their shade, and the grounds around were full of sunny early summer flowers. He looked at the house, then at her. She nodded. They left the car behind the house and walked through the flowers to a copse of other chestnuts.

"And did you feel the solstice pass?" she asked later.

"And now it's summer."

"And the days grow shorter."

He wanted to marry her. They talked about marrying the rest of the way to the cousins'. She would like living in Raleigh, he said. Interesting and important people to see and know. Other literary people she might meet. That Walter Hines Page was from there and had connections with magazines and publishing houses in New York and Boston. He'd met him. Good, sound man. She'd like him, could let him see her poems. She said wait.

For the rest of the summer, they saw each other every chance and lived in a kind of ecstatic elation. They had found each other. Then she stopped seeing him. He'd call and she wasn't at home. He'd write and get no answers. Then a letter came. She was going to Philadelphia to study art at the academy. She would explain later. Don't try to follow her.

He tried anyway. Made three trips to Philadelphia but never found her. The address was always wrong. True places never are on the map, he remembered she once said. Something she'd read and liked. He tried the academy. She had been seen, they said, but no one knew where she was now. Maybe she's a ghost, one of the students said, smiling.

His practice began to suffer. Several of his law friends asked what bothered him. Woman trouble—aye? Get over it. Plenty more out there for a good man like him. Then his cousins began to talk. What he needed was a wife with the right connections. Right wife could do wonders for a man on the rise. We know the one for you. Mary Lee Danforth. Good looker. Rich papa with political influence. Quite a politician herself. Mixed with all the right people at her papa's parties. Lots of suitors but just waiting to be taken by the right man.

To humor his friends and keep up with business, he went with his law friends to a Danforth evening and met Mary Lee. She was all they said she was. They must have talked about him to her. She was cordial, even attentive. But he still wanted to find Greneda. Not even calls and letters to Titus and Joanna helped. He thought their answers, if they gave any, were evasive.

The year wore into winter. Still no answers. Somehow his friends managed to place him next to Mary Lee at dinners. They talked and were easy with each other. Out of the side of his eye he could see her delicate profile, graceful neck, and outlines of a fine bosom. Sometimes she touched his arm or shoulder in an inviting, almost intimate way. Then he was invited to her father's country house north of Raleigh for a weekend. Others were there, but Mary Lee and he had fine walks together through the winter-bare gardens, laughing at the chill and the birds and squirrels scurrying to find winter food. He got the feeling she was waiting for him to speak about serious things. On Sunday afternoon, as the weekend was beginning to break up, Mrs. Danforth took him aside and said how much they had enjoyed having him there and hoped he'd return soon. Mary Lee held his hand longer than she did others' and said she would see him in Raleigh.

His friends began to ask how things were with him and Mary Lee. People were beginning to talk about them together in the same breath. Got something going there? Then they began to say he ought to declare himself. Everything to gain if you do. Everything to lose if you don't.

If he'd lost Greneda, he thought, there was Mary Lee. She'd do honor to a man. Everything was right about her except the deep feeling he'd had with Greneda. And he had the rest of his life and career to think about. So he proposed marriage to Mary Lee. She said wait ten minutes so she wouldn't seem too eager. Then she said yes. Of course he would have to ask Papa, but she'd tell Papa what to say. The Danforths announced the engagement of their daughter Mary Lee to Mr. Lawton Peter Harvey of Raleigh and Cromwell, the wedding to occur the following June. His friends slapped him on the back and congratulated him.

His cousins said he'd made the right choice. Marrying a cousin didn't look right anyway. (Maybe she wasn't really a close cousin, but the sister of his half-sister's husband. In Cromwell usage, though, she was a cousin, even if by several removes of kinship through the Pattons.) His enemies, and he was sure to have some if he got into politics, might try to make something nasty of marrying a cousin. Better this way. The Danforths were solid, respectable, and powerful.

In May, a letter came from Greneda. Come to Philadelphia. He'd find her at the address in the letter. She had something to tell him.

The address was that of a restaurant near the academy. Dark wood inside, the smell of heavy food. A waiter with a big handlebar mustache showed him to a booth where Greneda was waiting. She looked more like an art student than the proper but mischievous daughter of Ferguson Bruce, he thought. Same perfect face, but hair covered by a beret-like cap. Eyes—he couldn't decide. Soft and welcoming, but maybe sad. She smiled. He sat down across from her. The waiter asked if they wanted something to drink before they ordered and brought her a light wine, him a bourbon and water. He sat and looked at her. She smiled again and told him.

"We have a daughter. Beautiful thing. Born last March."

"Why didn't you tell me? Marry me? Where is she? I would have loved you both. My God!"

"She's gone now. I gave her to a couple. They'll give her a good life."

"Who?"

"I promised not to tell."

"I have to know. She's my daughter too!"

"It's better this way. She'll be happier never to know about us. I made a promise, gave my bond."

"Bonds are obligations to appear, not vanish."

"You've given your bond. They sent me clippings about your engagement. Next month, isn't it?"

He looked at her more closely. Still the perfect face and eyes like a Madonna, but not shining now. She smiled, but her lips trembled.

"Oh God! I wanted not to cry."

He reached in his pocket for a handkerchief. "I can break that bond."

"No."

"Let's make a better bond."

"I want that too."

"When can we meet?"

She looked at him, now sad, then thoughtful. "In a better time and place. Not here. Let this meal be our communion and our bond. Our rehearsal for a better communion when we'll have earned it by our pain."

They looked at each other a long moment.

"Would you be getting ready to order, sir?" The waiter stuck his head between the curtains.

Greneda's face took on a bright look, and she began to smile. "Ask him if he has any lamb."

"No, sir. No lamb today."

"We'll have to wait for the lamb, then." She began to laugh quietly to herself, then almost aloud.

He and the waiter looked at each other, puzzled. He ordered something for them both—he couldn't remember what.

They waited to be served. "I'm leaving for Chicago tomorrow," she said suddenly.

"What? Why?"

"Work at the Hull-House. It's what I want to do now."

"Does your father know? How will you live? Will he send money?"

"I have that small inheritance from Grandpa."

"It won't last. I don't know how much it was, but it couldn't have been much."

"I'll make it last."

"No. Not good enough. I'll deed you that property by the railroad. It pays good rents."

"I won't take gifts."

"I'll exchange it for that inheritance."

"What will your wife say?"

"I'm not married yet. It's all mine."

"Well then . . ."

Before they left each other, he took her to a jeweler down the street. He wanted her to have something to remember this day. She chose a necklace with a pendant.

"That's a strange figure on the pendant. What is it?" he asked.

"I'll think of it as a lamb."

After that, they walked away in different directions, but each looked back at the same time.

So she went to Chicago, and he married Mary Lee Danforth, big wedding and all. No word from Chicago.

After Ferguson Bruce died, she returned to Cromwell. Ten years after his marriage, Lawton came back to Cromwell as circuit court judge, appointed to fill an unexpired term and fairly certain of reelection at the end of term. He was still the local hero come home. Not bad for a forty-year-old lawyer, but he knew he had backed the wrong wing of the state Democratic Party, and his prospects for state office were not bright. He and Mary Lee settled into the big house with their two children. He ran a tight court and began to earn the reputation of a lawyer's judge. And looked after his investments. They grew as Cromwell grew.

A week after he had settled into his work, Titus came to his office. "Your clerk said you could see me now if I took only half an hour."

"Titus, come in. Good to see you. How's Joanna? Been a long time."

"She's fine. We have three girls now. Don't know if you knew."

"Three girls. They must be close to the ages of mine."

"All girls?"

"Boy and girl. Howell and Amanda."

"And your wife?"

"She's fine too. Learning to live the Cromwell way."

"We have someone else living with us. Don't know if you knew."

"Yes?"

"Greneda."

He felt his insides turn over. Still Greneda!

"I'm here because of her." Titus unbuttoned his coat, and the Judge could see his hand shook.

"I see."

"She says it must be a strange fate that brought you both back to Cromwell. And have to live in the same town. She hopes you will not try to see her. If you meet in public, silence is the rule. No blame, no shame. She has her life. You have yours. Best to keep them separate. Agreed?"

"Agreed."

"That's all. I can give your clerk back part of his half hour."

But in a town the size of Cromwell, people of a certain class have to meet, at least in passing. The Judge and Greneda kept their bond and seldom spoke. But their eyes did, and he knew their other bond was not forgotten. Her pendant and his pain kept it real. He might go for years and know only through others what she did. He doubted they knew what she felt. When he met Titus and Joanna, they were civil but not cordial. When they petitioned to open her grave, he hated to deny them, but he did it for Greneda. That pendant belonged with her.

***

"Now, Roy, let's turn to the 'old friend' question. I hope I've not kept you too long."

"I feel like the wedding guest in that poem they made us read in school."

He laughed. "Not that bad, I hope."

"Who do you think he is?"

"I don't know, but I suspect it's Horace Bogart. He has the motive. Jilted lover and all that. Even more, rejected social climber. Old Mr. Bruce is dead, but Bogart probably thought he still had Greneda to hurt. He could get even with the Bruces and make a profit too by getting that property and selling it to the railroad. Now Greneda is gone, but he can hurt Titus and Joanna."

"How did he know about the baby? You didn't know."

"Good question. He probably learned about her being pregnant from some traveling salesman. He buys art supplies from Philadelphia. Has a good stock of them, too. I've seen the

Philadelphia mark on art things my children brought home. This hypothetical salesman could have seen Greneda there and heard she was from Cromwell. Next time he was here, he could have mentioned it to Bogart. You know how travelers like to carry gossip from one town to the next."

"That's as good a guess as any. But that was a long time ago. Why didn't he do something then?"

"He wasn't ready. He still had a fortune to make. He could carry that knowledge in his pocket for years. It was good as money in the bank. Maybe he thought it accrued interest as Greneda made a reputation for good works. He could wait for the right time."

"Does he know what happened to the baby?"

"Probably not."

"Does he know you're the father?"

"Probably doesn't know but suspects. No doubt he'd watch Greneda after old Mr. Bruce turned him away. He'd watch to see if there was somebody else in the picture. She was sent away to her cousins, but I was there when she came back. He knew when she was pregnant, and he could count back. He knew she'd gone away and could guess why." He laughed ruefully. "He probably knew more than I did at the time."

"This is all speculation about speculation. Can he prove it?"

"Nothing in writing I know of."

"There's the land record at the courthouse. If I could find you owned the land before Miss Greneda did, he could too."

"And probably did. But that's not proof."

"His son Derek has the Bruces all upset as if he has proof."

"So you told me. He's bluffing."

"What do you think should be done?"

"Wait and see. To make a move, he'll have to come out of his corner. He'll have to show himself then."

"You don't think Derek's offer is that move?"

"I'd say it's a gambit to prompt the Bruces to make a move."

"Like what?"

"Don't know. I'm not close to Titus and Joanna any more. You are. They have to be patient."

"Meanwhile, we're agreed Jackie is not to be told about you?"

"Agreed."

As I got ready to leave and shook his hand, I thought this was a different Judge Harvey from the one I'd expected. I didn't suspect I was in for another surprise.

Chapter 7

A couple of days later, I got a note from Mollie: "Come quickly." Strange. Why had she sent a note instead of calling or coming by? Why such a terse note? If she wanted something quickly, why wait for a note to be delivered? I went to the Bruces' with a feeling something bad was about to happen, or had happened.

I'd hardly gotten in the door before Mollie turned on me, put her fists on her hips, and glared at me.

"Roy, I'm disappointed in you. All right, I'm angry. Why didn't you tell me you knew Aunt Greneda had a baby? Why do you keep secrets from your friends? That's no way to show trust! And you've known a long time!"

"Who says?"

"Mama and Papa. They say you knew before they tried to have her grave opened. And that Judge Harvey turned them down."

"It was a professional confidence."

"So—are you a friend or an undertaker?"

"Both, I hope."

"Well, you're not our friend any longer. You can stop coming here. I cringe when I think how I told you I believed it and you kept quiet. I thought we were close then. Now I know better."

Suddenly she was crying instead of angry. I pulled out my clean handkerchief. She grabbed it and turned away. I stood there. The house was quiet, I noticed. No voices in other rooms. Were they listening, or was this Mollie's solo accusation? I put my hand on her elbow. I wanted her to face me.

"Don't touch me. Just go!"

"Can we talk?"

"Just go!"

I left without the handkerchief.

In the midst of the dismay following Mollie's dismissal of me, I had a call from cousin Victoria McMillan. She was one of Mama's friends from a long time back as well as cousin. She said she had a chest full of Mama's old notebooks, school books, some pictures she'd drawn and colored, some of her favorite books they'd read together when they were both girls, some letters she'd kept, some old jewelry, and lots of other girl things. Did I want them? She was getting ready to move in with one of her daughters and had to get rid of things that wouldn't fit in the daughter's house.

I said I did want them and would send around a truck for the chest. Thank you, Cousin Victoria.

A couple of days later, the phone rang. Cousin Victoria again. "Well, young Roy, thank you very much. All my neighbors have been calling. They want to know who died. They peeked through their curtains and saw two men carry out that chest to your truck."

I started apologizing, and she started laughing. "Don't apologize. That's the best thing that's happened in weeks. I wish Martha could know about it. She'd laugh too."

What a fishbowl we live in, I thought as I hung up. Nothing gets by the folks in Cromwell.

When Dr. Kathleen called me to come by, I guess I was still stung by my session with Mollie and wondered if I was in trouble again. Dr. Kathleen and I had knowledge kept in confidence. Had I kept too much? True, I hadn't told her yet about my long talk with Judge Harvey. I thought that would keep until George came back to town.

But this time she was adding confidences. She said Horace Bogart's wife Lauralee had come to her to be examined for pains she'd been having. It didn't take long for Dr. Kathleen to realize she was dealing with cancer. She told Miss Lauralee that she worked mostly with children, she ought to see another doctor more familiar with cancer. Maybe he could tell whether surgery would help. Miss Lauralee said she suspected cancer but came to Dr. Kathleen for other reasons. Dr. Kathleen said she might not have long to live if she didn't get treatment soon. Miss Lauralee said she thought so too.

Then she talked about the other reasons. She wanted to make peace between her husband and the Bruces before she died. She knew Horace had threatened the Bruces with something scandalous. And she knew Derek had threatened the Bruce girls. She thought the town was too small for its people to keep grudges. Yes, she knew her husband had wanted to marry Miss Greneda and had been sent away by her papa. That didn't bother her. It was all so long ago. She wanted a good life in Cromwell for her grandchildren, a life unclouded by old grudges. She wanted Dr. Kathleen to work with her to clear up the past. Dr. Kathleen knew the Bruces—she didn't—and had worked with Miss Greneda. Would she act as a go-between so, woman-to-woman, they could heal the past before she died?

Miss Lauralee also said she thought Horace was about to threaten Judge Harvey with scandal. She didn't know if it was linked with the Bruces. But she'd heard Horace say things about the Judge and knew he was about to do something.

Dr. Kathleen asked her if she'd agree to let her tell her fears to the Bruces and the Judge and to me. "Why Mr. Vance?" she had asked.

"He's already familiar with most of what you've told me. From the Bruces." She gasped but agreed.

Then Dr. Kathleen put her hand on my arm, smiled, and said, "Roy, you're the real go-between in this town. You know more about most people's business and hopes and secrets than their preachers and priests do. You ought to run for alderman. I believe most folks would support you. They trust you."

I laughed and said no thanks. The best way to lose friends was to go into politics. Somebody always loses in politics, and losers get sore about losing.

"Think about it," she said.

Next time I saw the Judge, he told me Dr. Sullivan had told him to watch out for threat of a scandal from Bogart. He'd told her, he said, Bogart had already done so, but he had no proof. I thought the Judge looked a little less confident than he had earlier. His eyes looked tired, and he looked grayer than I remembered. He said he hoped for the Bruces' sake no proof existed.

During those weeks, I still wasn't clear how I stood with the Bruces. I still didn't know whether Mollie's anger was hers alone or the family's. In any case, we'd had no reason to talk, and I didn't think I should risk visiting unless I had a practical reason. I wondered if I was right to keep relations on a basis of practical action instead of feelings. I was pretty sure Mollie wouldn't relent.

Then I began to get a clearer view. As I was standing beside my Ford, ready to get in, Sally rolled up in the Bruces' car, stuck her head out the window, and said come closer. It was a relief to see that tanned and smiling face at the car window.

"Hello," I said. "I'd guess by the sun on your face you've been riding the trails again."

"Riding the roads is more like it. If you have a minute, I'll tell you a story."

"I like good stories."

She and William Walker, she said, had been riding William's horses on one of the back roads and came across Derek Bogart's car in the ditch. He was sitting on the edge of the road. Had a gash on his head and was acting kind of groggy. They checked him over, decided he was not badly injured, and told him to stay put, they were going for help. She got William's car and took Derek to Dr. Brandon's. William got his heavy horses and pulled Derek's car out of the ditch and took it to Roy Willard's to be worked on. It was there now.

"How's that for a turn of events?" she laughed.

"What did your folks think about it?"

"More interesting, what did Derek think about it? By the time I got him to Dr. Brandon's, he began to realize who I was. Started acting real embarrassed. Said he hoped we didn't hold it against him for what he'd done. It was just business. He worked for the railroad and had to do what the railroad wanted."

"Did he mention his papa's part in it?"

"He said Mr. Bogart was just trying to look out for us."

"Did you believe him?"

"I tried to keep from laughing."

"So?"

"So somebody behind me is trying to get by. I'd better move on. Thought you'd be interested." She was wearing her hair in what they call a ponytail, and it was swaying nicely as she drove away.

Then a week later, I met Livie as I was going into Goodman's department store and she was coming out. "Hey, Roy," she said and stopped. She was smiling, mouth and eyes too. I took that as a good sign, stopped, and asked how she was. We stepped to the side to let some shoppers get by. After asking about Titus and Miss Joanna, I asked how she and Derek were doing since Sally and William had rescued him. She laughed and said not good. They'd had a quarrel after she had gone to a dance with Charlie Bains. But that was okay with her. Charlie was a neat dancer and lots of fun. Did I know him? I knew his family. I saw she'd let her bobbed hair grow out to short blonde curls around her face.

I asked her what became of Derek's offer to buy the property down by the railroad. Nothing, she said. Papa and Mama had told him they'd think about it, but that was their way of putting off a decision. She didn't know what they really thought. They had so many things to think about. Then she gave me a conspiratorial look out of the corner of her eyes. What about the threat he mentioned? Nothing more had been said about it since Sally and William helped him. She didn't know what his silence meant. Anyway, he's out of town. Gone on railroad business, he said. Away she swished, her trim figure and swaying skirt turning men's heads as she walked. A pretty girl is like a melody, or something like that. I watched a moment, then went on in to buy some new handkerchiefs.

The next weeks were full of business, and I found little time to think about Mollie or the Bruces and their problems. It's sad sometimes to find out how unprepared some folks are for the inevitable. Several supposedly well-off businessmen had died, one playing golf, another cranking his car, and had left their financial affairs in a mess. Their widows knew next to nothing about where their money for living came from, and after the funerals I had to help them find lawyers to sift through the papers and find out whether they were solvent or broke. Of course, the lawyers made sure they got their money, and I did too. Everybody has bills to pay.

One of the men who died was a city alderman with a year and a half remaining on his term. They began to talk about holding a special election for a replacement to serve out his term. Judge Harvey came by, said he'd talked with Dr. Sullivan and several others, and they wanted me to run for the office. Again I said no thanks, I had things to do, things to do. He said they would be disappointed, I was the right man for the job.

Derek was out of town all right, but not out of the Bruces' thoughts. I learned that when I met Mollie coming out of the town library near the railroad depot. We either had to meet or ignore each other. She chose to meet. She had books in her arms and held on to them without shaking hands or touching. I thought she looked taller and prettier than ever, blue eyes and brown hair above her armful of books. She smiled with all the cordiality of a distant neighbor and said hello. I asked how she was. Just fine, thanks.

"Going to do a lot of reading, I see."

"Yes, they have some new books I wanted to look at."

"How's the school year going?"

"Be over soon."

We stood there. "Well," I said, "I'll be—"

"Wait," she said. "I have some news to tell you."

"Good news, I hope."

"Interesting, anyway. The news is that Derek met Amanda Harvey on the train from Richmond, and they're much taken with each other."

"Oh?"

"She was on the train with her mother when they met. Seems Mama Harvey is not as impressed with him as Amanda is. Thinks he's a presumptuous parvenu. I think that was the phrase used."

"How did you hear that?"

"Two ways. Mrs. H. was talking to the ladies. Mama was there. And Amanda told Livie."

"What did Livie say?"

"Take him and God bless you, or something like that."

"What about the Judge? What does he say?"

"She didn't say. Mrs. H., that is."

"What about Horace Bogart and his wife?"

"Haven't heard. They'd like that, wouldn't they? It would add a bit of class to their money, wouldn't it?"

Damn, I thought as she walked away. More things you couldn't tell. She must not know Bogart's scandal threat involves the Judge. Or that Bogart's wife was trying to patch up things.

I was a bit surprised, then, when Titus came by the office a couple of days later. "Come to supper next Friday," he said. "Livie won't be there, but Sally and her William will. And Mollie, of course. We'll laugh and tell gossip about our neighbors." I said I'd be there.

The talk was as good as the dinner at the Bruces'. Miss Joanna set the tone when I gave her a bottle of French red at the door. "Wonderful, Roy!" she said. "I won't ask where you got it." I didn't tell her about Dan Blue and his connections.

Mollie and I sat side by side, Sally and William across from us, Miss Joanna and Titus at the ends. I wondered if the seating meant anything. Actually, I'd rather have sat across from Mollie so I could see her better. But we could talk and pass the dishes and touch hands when we did. I began to relax. We sipped the red wine with our veal and vegetables. Titus told another of his droll stories, and Sally rolled her eyes and looked at Mollie. I supposed Mollie rolled her eyes, too. The sisters looked conspiratorial, I thought. Wonder what's up.

After Auntie Mae removed the main dishes, we sat back to enjoy the coffee. "Coffee's the American brandy these days," Titus mused. So we speculated whether Prohibition was ever going to be repealed.

After some more talk about the times, Sally turned to me. "Roy, here's more on what Mollie told you about Derek and Amanda."

I glanced at Mollie and waited.

"Will and I've seen them a couple of times riding the back roads in Derek's new car. They looked like they were more interested in each other than in cars."

"Did they see you?"

"They waved as they passed us."

"What did your horses think of the strange car on their road?" I asked William.

"They're getting used to cars now. Pay them no mind."

"Why the back roads?" I wondered.

Miss Joanna answered. "I've heard from several of the ladies, Derek and his papa have had a falling out. No one says why. No one really knows, but we guess Mr. Bogart disapproves of a connection with the Harveys." I saw her look at Titus.

"I don't know why," Sally said. "They're good family."

"Better than his," William said.

"Would it have anything to do with that railroad deal?" Mollie wondered. "Maybe Derek is more a railroad man than a son in something like this."

"Well, he's sure in a position to influence the purchase. Or not," Titus thought.

"So Derek doesn't want Mr. Bogart to know he's seeing Amanda. Is that it?" I asked.

"Something like that," Miss Joanna said. She almost looked at Titus again.

We stayed around the table to talk. I liked that. Getting up and going to the parlor shakes up the talk, and you hardly ever get it going right again. I'd seen that in the army. Best talk was always right in the mess, drinks and elbows on the table. Miss Joanna got going on family genealogies. Sally and Mollie rolled their eyes again. By the time she finished, she had the Bruces and Millards related to half the families in the county. The better families.

When it was time to leave, I thanked Miss Joanna and Titus for the pleasant evening. They said please come back. Mollie walked with me to the door. She offered a handshake instead of a hug.

"So Bogart disapproves of a connection with the Harveys," I said. "Do you disapprove of a connection with the Vances?"

She just smiled and said, "Good night."

While I was trying to figure out what Mollie was really saying, Ed Braswell came by late one afternoon to arrange for the burial of his brother Lawrence. At first, I thought he had come to collect information for *The Cromwellian* on one of the citizens we had recently buried. But he had come to talk as much as to make arrangements. I thought he looked sad. He usually had a half-cynical draw to his mouth under that mustache. Now he looked sad.

Lawrence, he said, had died in Raleigh, and his brother's death left him as the last of the Braswells. He wanted to have his brother's body brought back to Cromwell for burial with the rest of the family. He said Lawrence had died of a heart attack, at least that was what the medical report would say. But he knew his brother drank himself to death because of despair. At that point, I put down my pen and pushed back the record form. I had the sense that this was one of those sad sessions when you hear the dark memories that don't get into public records.

Ed said he knew lots of untold stories about folks in town, stories he couldn't put in his paper, but this was real and close to him, and he wanted to tell me since he had no family left. I nodded, and he told.

Lawrence began drinking heavily back in '18, he said, and managed to get his liquor even after Prohibition was passed. He was a lobbyist for the railroad in Raleigh and had lots of connections. He didn't know, maybe Lawrence got hold of some bad stuff, but he didn't think that was what killed him. He began that drinking after he was disappointed in love, rejected by Greneda Bruce. At that name, I sat up straighter and listened harder. He said since Greneda and Lawrence were both gone, there wasn't any reason to hold back.

Lawrence was a lawyer for the Eastern and Southern back in the war years. His wife had died back in '15, and he had been going through the motions of living, though their marriage hadn't been a close one and they had no children. Even back then, the railroad had its eye on Greneda's property. The war business was good, and the railroad was looking to expand after the war. He was the one the railroad sent to explore the opportunity of buying her property.

He called on her several times to talk about the purchase and had to pretend interest in her work with the children. Before long, he got really interested in that work. The railroad encouraged his interest because Greneda was working with the children of railroad laborers as well as with mill children. Several of the railroad families were barely scraping by after a lot of the men were drafted into the army, and those left had to travel all up and down the line to keep the tracks clear and the trains moving. In fact, he put some of his own money into her school.

Before long, Lawrence was calling on Greneda every time he came to town, and Ed realized Lawrence was in love with Greneda.

She was more alive than his wife had ever been, Lawrence told him. They became closer. She even showed him some of her poems. Lawrence had tried his hand at some poems when he was younger, and though he was no poet, he knew good poems when he read them. He wanted her to let him get them published, but she said no, they were too personal. And some she wouldn't show him at all.

Lawrence kept telling Ed how beautiful and gracious she was, how lively and imaginative. He wondered sometimes why she hadn't married when she was younger, but he wanted to marry her now. They still had a good life to live together. But she said she couldn't marry and wouldn't say why. He asked her several times and told her how he could offer a free and fairly wealthy life, but she still said no. Once she said she had gotten the habit of renunciation. He couldn't tell whether she meant refusing his offers or something else.

About that time, Ed began to tell Lawrence not to pursue Greneda. True, she was sharp and quick, but strong-minded. She had her quirky way of thinking and wouldn't change or discuss her ideas. She would be bad for his career.

Lawrence persisted in his courtship, though. Finally he wrote to Titus Bruce and asked him to speak for him to Greneda. He thought some brotherly advice might sway her. The last time Ed had a real talk with his brother was when Lawrence told him he had a meeting coming up with Titus. He would let him know what Titus was able to do.

But Lawrence never told. He suddenly moved to Raleigh and wouldn't tell why except he was going into a new line of work. And he began to drink.

"Tell you the truth, Roy, I'm both glad and sorry he didn't marry Greneda. Glad because she was unknowable. He was besotted with her and would have done any crazy thing she wanted. Sorry because—well, he was only half a man after she turned him down. Sorry too because he was lonely, and I reckon she was too. Far as I know, she never had a friend in her mysterious sorrow. Couldn't marry. I never figured that out."

A couple of days later, Lawrence's body came to town, and we held a private graveside service. Ed invited Titus and Miss Joanna, and they came and cried real tears. Reverend Benfield said prayers that seemed strangely personal.

I was still wondering what Dr. Kathleen and Miss Lauralee were doing to patch up a peace between Horace and the Bruces, and whether I was supposed to be doing something to help their effort, when I had a call from the Judge. Could I come by his house? He had a new development to talk over with me.

By then, I knew to go to the porch door that opened to his office. He motioned me to a chair, and I watched as he went back to his chair. I thought he moved slower than usual, head bent down and shoulders sloped, like a man deep in thought about a problem.

"Well, Roy." He paused and thought a minute. "It's happened. Horace Bogart came to me yesterday and said he knows Jackie's my child and he has proof."

"But does he?"

"This time he's got it. He was smug, I thought, when he told me. Like I'd hidden something and he'd found it."

"What's his proof?"

"A letter. A letter Greneda wrote to Titus and Joanna. It seems Greneda did put me in a poem. Written when she knew she was going to have the baby. Joanna found it after Greneda left for Philadelphia. You might guess how cryptic the poem was. In itself it wouldn't have been definite, wouldn't have made a definite identification. But Joanna asked for an explanation, and Greneda made the identification clear in a letter. Well, almost clear. Clear enough. Even Greneda's letters could be cryptic."

"Didn't Titus and Miss Joanna know why she was leaving?"

"Apparently so, but they didn't know the father of the baby."

"Couldn't they guess? They must have known how close you had been."

"They wanted more than guesses. They probably thought they were entitled to know. They were her link with Cromwell. Probably the ones who sent her money to live."

"Her papa didn't know? Didn't pay?"

"Nothing to indicate he knew. No doubt he suspected. You realize, don't you? She didn't come back to Cromwell until after he died."

"Did she say she was giving the baby to the Carters?"

"No, the letter was written before the baby was born."

"So how did Bogart make the connection with the Carters?"

"Same way George Landry did. Derek went to Philadelphia and checked the birth and adoption records."

"How did he get the letter from Titus and Miss Joanna?"

"He wouldn't say specifically, wouldn't name names. But from what he did say, I gather he had a cleaning woman take it from Joanna's desk. Something about an open box of letters."

I remembered Miss Joanna saying she sometimes lost track of things. Mollie had to help her keep up with her papers.

"How did he get the cleaning woman to take the letter? She was taking quite a risk herself."

"I can only guess at that. My guess is she was in debt to him some way. I've heard he can ride his debtors pretty hard. She'd do it to get out of debt to him."

"Did you see the letter?"

"Not in my hands. He held onto it and read it aloud to me."

"So he's got the goods at last. What are you going to do?"

"Just wait for right now. Bogart's holding the letter as a threat. Once he uses it, it's used up. With the letter in hand, he thinks he can control me."

"How?"

"Don't know. Maybe he has a case coming up in court."

"What kind of threats did he talk about?"

"I'm coming up for reelection in a year. He hinted he could pass the evidence to an opponent. Or make it public and hurt the family. Also said something about telling Jackie who she is. I'd hate that. She's had enough trouble with that auto accident. She needs to be able to turn to the Carters for support and comfort."

"Did Bogart act like he's about to do something now?"

"No. I think he's enjoying the situation too much to change it."

"If he's been waiting twenty-five years, I reckon he can wait some more." He smiled ruefully at that.

We sat in the office several minutes, quiet and thinking.

Then I said, "What do you make of this new attraction between your daughter and Derek Bogart?"

He looked up. "Didn't know you knew about them."

"Sally Bruce told me. She said they're seeing each other on the sly. Said Horace is put out with his boy for that. Doesn't approve of a connection with the Harveys."

He laughed. "Mary Lee doesn't approve, either. Works both ways."

"What do you think of Derek?" I asked.

"Haven't met him yet. Mary Lee has, of course. She doesn't have much good to say about him, mostly because of his family. Now, Amanda's view is another thing. She looks at the young man, not his family."

"You know anything about him? Besides family, I mean."

"I've asked around. Several of the lawyers think he's pretty sharp. So's his father, of course. But things they say make me think he's not like the old man. Didn't have to scramble to make a place for himself. Maybe more like his mother. A decent woman. Not much class, but decent."

"Sounds like we're still talking about family."

"Yes. You can't escape it. But that doesn't mean like father, like son."

"So he's still a question mark."

"I suppose so. I'll have to meet him soon. If Mary Lee doesn't bring him in, Amanda will."

"That'll be interesting."

"Especially for him and Mary Lee. Women have a way of getting what they want, or don't want."

"So wait and see?"

"Wait and see."

The Judge has a problem, I thought as I left. Is that what the judges call "prayer for judgment continued"? But is he the judge or the accused?

As it turned out, the women had been at work. Dr. Sullivan told me one day she and Miss Lauralee had persuaded Horace to wait and see what happened with Derek and Amanda. And let the secrets remain secret. I thought it not wise to ask what pressures had been put on Horace, what arguments used. I could guess. I could see Dr. Kathleen telling him about his sick wife and making him feel guilty about anything that might upset her. I could see Miss Lauralee pleading the happiness of their one remaining child and their grandchildren. Maybe Horace didn't have a chance.

About two weeks later, Will Ford told me the Eastern and Southern had dropped its appeal of the train and truck judgment over in Johns County. Why? I asked. The railroad was afraid the suit would block its purchase of Miss Greneda's property, he said. The railroad wanted that property a lot more than the money they would pay on the judgment. I congratulated him and said I was glad for the folks in Johns County.

As I walked away, I wondered how Will knew about the proposal to buy Miss Greneda's property. Maybe that was more general knowledge than I thought. Or maybe Titus and Miss Joanna had told him after they petitioned for the hearing to open her grave. Something as important for the town as the construction of a major railroad facility probably had most of the businessmen talking. But why hadn't I heard it from some of them? So much for the Judge thinking I knew what was going on in town.

What I hadn't known about was the fine hand of Derek Bogart at work. Titus filled in the blanks for me. He came to the office looking happier than I'd seen him in a long time, face and eyes smiling, and put a stack of papers on the desk.

"Well, Roy, things are beginning to break our way. You see before you an offer by the Eastern and Southern to buy Greneda's property at twice the money they offered before. Reckon I ought to say the girls' property now."

"How'd that come about?"

"Derek Bogart's the man behind it. He was the one got the railroad to drop that appeal. Stop delaying and get down to business. Seems that clearing the mortgage on Greneda's place and freeing Roy Willard of the threat of bankruptcy is what broke things loose. Value of that property went way up then. Derek told them they better get the property now before it doubles again in value. You know how prices are going these days."

"And they believed him?"

"Not everybody. Old C. K. Whittington is disgusted, they say. He'd still rather fight. Thinks he can deal with Horace Bogart, but Derek's got the angle on him. He's inside the company."

"So the Bogarts are still at odds with each other?"

"Sort of. Old Horace is kind of lyin' low these days. Don't know why. Hope he can't spoil the deal."

"What's going to happen to Miss Greneda's school?"

"That's part of the deal. Railroad's going to build a new school on top of that hill overlookin' the town. And here's the funny part. They want to call it after the railroad, name it the Eastern and Southern School. Derek says that's their way of covering up for their cave-in on the price. Want to take credit for being the town's benefactor."

"Sounds like the railroad's coming up with a lot of money all of a sudden."

"Oh, they'll make a profit. Never doubt that. That switching yard will handle lots more traffic, and every car they handle carries a profit."

"What's all that traffic going to do to Cromwell? We'll be living with the sounds of trains rolling and thundering when they connect. All day and maybe all night."

"The business folks love it. Sounds like money to them."

"So Derek was behind it all? What got into him? I thought he was trying to make trouble for you."

"Money, for one thing. He can see a profit as well as his daddy can, maybe better. And after Sally and William helped him, he might have been skittish about bearing down on us."

"But we're still guessing, right?"

"Reckon so. It's all we got to go on."

I looked at the stack of papers. "I reckon you're going to take that offer?"

"Seems best to. Property values can go down well as up."

I nodded and thought how this deferential, almost apologetic man generally seemed to come out right on money matters.

I shook his hand, congratulated him, and wished him well. I still wasn't sure what Horace Bogart would do. He still might make trouble. He still had the letter against the Judge and might still use it to get him. But how would that affect Derek's courting the Judge's daughter? Looked like the old man and the son were working against each other. Maybe Dr. Kathleen and Miss Lauralee needed to make peace between Horace and Derek.

Then I wondered how serious Derek was about Amanda. Was he using her, the way he'd used Livie?

I lived with those puzzles for maybe a week. The funeral business was quiet, and I had time to walk around town and think. And look. Several new Fords were on the streets. Lots of folks going into and out of the banks. Robbie Green, the stockbroker, had cars parked at his office most of the time. Chestnuts along Main Street looked peaked. City ought to do something about them. I tried to see Mollie, but Miss Joanna said she was doing a program at school and spent all her time there.

Then Judge Harvey surprised me by coming to my place one evening. I didn't say anything about the change. If he wanted to come to my place, welcome. We went up to my quarters, lit cigars, and I took out a bottle of Dan's brandy. The Judge was more relaxed than he was last time we met. He sat in the big chair, legs crossed, but still looked alert and, I thought, judicial. We swapped opinions on baseball and agreed the Yankees looked strong again, maybe the pennant this year. And what's that fellow Mussolini think he's doing in Italy? I began to wonder the purpose of his visit. Finally, he talked.

"Had a visit from Horace Bogart last evening."

I sat up straight at that. "Horace?"

"Yes, Horace, not Derek."

I waited.

"Seems he wants to strike a truce. Says he's reconsidered his views of the other week. 'Take back what I said' were his words, I recall now."

"How's that?"

"He's withdrawing his threat. Fact, he handed me Greneda's letter, said I could keep it or tear it up. Or give it back to Joanna."

"That's the fact. What's the reason?"

"Said if we were going to be family, he didn't want any scandals in his family." He laughed.

"Wasn't that a big 'If'?"

"No. Two evenings before, Derek came to ask for Amanda, and I said yes."

"Wasn't that a big surprise?"

"No again. Mary Lee told me he was coming, and we agreed what to say. Rather, she told me what to say."

"She changed her mind, then?"

"Yes. Amanda worked on her and told her how it was between her and Derek. Mary Lee saw she couldn't stop it and decided she liked it. She wants our daughter to be happy and decided Derek's money, actual and prospective, brings him up in the world."

"And?"

"And she also knows about Horace being sent away by old Ferguson Bruce. She didn't want a repeat of that."

"Well, the world does change."

"Indeed it does. And stays the same, too."

"So if Horace couldn't marry up, he gets his due by seeing his son marry up."

We sat there and grinned at each other. "Strange, isn't it?" the Judge said. "Who would have thought twenty-five years ago things would turn out this way?"

"A lot has happened since then."

"Yes. Greneda."

I saw the Judge was having his own thoughts and didn't interrupt. I wondered if Miss Greneda would have smiled at the match. It felt almost like she and old Ferguson were looking over my shoulder and laughing quietly through the years. I almost looked around. Maybe we'd better, I thought, go about our daily business with the notion that someone down the years will look back and judge us for how small or large we conducted ourselves. That was a fearful prospect.

"Well," the Judge said, getting up. "Tomorrow comes early. Back to the problems of the day. Thanks for the cigar and brandy. I won't ask where you got it."

Chapter 8

Three weeks later, Judge Harrison confirmed the probate of Miss Greneda's will, and Titus, acting as agent for his daughters and Jackie Carter, sold their property to the Eastern and Southern. John Gentry at the bank grinned as he handed each of the Bruce women a hefty check for her part of the payment and urged them to open accounts at his bank. Titus had invited me to the handover as an interested party.

Sally said she already had plans for hers. As soon as she and William got married, they were going to build a nice house out at the horse farm and keep that property debt-free and separate from his business. They didn't wait long to have a quiet and quick wedding. The only tears were Miss Joanna's. She was disappointed she didn't have a big wedding to show the kin.

Livie said she wanted to buy one of those new touring cars, but Titus talked her into waiting for the next year's newer model.

Paternal subterfuge, that was. He wanted her to wait and see what developed with Charlie Bains. He thought they were getting serious, he told me. They had dined often with Will and Kate Ford and Emma and Harry Bains, Charlie's older brother, and he thought they would be a good influence on his exciting but flighty daughter.

Jackie had come back for a short visit and to get her part of the inheritance. She said she wanted to wait and see what George said. Mollie told me later George had said "Marry me?" and Jackie gave the right answer. But they had to negotiate. George agreed to join the Episcopal Church, and they would marry in the Carters' church in Richmond with, Jackie said, all the bells and smells. Jackie agreed to move to Philadelphia. She said it wasn't home to her, but she'd make it feel like home.

Mollie said at last she was free to move to New York, and maybe later to Paris. She would find out if she could write well enough to sell her stories. Just think of this money as an investment, she said, laughing. I tried to laugh too. What kind of stories? I asked. She got serious. Satires and exposés about places like Cromwell, she said. Sinclair Lewis had already shown there was an audience for stories like that, and she knew a few things he didn't.

Along with Titus and Miss Joanna and Livie, I went to the train station to see her off. This time she hugged me briefly before getting on the train, but she was hugging everyone. Almost hugged the conductor, she was so eager to be on her way into the world. Then, just as the train was pulling out, she leaned out the door of the car and looked a long moment at me. I thought she was about to say something, but no words came. We looked back at each other as the train moved away.

"I do hope Evelyn is at the station to meet her," Miss Joanna said as we walked back to the cars. Evelyn Jobe was one of Mollie's college friends. She was a secretary for one of the publishers and was supposed to help Mollie meet the right people and hear about the right opportunities. They were going to share an apartment. Titus walked glumly on. I guessed he felt he had just lost a daughter.

So how to live without Mollie? Tend to business, for one thing. Most of it was routine by then. The ministers in town and I had our procedures pretty well worked out. I knew their preferences, and they knew my possibilities. Mostly the funerals were in churches, but I had noted a small increase in the number of families who wanted services in the funeral home chapel. One reason, I saw, was that more families were asking for cremation of the remains, and several ministers couldn't bring themselves to talk in their churches about resurrection of the ashes. They just did a memorial service in the chapel.

Then came the day when Winston Eller died. He and his family were new in town and hadn't joined a church. Said they didn't think they would. I suggested several ministers the family might ask to do the service. They said no. Mrs. Eller said they had been married by a justice of the peace. Couldn't they get someone like a justice of the peace to do the funeral service? I said justices of the peace didn't do funerals. She said, "You do it." I said I wasn't a minister. She said they didn't need one, they just needed someone to say Winston had been a good man and was gone. You don't have to have a license to do that, do you? I said you just need a license to prepare and bury the dead. Well, then . . . , she said.

Winston couldn't wait, and that meant I couldn't either to decide. So I spent a good part of that evening trying to think up a proper service to fit the Ellers' needs. But mainly, I guess, I put in things I'd wished the padres had said for the soldiers we put in the ground. They had made journeys from places in the States to a country they knew almost nothing about. Then they made another journey to somewhere they knew less about. I put in some Shakespeare, a little Ecclesiastes and Job, some Housman that Mollie had shown me, and a bit of the spirituals I'd heard out west. The best part, I reckon, was it was short. And I was able to say it from memory.

After I finished the service, the Ellers and their friends just sat there. I knew I had bombed. But after the burial, Mrs. Eller hugged me and said she had felt the service more than any other she'd ever heard. "Keep that," she said. "I want you to say it for me." Then I really wondered what I'd done.

The Ellers' friends didn't hug me, but they must have talked. A couple of weeks later the Methodist minister came up to me on the street, slapped my back, and said, "Roy, I hear you've gone into doing services now. And the Johnsons said you did a fine job." I said don't worry, it was a onetime thing for the Ellers. Then the Baptist minister told me after a funeral he'd heard I preached a good funeral, maybe a little short on spiritual truths. We laughed at that. Somehow the word of my weak moment got around. I tried to be more professional and technical after that, let others say the big thoughts.

When Titus came to the office, I hoped he had some word from or about Mollie. But he said he'd come to talk about my future. He and several others in town wanted me to run for alderman. I said I'd already told Judge Harvey and Dr. Sullivan no thanks. He said things were different now. Jake Borden was going to run, and everybody in town knew he was in the railroad's pocket. Let him get in and Cromwell would become a company town. Besides, he was an unsavory character and had worse friends. Word was they had links with the Chicago Mob. How about it? Several folks in town had said I had shown I could speak in public.

I told him I'd hoped he would tell something about Mollie. "Oh, she's doing fine," he said. "She's writing but hasn't sold any stories yet. Making lots of useful friends. Meeting some important writers. Learning her way around. Learning how expensive New York is, too," he said ruefully.

I thought about Titus's visit a few days and decided I'd try for it. The business was coming along all right, and with Johnny Dayton to help, I could probably juggle town business and funeral business. I had lots of empty evenings with no Mollie to see. Maybe a little town politics would fill my days. So I paid the filing fee and declared myself a candidate.

The campaign went well, better than I expected. Titus and his friends made sure I had good crowds when I made a campaign pitch.

My promise was to keep town business public and on the table where everyone could know what was going on. *The Cromwellian* was careful not to take sides but said I had a good plan. Several folks came up to me on the street, shook my hand, and said they looked forward to voting for me. Jake Borden and I shook hands at several meetings, and he was civil but cynical. Said in so many words I didn't know how real business was done. Some of his men laughed when he said that. I saw they hung around the edges of my crowds as well as his.

A couple of days before the election, Titus came to my office looking worried. He said things didn't look good. Jake's crowd was passing around rumors I had "worked on niggers" in my embalming room. "Do you want your mother on a table where a nigger's been lyin'?" they'd say. "Do you want a nigger-lover for your alderman?" I said it was true, I'd helped get the folks who were killed in that train wreck in Johns County ready for burial. He said he appreciated that but didn't think the folks in Cromwell would like it. Couldn't I do something?

The newspaper was due to come out the day before elections. I thought, since my campaign was based on being aboveboard, I'd better tell the facts and wrote an open letter for the paper. It was published the next day with the headline "VANCE TELLS FACTS." I said yes, I had helped the plain folks in Johns County in their time of need. The Eastern and Southern had rolled right along and didn't help.

The election count the next day was close, but when the count was reported, the railroad won. For several days after, folks came up to say they were sorry and better luck next time.

The one good thing to come out of the election was that I got a letter from Mollie. She said Titus had told her how the election was lost and she was sorry. She felt partly responsible. If she hadn't stirred up the railroad about that suit in Johns County, maybe the railroad wouldn't have been out to get me. She also said things were going pretty well for her. She hadn't sold anything yet, but she was learning what made a sellable story. One of these days, I'd see a story of hers in print.

I didn't think her point about the railroad's revenge was right, but I was glad to see she thought we were still linked in the town's and railroad's thinking. You grab at whatever straws you can.

Politics took a new turn in early spring when Will Ford agreed to run for county commissioner and asked me to help with his campaign. As in most counties in this part of the state, the real contest was the Democratic primary, tantamount to election, the papers said. There weren't enough Republicans in the area to make the general election much more than a formality, even if Republicans held office in Washington. But the Democrats ranged from more conservative than the Republicans to almost moderate. Forget about liberals. They were in the Midwest and Northeast. And in Ireland County, the fight was more about local issues than state party politics. Raleigh was farther away in folks' thinking than it was in miles.

I told Will I still had the Negro question hanging around my neck and might be more hindrance than help. He said folks didn't have to vote for me, but some wished they had after seeing how Jake Borden was acting. Jake said the business of Cromwell was railroad business and was making it stick. More and more businessmen in town were beginning to feel left out. Railroad contracts were going to Jake's friends. And folks out in the county were beginning to say the gap between town and county was growing. They felt like the poor relations of the town folks. Will thought he could swing the county vote behind him but needed me to help swing the town vote. So I agreed. It's your campaign, I said.

I understood from Will I should work behind the scenes. Provide no target for Jake's man Ed Bromley. I couldn't campaign from my business, but I could drop a good word for Will when I was buying supplies. A customer is a valuable friend to a merchant when he's buying. And I could agree with farmers and businessmen, without mentioning names, about how wrong things were getting in town and out in the county. I still had some credit with folks I'd helped when a death in the family had thrown their affairs into confusion. Sometimes they'd remember, but I knew by now folks voted for what they thought they'd get rather than what they'd gotten in the past. Or voted out of fear of what they thought might happen.

Finally I realized I was just getting scattered support here and there. What Will needed was blocks of votes. What were the blocks in Ireland County? And who controlled them? Some of the biggest and oldest, I thought, were the McDonalds and McMillans, Will's mother's folks and my mother's. I knew who had the big voice among the McMillans. Uncle Jeremy. Who among the McDonalds? I'd better ask Will. Ireland County clans! Maybe we'd find out how strong they were.

When I went to see Will, I met Kate. Now there was a real woman. Tall, dark-haired, blue eyes, one of the handsomest women in town. And had a fine sense of humor, ready to laugh with you or at some of the quirks of Cromwell. She said Will was due home for dinner any minute. She'd wait with me till he came. Their two boys were at school and had their lunches. Our talk didn't go on long before she asked how Mollie was doing. I told her I hadn't heard lately. Mollie was busy in New York learning to become a famous writer. She looked at me a minute, then smiled.

"She's coming back."

"When?"

"When she's ready. She has to prove herself first. Has to earn her independence. She won't want to go from her papa's house to her husband's without becoming a woman in her own right. It makes for a good marriage later, I've always thought."

"Sounds like you know her better than I do."

"We women talk."

About that time Will came in. "Good morning, Roy. I hope you're getting good advice from Kate."

"Best kind of political counsel. And about that, I need to ask your advice."

I told him my idea and asked if someone in the McDonald clan had sway over McDonald votes.

"Cousin Malcolm McDonald. He's your man."

"Will he talk to me?"

"Think so. Tell him Kate sent you. She's got all kinds of pull with him. He wishes she was a McDonald."

"Don't forget the McClouds," Kate said. "They wish Will was a McCloud." I remembered Kate was old Judge McCloud's daughter. Nice match, the McClouds and McDonalds. Will and I were the outsiders. Our papas were from outside Ireland County and had married into the clans.

"Uncle Jamie is the one to see," Kate said. "Talk about the war in Cuba, and he'll be your best friend." She was a smart politician herself, I thought. She'll be good for Will.

The election was coming on, and it was soon time to see Uncle Jamie and Cousin Malcolm. They were both amused when I called on them, but they promised to do what they could. They said, oh no, they didn't have much influence with the kin, but I soon saw they were droll masters of understatement. Uncle Jeremy was another thing. Since our disagreement over Mama's burial place, we had been civil but never warm. He still mentioned her being buried on the other side of the hill. Like maybe she didn't have a sure entry into the McMillan heaven.

I finally built up my courage and went to see Uncle Jeremy. He was sitting on his side porch, puffing his black pipe and watching the neighbors go by. A paunchy old man now, almost bald, but with eyes that looked into the distance. I had sent word through his son Jack that I'd like to visit, and he was ready for me.

"Come sit down, young Roy."

"Thank you, sir. How are you?" We shook hands.

"Pleased you're here."

"And Aunt Myrtie?"

"She's fine. Doin' women things in the house. Says her back ails her, but she don't stop."

"Give her my best, will you?"

We agreed the days were getting finer and the times getting worse. A man could hardly make a living anymore. I saw a new car just outside his garage.

"Jack says you want to talk. Goin' to run for office again?"

"No sir. A better man is."

"You talkin' about Will Ford?"

"Yes sir. He's the man."

"You workin' for him? What's he want? Thought I heard he has the McClouds and McDonalds all locked up to vote for him."

"He needs the McMillans, too."

"Does, eh?"

"I thought you might be able to speak to some of the kin. Maybe they could see their way clear to vote for him, too. A gathering of the clans, so to speak."

"That would be a sight. Ornery as some of 'em are, they're still kin. Blood tells every time."

"I thought the clans might come together for this the way they did in times past."

"Times not what they used to be."

"No sir. Times change. This Jake Borden's making sure of that. His man Ed Bromley is not real Ireland County. He and his Chicago friends want to move in on us and sell us down the railroad."

"Wouldn't like that."

"No sir. They say he's got some Chicago toughs working for him. Types that carry guns under their coats."

"Don't need that in Ireland County."

"Comes down to the clans against the Mob."

"That bad, eh?"

"Looks like it."

We agreed he'd better talk to the kin. Wouldn't want outsiders taking over. Folks here know best what they need. Before I left, he sprang his surprise.

"May need you to look for some plots on the other side of the hill. McMillans are multiplyin' so fast we're runnin' out of room on the old side. Think you can do that?"

I told him I'd be glad to. Thank you, Uncle Jeremy. I wondered how many of those multiplying McMillans would stay around to populate the other side of the hill.

I thought my politicking was about done. I still dropped a good word for Will when I had the chance. You could tell things were tensing up for the election. A kind of undercurrent of talk was going through town. Folks would sit in twos and threes at the cafes and talk, then stop when some of Jake's men came in.

I was sitting in the office going over some overdue accounts when Johnny Dayton stopped in the door, coffee cup in hand, grinned knowingly, and said, "Brace yourself, Roy. You have company. You couldn't guess who."

I put the books away, got up, and started for the door, when Horace Bogart appeared there. In his dark suit, white shirt, and dark tie, he looked more like an undertaker than I did. He smiled quickly, a flash of white on his dark brown face. "All right if I come in right now, Roy?"

"Mr. Bogart. Come in."

"Call me Horace if you will. We've done business."

"Yes sir. Won't you have a chair?"

He sat there a minute and looked at me. I lifted my eyebrows.

"I hear you're drumming up votes for Will Ford."

"Trying to, yes."

"That's risky business."

"I thought we were making a little progress."

"Not that way. Risky. Jake Borden's men are out to get you."

"What do you—?"

"Let me talk. I'll tell you how."

He said Jake Borden's men were aiming to burn down my place. He'd heard it from Derek, who'd heard it talked about at the railroad office. Jake was scared about the election. Things didn't look as promising as when he'd put up Ed Bromley for commissioner. He'd heard I was mobilizing the clans to get out and vote for Will. And Jake still held a grudge against me from when we ran against each other. Didn't like things I'd said about shady business deals. Besides, he thought I was vulnerable. I didn't have a clan to stand beside me the way Will did. And my business had more to lose than Will's office did. And stood alone without other businesses in the same block.

Why had Bogart taken sides with me? He knew Judge Harvey and I were friends, and he and the Judge were same family now. Said we knew some of the same dark secrets of Cromwell. He grinned.

Again I thought of Miss Greneda and old Ferguson looking over my shoulder.

"This is pretty bad," I said. "Do you know any details? When do they plan to do it?"

"Saturday night. They think you'll be away then."

"How many? Did you hear?"

"Four, I think. They plan to burn your car sheds, too. Won't look like an accident if they hit both. But they don't mean it to look like an accident. Mean it to look like a warning. Mean it to show who's got the power."

"Are they the toughs from Chicago?"

"Right. They'll be out of town before the fire truck gets here."

I thanked him for the warning and said I'd try to be on guard. He said better see if I had any friends with fire hoses.

"And by the way," he said, "I'll see if I can persuade some of my hands to vote for Will Ford. They ain't kin, but they know a boss when they see one." He grinned again. There's more than one kind of clan boss, I thought.

Before he left, I asked about his family. "They're fine," he said. Then, "The wife's not doing well. Worried about her. But we'll manage." I wondered how much Miss Lauralee had told him.

After he left, I sat there, drumming my fingers on the desk, trying to decide what to do. If I asked Sheriff Johnny Patterson to help, he'd do it for sure. But if he brought deputies, somebody would talk, and the Chicago tough boys might ambush them. I didn't know how far Jake Borden reached into the law men. What I needed was help from somewhere they wouldn't expect. But who had enough hands to scare off the goons and maybe fight a fire if one got started? It sounded like time for a clan action. That was it. Blocks of guns instead of blocks of votes. Maybe I'd better see what kind of influence Uncle Jeremy had over guns. But what about the sheriff? He wouldn't take kindly to guns shooting in his county without his okay. I'd have to talk with him, too.

Uncle Jeremy looked surprised when I went to see him. "You got plots already located?"

"No sir. Got another kind of plot to tell you about."

He chuckled, then chuckled some more, when I told him about the fire threat.

"Roy boy, that's what families are for. Help each other out. We got half a county full of young hellions who'd rather shoot at outsiders than fence posts and road signs on a Saturday night. How many you need?"

I told him about ten, but they'd have to keep quiet about it and stay off liquor that night. The sheriff would come sooner or later, and he couldn't go along with shooting and drinking both.

"They know how to do. They know the woods. You won't know they're there till the shotguns start goin' off. I been out there to watch 'em run the dogs and hunt coons. They're right at home in the woods and the dark. As I remember, you got some trees and bushes round your place, eh?"

So we agreed they'd come to town in twos and threes just about dark. Look like they were in town for a good time. One could bring the shotguns in a car and park behind my car sheds. They could slip along the streets and alleys and get to my place. I told him it would be better not to get anybody killed. Just hit their legs, knock them off their feet. Disarm them. Keep them for the sheriff. They might have interesting stories to tell.

Uncle Jeremy said he looked forward to a visit and a good story from me when it was over.

When I went to see Johnny Patterson, he looked worried. He was a good sheriff, but ten or twelve years of keeping folks out of trouble was showing on him. His eyes looked tired, and his face was beginning to sag. He hated to think something like arson could happen in his town. He thought his deputies were all right, but he reckoned I had a point. Somebody could talk, might let the secret out whether he meant to or not.

"Tell you what I'll do," he said. He'd send two of his deputies out to the east part of the county to check on a still they'd heard about and keep one handy in town to show the law was there on a Saturday night. He'd deputize the McMillan boys for temporary service overnight, but they had to realize their deputy time was over soon as the Chicago boys were taken care of. And they'd better mind what he told them. He didn't want them to get on the wrong side of the law. Remember, no shooting unless the arson boys refused to stop and tried to resist arrest. I told him I'd get the word to Uncle Jeremy.

Saturday evening came on as usual. Weather was clear, but the moon was thin and didn't give much light. I looked at my place and wondered if I'd see it still standing in the morning. It showed white against the dark trees behind it, and there were lots of shadows from the trees and shrubs in front and on the sides. I had left a light at the front entrance to show I was away. No bodies were inside waiting to be viewed.

At good dark, I began to hear rustling in the bushes and thought I heard someone climbing one of the trees. Once I thought I heard a low laugh out by the car sheds. Then quiet. Sheriff Patterson came up through the shadows, and I hissed him over to where I was waiting.

"Remember," he said in a low voice, "I got to call 'em to stop first. It's the law." Then he said in a voice you could hear about ten feet away, "All right, boys, raise your right hands and I'll deputize you." I realized he said it for the record. Maybe one or two heard him mumble the words.

About ten o'clock, sometime late like that, a car pulled up in the driveway and backed into the shadow of a tree near the street. Sat there a minute. Then four man-size figures got out, went to the rear of the car, and started toward the house. Each had what I took to be a gasoline can. They walked quietly but didn't try to stay in the shadows. Sure of themselves, I thought.

One of them swung his arm around and pointed toward the back. One figure veered off to the back of the house, toward the car sheds, I guessed. I hoped Uncle Jeremy's boys were in place back there. The three remaining stood together a moment, then started for corners of the house.

"Stop right there!" shouted the sheriff. "Drop your cans and put up your hands. This is the sheriff." I heard him drop to the ground soon as he said his piece. He didn't think they'd stop either, I reckoned.

The figure on my side—the boss man, I thought, the one who'd motioned the fourth man to the back—froze a second, then whirled around with a pistol and started shooting into the dark where the sheriff's voice had come from. He got off maybe two shots. Then a shotgun blasted from the tree above me. I saw the man's hand jerk back, his pistol fly up and away, and heard him scream, "Oh, goddam!" Then another shotgun blast from near ground level knocked him off his feet. I saw his coat fly open and his hat fall off as he went down.

The figure from the front of the house was running toward the car. A blast from one of the bushes took him off his feet. I heard him yell, "Louie!" when he went down.

The one at the back corner had dodged behind a shrub. He was quiet. And dangerous, I thought. He hadn't fired. He was waiting. I hoped none of Uncle Jeremy's boys would show himself.

Shots from out near the car sheds and then a whoop made me think the boys back there had hit their man. But I decided to wait to find out.

A scurrying out near the car puzzled me. Had they left a fifth man there? Then three figures were pushing the car out into the street. The car rolled out of the shadow and into the open. One figure dodged from the car, ran to the downed man, grabbed the gasoline can, hit him over the head with it, and ran back to the car. I thought I heard laughs, a gurgling I thought but wasn't sure, then a lighted match arced to the car, and it broke out in a ball of fire. I hoped to hell nobody was inside.

The man at the corner of the house, behind the bush, was still quiet. I wondered if he had been hit. Strange, I hadn't seen or heard any shotgun blasts from that direction. We all waited too.

"Come on out, hands up!" the sheriff called. "You're trapped."

Still quiet.

Then a gurgling sound? I hoped he wasn't going to get a fire started there. But how could he light it without showing his position? I realized it was darker on that side than the others. The shrubs were closer to the house.

Then a crashing in the bushes. Two pistol shots from the man at the crashing sound. Then three shotgun blasts. A small fire began about ten feet from the house, I judged from the angle of light.

"What's going on there?" I shouted.

"Come on. We got him."

Then another voice. "You gotta come here. We cain't go there." Oh no, I thought. Not somebody hurt.

Sheriff Patterson and I worked our way around to the dark side, careful to keep in shadows. A body in city clothes was lying behind a shrub. Three of Uncle Jeremy's boys were standing in a group around the fire and laughing. I heard a hissing.

"Come on," one called. "Fire's out."

The sheriff and I looked over the ground. Our best guess was the man had poured gasoline at the foundation, then tried to make a trail of gas off into the bushes, planning to light it off from behind a far bush. He must have known there were shotguns there too. May have suspected it but was desperate by that time and had to take a chance. But his trail had missed some spots while he was creeping around shrubs. When the shotgun boys used the old trick of throwing a rock behind him, he shot instead of getting a good light on the gas trail. That was his last mistake.

"Send one of the boys for Doc Brandon," the sheriff said. "We got to make a report on this. We'll need him to sign the report. Cause of death: playing with fire." He smiled wryly.

By that time the town's fire truck had come up, and men started hosing the burning car. Not much of it was left, though. When I looked over the car later, I could imagine what my house would have looked like.

The boys from the back at the car sheds brought up their man. He had buckshot in his legs and one arm but was not bad hurt, more scared than hurt. He limped when he walked.

"Keep those yahoos away from me!" he called. "They're crazy."

They laughed and pushed him along. "Here's his gun and here's his can," one said. "Didn't use nary a one."

He's our man, I thought. We'll get him to talk.

As the rest of the shotgun boys came out of the shadows, I looked around at them. Not all of them looked like McMillans. All young, all with a hell-for-leather look in their faces. Bet the McMillan boys brought some of their friends in for the Saturday night fun.

"All right, boys," the sheriff called. "Shootin's over. You can turn in your badges now." They hooted at that. It was probably the closest some of them had been on the right side of the law. I realized then he said it for the record. He said they could go home now, and thanks for their service to Ireland County. They hooted again. I reckoned the fence posts and road signs would take another beating before they got home.

I told them thanks and to listen for word from Uncle Jeremy about a big barbecue I'd throw for them and their friends. They cheered at that.

By that time, Doc Brandon had come up and started patching up the Chicago toughs so the sheriff could take them to jail. He told the sheriff he'd have to take the one with the damaged hand to his office for more patching. He gave shots of morphine to all but the one from the back of the house. After Doc certified him, a couple of the boys and I took him to the embalming lab to wait for word on disposition of the remains. They looked around the lab, shivered, and left quickly.

Lights had come on at houses along the street, and in a few minutes, when folks were sure the shooting was over, a small crowd began to gather around the burned-out car and stare at the men Doc Brandon was still working on. I told them how they had missed seeing a big fire. They didn't want to believe it could happen in their town.

Needless to say, the town was buzzing for several days after that. Folks telling their own versions about what happened. Most of them hadn't seen the country boys, and word began to build up that Sheriff Patterson and I had taken care of the outsiders. I laughed when they congratulated me and told nothing. I didn't want the country boys to be implicated in any inquests that might be held. I wasn't sure how Jake's aldermen would act.

Sheriff Patterson ruled that the man lying on the lab table had been shot in self-defense while resisting arrest. The man taken back by the car sheds saw no railroad attorneys or aldermen were coming to his defense. He told his story to the county attorney, identified the boss man as Louie Lugg, the dead man as Kurt Holz, the other as Bertino Fazzi, and himself as Peter Flinn. A real Chicago Mob mix, I thought. No, he didn't know who gave the real orders. He just did what Louie said. He pleaded guilty to conspiracy to commit arson, not arson while armed, and received a reduced sentence. Nobody contested the sheriff's ruling. The other two stayed in jail to wait trial. Judge Harrison ruled that they were not acceptable subjects for release on bond. And for their own protection. Too many Chicago friends. No attorney contested his ruling.

I learned later that Sheriff Patterson told Jake Borden he'd better take a good, long vacation—a year or two in Europe would be about right. Anyway, stay out of Ireland County. The county attorney would have to follow up on Flinn's confession, and Jake would have some hard questions to answer.

The attempted arson was still heavy on folks' minds when the election was held, and Will Ford won by a big margin. The clans had come through with big votes. Folks in town and county said "Let's clean up this mess." Jake Borden and his friends stayed out of sight and hearing. I reckoned his chances for reelection had slipped some.

I went to thank Uncle Jamie and Cousin Malcolm and took each a bottle of Dan's best. They said much obliged and looked but didn't ask where I got it. I took a bottle to Uncle Jeremy too, and told him I wanted to treat the boys right for what they did. He took his black pipe out of his mouth, chuckled, and said they had a good time. Their womenfolk said it was hard to calm them down when they got home. We agreed a barbecue out at Seven Oaks campground would be about right. I'd get the pigs out there a couple of days early so they could get the slow roasting started. The fixings would come out early on the big day. Tell them to bring their friends too, as well as their women. I thought we'd better have lots of folks there so no one could say which ones had come to help me on a Saturday night.

On the big day, I left Johnny Dayton in charge at the home and promised to bring him a big basket of barbecue and fixings. When I got out to Seven Oaks, I found the party already going on before the party started. I unloaded fixings from my extra truck and got lots of hurrahs and comments they were glad the meat was already there. Several women set out the tables. I brought lots of urns of lemonade but was soon aware the lemonade several were drinking had unusual power. The eating started by noon and kept going on as more folks came. Getting close on to a hundred by then. Cousin Lucius came up with a plate in one hand, a drink in the other, and said I ought to go into politics. A spread like this would elect me for sure.

We were all feeling full and good when Cousin Paul McMillan came up. Dark and smirky, I thought. Not one of my favorite cousins. What was he doing here? He ran the book shop in Cromwell and said he'd been up to New York to look at books the publishers were going to put out in the fall. He'd seen Mollie Bruce. Didn't I know her? I knew he knew I did. Why was he playing coy? He said he'd seen her at a restaurant with one of the big writers, and they were mighty cozy. Just chatting away. And he thought he saw the man's hand rest on her knee but couldn't be sure because of the tablecloth. Anyway, he saw her foot jerk. I said I reckoned she was learning a lot in New York. I didn't feel as good after he wandered away.

Chapter 9

After he was elected, Will Ford asked me to be one of his advisers. Not for playing politics, he said, but to keep him up on what folks were saying, what their fears and ambitions were. What the mood of the town was. He knew my work gave me a listening post for talk folks wouldn't say in public. He didn't want to hear family secrets. I wouldn't need to worry over being asked about those. What were they saying about the effect of the railroad on town life? Were folks really feeling as flush as the papers said? What were folks saying about that evolution trial out in Tennessee? Where did they need more roads in the county? That sort of thing. I told him I'd try to remember what I heard.

As winter wore on, I learned that both Will and Judge Harvey had invested money in Roy Willard's truck repair business. They didn't keep their investment a secret, but they didn't shout about it, either. As Will told me, Cromwell and Ireland County needed to make sure they weren't completely dependent on the railroad. He also said Willard's looked ready to grow. They might double their money in a few years. Trucking looked like a rising competitor to the railroad. They might even put some money into Acme Trucking. But most folks in town still believed in the Eastern and Southern. They could see that school being built with the railroad's name on it and thought the switching yard being built was a sure thing for the future of the town.

Titus stopped me on the sidewalk one day and told me Sally and William's house out at the horse farm was coming right along and was going to be a handsome place. I ought to go out and see it. Yes, they got letters from Mollie. She said things were coming along fine. She still hadn't decided whether to go to Paris. Why didn't I come to visit more often? He and Miss Joanna wanted to hear my story on the big fire that didn't happen.

In the early spring, I found a brown paper package in the mailbox. New York postmark, I saw. Inside were two magazines, the *American Mercury* and *Collier's*. I opened to the table of contents of the first one, ran my finger down the page, and saw the author line "by Mollie Bruce." Same for the other magazine. I had a family coming in about half an hour to make funeral arrangements and decided to wait for a better time to read the stories.

When I had a chance to read the stories that evening, I was surprised at what I found. The stories didn't look much like that new kind of writing Mollie had said she was going to do. They were stories about folks in a small southern town, and I thought I recognized some situations and folks like those in Cromwell. Well, Mollie, I thought, what's changed with you?

A couple of days later, I found a letter from Mollie in the box. She was coming home to Cromwell, she said. She had done what she needed to do in New York, and she was coming back. Did I get copies of the stories she'd sent? What did I think about them? They showed the way she wanted to write now. They were about the kind of life she knew, and she wanted to come back to the source for her stories. She had written some other stories like those she sent. They had sold and would be published soon. Better still, she had an agent who believed in her and had gotten her a contract to write a novel like the stories. She wanted to come home to write the novel. She wanted to see me when she came back.

I want that too, I thought.

To heck with the mail, I decided. Send a telegram. JUST SAY WHICH TRAIN TO MEET ILL BE THERE ROY.

When I went to meet the train, I was puzzled not to find Titus and Miss Joanna there, too. Wondered if I got the wrong train or day. But when the train rolled to a stop, she stepped out. There was funny, quirky Mollie. She had one of those cloche hats circling her face, and her eyes were bright. Trim skirt and trim figure. I held my breath. She looked around, saw me, smiled, and ran into my arms.

"Oh Roy," she said. "Hold me tight."

"Well," I said, "this is better than a letter." She kicked my shin.

"New York manners?"

"It was for that awful rhyme."

I soon realized Titus and Miss Joanna weren't supposed to be there. Mollie had told them she'd arrive on a later train. She wanted me to meet her. And not have to share the hugs. We'd surprise them, she said. I could hardly get her luggage collected because she wanted to hold my hand all the time.

We surprised Titus and Miss Joanna, all right. Not only Mollie but me at the door. After a quick look, they understood. I wondered if Mollie had told them more about her feelings than she'd told me. Who cared?

In the next several days, Mollie settled back into her room at the Bruces'. But she said she wanted to get a big table placed by the window. That was to be her working place. Would I help find one?

We took most of a day to find that table. We had a lot of talking to catch up on. We sat a long time at the hotel dining room table after the waiter had taken away all but our coffee. She'd learned by being away from Cromwell how real it was to her. She saw things clearer now. New York had been all right, good for learning to publish, but it couldn't be home to her. The things and people she wanted were in Cromwell.

Then she looked at me a long time and smiled.

"I know you never really proposed," she said. "But I accept anyway."

"I was about to when something came between us."

"I know. Aunt Greneda."

"That was a real kick in the shin."

She laughed. "I've found out a lot since then. Mama and Papa told me but made me swear never to tell. Not even Sally and Livie. They still think Jackie is their Richmond cousin. Or maybe Philadelphia by now."

"The burden of knowledge."

"Oh, don't get philosophical. That's my corner to work."

"I don't know if you'll fit into my corner now," I said. She looked startled, then flushed.

"I'm going to have to move my living quarters out of the upstairs at the funeral home," I continued with a poker face. "The Ellis place several doors up the street looks like where I'll live. You think you could live there?" I felt another kick in the shin under the table.

"Would you?" she said and laughed. "I love that place."

"It needs a woman in the house. And in the bed."

She smiled. "It needs a few formalities first, but I think I could do it. Is there a place for a writing table, too?"

"By a window overlooking the street."

"A bed and a writing table sound like the main things to me."

"We might have to share the kitchen with Auntie Flo. She goes with the move."

"Two women in the same house! You are brave!"

"She doesn't sleep there."

"Good. Don't want another woman looking over my bed or my table."

"By the way," I said. "Will you marry me?"

"I thought you'd never ask. Wait till we get home, and I'll give you a real answer."

She sat silent, looking at me. "I don't want to give up going to your office, though. That's the real window to living and dying in Cromwell. Could I do that?"

"I'm always behind on my paperwork."

"I want to meet the families, too."

"We could set up a receptionist and secretary's desk. Everybody knows secretaries really run a business."

"I think so too."

"You'd learn a lot. Some of it not happy stuff."

"I want to tell real things about living in Cromwell. The bad as well as the good. I might have to publish under another name to keep from hurting people. I'd need to change the name of the town as well as the people. I'd need a nom de plume. Can you think of a good one? Something simple."

"What about la plume de ma tante?"

"Yes, I know," she said. "Aunt Grenada."